THE RAMPART GUARDS

Also by Wendy Terrien

Novella: *The Fate Stone*
One of seven stories in the anthology,
Tick Tock: Seven Tales of Time

THE RAMPART GUARDS

CHRONICLE ONE IN
THE ADVENTURES OF JASON LEX

A NOVEL BY
WENDY TERRIEN

CAMASHEA
PRESS

CAMASHEA PRESS | DENVER, CO

TEEN

THE RAMPART GUARDS

Chronicle One in the Adventures of Jason Lex

Copyright © 2016 Wendy Terrien

Published by Camashea Press.

All rights reserved. All logos are owned by Camashea Press.

First hardcover printing, February 2016.

ISBN 978-0-9969031-0-3

Camashea Press

PO Box 621252

Littleton, CO 80162

Library of Congress Control Number: 2015919229

Printed in the United States of America

For Kevin
Thank you for being proud of me

ONE
The Disappearance

Jason stopped at the kitchen doorway and watched mom stare out the window, her lips moving like she was counting the snowflakes.

He took a deep breath. "G'morning."

She didn't respond.

"So, I'll see you and Dad at the basketball game this afternoon?" Jason ducked into the mudroom. He grabbed his uniform and sniffed it. *Clean enough.* He stuffed it in his backpack.

Dad refilled his coffee. "We wouldn't miss it for the world." He smiled and blew on the steam rising from his cup.

Jason could always count on Dad. Mom, not so much anymore.

"Right, Adrienne?"

She didn't answer.

"Adrienne?"

Mom jerked like someone had snuck up behind her. "Oh. No. No, I won't be there. I need to be here."

Jason huffed. "Why?" He snatched up an orange and shoved it in his pack. "What's so important here? Will the house fall down without you or something?"

Dad stepped close to Mom and leaned his head toward hers. "Honey, please don't miss another game. The coach is really

1

impressed with Jason. I have to admit, he's got skills." Dad winked at Jason. "Come tonight. Show your support."

"No. I can't." She shuffled away from Dad. "You understand. Don't you, Jason?"

He shook his head. "Sure. Whatever." Jason moved toward the doorway. After weeks of her weirdness, he was over it.

"Wait. Do you have your lunch?" Mom reached for the refrigerator door. The handle zapped her and she yanked her arm back. "Damn static electricity." She stuck her finger in her mouth.

Jason rolled his eyes. "Okay. Well, I already have my lunch." He walked out of the kitchen and yelled upstairs. "Della—let's go."

Jason's younger sister bounded down, her blonde curls springing on her shoulders. She ran toward the front door.

"Kinda hard to walk you to school if you don't wait for me." Jason quick-stepped to catch her. "And I don't remember fourth grade being so great that I'd hurry to get there."

"My fourth grade is better than your fourth grade." Della put on her coat and scooted out the door, her pink and black backpack rolling behind her.

* * *

After the game, Jason bolted into the house, Dad, Della, and older brother Kyle close behind.

"Mom, we won." Jason rushed into the living room, the kitchen. No Mom. The office. No Mom. The back patio. No Mom. He looked at Dad. "I thought she had to stay home tonight?"

Dad picked up a note lying on the entryway table. He read it aloud. "On a walk. Be back later. Love, Mom." He crumpled it and walked into the kitchen. Jason, Della and Kyle followed.

"She goes for walks, like, every day. By herself. She never used to do that." Jason wiped his neck with the towel draped over his shoulder.

Dad tossed the note in the recycling bin.

"Yeah, why doesn't she take us on walks anymore?" Della asked.

"Because she doesn't like us anymore." Kyle talked like he knew the answer to everything. Apparently starting high school did that to you.

"Kyle, that is not true." Dad turned to Della. "She loves you all very much. There are just things . . . she's had a lot on her mind lately."

"Like what?" Jason chugged from his water bottle. The chill iced his throat."Grown-up things. Nothing for you guys to worry about." Dad took a pan out of the cupboard. "Who wants tacos?"

They all raised their hands, but Jason didn't stop wondering about grown-up things.

✳ ✳ ✳

She didn't come home before bedtime. Jason wrestled with his sheets more than he slept. He awoke to hear Dad talking downstairs. *Mom must be back.* Jason pulled his covers closer, buried his head under his pillow. But the talking kept him awake.

Jason eased out of bed and opened his door, stepping into the hallway. A dull glow from the room below climbed the stairs and dissolved into black where he stood.

Dad's voice rose. "I'm telling you, something is wrong."

No one answered."I already said she left about seven PM." Dad was on the phone. "Yes. We've lived in Colorado for eighteen years, we know about the damn mountain lions."

Goosebumps prickled Jason's skin.

"She knows how to take care of herself. She's not an idiot."

Another pause.

"As soon as you can, please get someone here." Dad's voice morphed from muscled to mouse. The recliner creaked. "Oh, Adrienne . . . "

Jason padded down the stairs. Dad sat hunched in his chair, the *Throne for the King of Comfort* as Mom had dubbed it. He held his head in his hands.

"Dad?"

He jolted up. "What are you doing out of bed?" Dad glanced at his wrist where a watch should be.

"I heard you talking. Where's Mom?"

Dad flinched. "I don't know."

"Wait, what? How can you not know?" Jason's voice scaled higher making him sound more like his nine-year-old sister than his thirteen-year-old self.

"Keep your voice down." Dad patted the air in front of him and stood. "It'll be okay. She'll be home soon. I called the police, just to be safe." He put his arm around Jason's shoulders.

"That's who you were talking to?" Jason shrugged out from under Dad's arm. "We don't need them. Let's go find her. Right now."

"Jason, it's dark. It's snowing. We can't do anything right now."

"We've got flashlights. Kyle and Della can help, too." Jason pushed his hair back. "We can't just sit here."

"She could be anywhere. Besides, she always comes home. Always."

"Effing stupid, but whatever." Jason fell onto the couch facing the picture window and the woods beyond. "Then I'm waiting for her right here." He crossed his arms and squinted, trying to X-ray the darkness and spot his mom.

"Do not say 'effing' anything, and go back to bed. It's a school night . . . almost day."

"No. Can't sleep." He tucked his fingertips in his armpits and stared at the night.

Dad breathed deep and blew it out. "Okay. Fine." He sat next to Jason.

Jason started counting backward from one hundred in his head. She'd be home before he got to zero.

. . . *three, two, one* . . . No Mom.

He gave her another hundred. *One hundred . . . ninety-nine . . .*

ninety-eight—wait—what was that? Something moved outside the window. "I saw something. Something moving." He popped off the couch.

Dad leaned forward. "Your mom?"

"Maybe?" He slid a side window open and shivery air shot through. There were things, lots of things, flying through the air, swooping close then away, left and right, swift, smooth, agile. One swooshed at Jason and he jerked his head back.

"Jeez." Jason thudded the window closed. "Bats."

"Bats? In January?"

Jason pulled a blanket out of a trunk behind the couch. It sputtered with static. "Guess so." He wrapped it around himself and returned to the couch.

A few minutes passed and Jason started counting down again. *One hundred . . . ninety-nine . . . ninety-eight . . . ninety-seven . . .*

✳ ✳ ✳

"Jason." Dad squeezed his shoulders. "Wake up, son."

Jason half-opened his eyelids and swiped at something winging past his face. "Aaaah—are there bats in the house?"

"No. You must have been dreaming."

"Mom?" Jason rubbed his sleep-glued eyes. The orange glow of the morning sun reflected off the glass coffee table. "Is she home?"

"Not yet." Dad stood and massaged his forehead. He took a deep breath. "Go upstairs and get ready for school. Make sure your brother and sister are up, too."

"But Dad—"

"I said go." His gaze zeroed in on Jason. "Now."

It was the voice you didn't question.

Jason stomped up the stairs and pounded on his brother's door. "Get out of bed," he yelled. He repeated the command at his sister's room then went into his own room and slammed the door.

He took a quick shower, threw on jeans and a sweatshirt, and flew back down the stairs to the kitchen. Kyle, Della and Dad were all in their usual spots at the round wooden table.

Mom's spot was empty.

Jason rushed past them. He grabbed a box of cereal, a spoon, and a carton of milk and *thunked* it all on the table.

"Dude, what is your problem?" Kyle glared.

Jason ignored him.

"Did you remember your homework?" Dad asked.

"Don't need it." Jason yanked his chair out from the table. He didn't sit. "I'm not going anywhere until Mom gets home."

Dad's eyelids flicked and his lips puckered.

"Mom's not here?" Kyle asked.

Dad rubbed both hands down his face.

"Dad?" Kyle's brows rose.

Della stopped eating her toast mid-bite.

"Everybody, relax. Your mom knows these woods. She probably got too far away to risk heading home in the dark."

Jason heard the words but they sounded empty.

"She's been gone all night?" Kyle asked. "What's her problem?"

Jason's stomach winched into his chest.

"Kyle . . . " Dad's eyes narrowed.

"Something's wrong with her and you know it." Kyle skidded his chair back from the table. "And now she's, what, lost in the woods?"

"There's nothing wrong with your mom—"

"No. I'm with Jason," Kyle said. "I'm not going anywhere until she gets home."

Della's spoon clanked in her bowl. "Me too." She wiped her milk mustache on her sleeve.

"Correction. You're *all* going to school."

"Dad, no." Jason gripped the back of the chair. *We can find her. We can help her. We can make her better.*

Dad shook his head. "I will handle this. You will go to school."

Before Jason had a chance to argue, the doorbell rang.

"It's Mom." Jason raced out of the kitchen.

"She wouldn't ring the doorbell, jerkwad." Kyle called after him.

"Maybe she lost her keys." Jason was almost to the front door, the rest of the family not far behind.

Jason pulled the door open. Two police officers in dark blue uniforms stood on the porch. A third man stood with them. He wore a dark blue windbreaker over a white shirt and a red tie. His stare traveled past Jason like he wasn't there. He looked at Jason's dad.

"I'm Nate Hughes from the sheriff's office. Are you Zachary Lex?"

"Yes, that's me. You're here to help us search?"

"Search, sir?" The man removed his sunglasses.

"For my wife. I called a few hours ago. She went for a walk last night and—"

The man raised his hand. "No, Mr. Lex, we're not here about your call. But we are here about your wife. Adrienne Lex?"

Dad didn't answer.

"Sir, is there someplace we could talk? In private?"

"Yes, of course. Please come in." His voice sighed through the air. "Kids, go upstairs. Please."

Jason wanted to stay, wanted to listen, but he trudged up the stairs behind Kyle and Della.

"I don't want to go to my room." Della twisted the hem of her shirt.

"C'mon, you can hang out with me." Kyle half-nodded at Jason, signaling him to get the scoop.

Della followed Kyle down the hall. Jason ducked into his room then sped back out, tucking into the spot where he could peek through the rails unseen. He'd used it many times before, successfully spying out Christmas gift placement and hiding spots for cash-filled Easter eggs, and eavesdropping on his parents' grown-up parties.

Dad and the three men stood in the family room. The two officers stayed a few steps behind the man in the windbreaker.

He spoke. "You reported your wife missing?"

"Yes, a few hours ago. I . . . I called it in a few hours ago."

"Why don't you take a seat, sir?"

Dad settled on the couch and Mr. Hughes sat next to him.

"Mr. Lex, early this morning, a runner out on the East-West Trail, the one through these woods out here, found a small day pack. Based on the contents, we believe it was your wife's day pack."

Dad straightened. "She probably dropped it. I was telling the kids I thought she walked too far and it was too dark for her to get home safely so she waited it out somewhere and now she's probably retracing her steps trying to find her pack so that's why she's not back yet—"

"Sir. Mr. Lex, please."

Dad shrunk a little.

"The runner also found a blood-stained jacket."

Dad tilted his head like he couldn't understand the words being spoken.

"Our officers searched the area. Not far from where the pack and jacket were found, we discovered blood, and signs of a struggle."

Jason didn't blink. Didn't breathe.

"There was no body, but—"

Dad leaped up. "Then she's alive. She's hurt and she needs help but she's alive." He looked from Mr. Hughes to the policemen then back again. "We need to find her. We need to hurry."

There was a different answer in Mr. Hughes' face. Jason's stomach pulled like it was lined with glue, the sides puckering and pasting themselves together.

"Mr. Lex, the amount of blood," Mr. Hughes said, his voice heavy, his hands upturned, "well, if it is your wife's blood, it's not good. It's tough for someone to survive with that amount of blood loss."

Two quick gasps forced their way into Jason's lungs. They shuddered out.

Dad tipped his head and teetered backward.

"It appears a body was dragged away from the scene. All signs point to a mountain lion attack."

Mountain lions? Mom? Jason clutched the railing, a post in each hand. The corners of the wood squares cut into his palms. His hands burned and he jerked them away. They were smoky and blue. Smoke wisped off the wood.

What?

Crackling filled his ears. He shook his head hard, wiped his hands on his pants.

They were wrong. Mom would be fine. She *was* fine. She'd be home any minute.

Their voices rumbled through his head, fighting with the crackling. He couldn't make sense of the words. He didn't want to make sense of the words. He wanted them to leave. He wanted the words to stop.

Dad crumpled. Mr. Hughes turned and grabbed Dad's arm.

Jason needed his mom.

But she wasn't there.

TWO

Changes

Mom didn't come home.

Weeks passed in a blur of tears and sleeplessness and fruitless searches of the woods. Grandma Lena drove in from Salton, the small town in Idaho where Mom grew up. Dad's dad, Grandpa Quentin, came from London where they'd moved when Dad was twelve. Grandpa Quentin, or GQ as they called him, rarely visited the US, but the *slog across the pond* wasn't going to stop him this time.

Jason kept up with schoolwork from home until Dad decided the kids should return to school. Grandma Lena said it was important for everyone to get back to their routines. Dad returned to work, and Grandma Lena and Grandpa Quentin headed home. Jason was glad to be doing something that resembled the old normal.

He heard the mumblings in the hallways between classes. "That's the kid whose mom disappeared," they said. Or worse. "Maybe she died." Or, "She probably got eaten." Jason tucked his head and sped up his pace.

His teachers randomly patted him on the back and his school counselor, Mr. Farnsworth, made sure to run into him every day, wearing his glasses on top of his head and a let's-try-to-be-upbeat-smile on his face.

10

"Jason. How's it going?" Mr. Farnsworth grabbed for his glasses before they dropped down to his nose.

"Good." Jason forced a neutral expression and swapped his math book for his history book. He snapped his locker shut. "I have to get to class."

"Of course. Good to see you." Mr. Farnsworth gave him one of those pats on the back, with a squeeze of his shoulder for good measure, and walked away.

Brandon, Jason's locker neighbor and friend since forever, thumbed over his shoulder at Mr. Farnsworth. "Dude, is he going to do that every day?"

"Sure seems like it."

"That's gonna suck."

"You should have been there Monday when he gave me the *Why You Shouldn't Kill Yourself* speech."

"You're thinking about killing yourself?" Brandon's mouth fell open.

Jason rolled his eyes. "No. He just thinks I might be thinking about it. But I'm not. Idiot." He shoved Brandon sideways. "Let's go."

But is that what kids do when their moms disappear? Or die? Or whatever? Wasn't it enough to feel like you're dragging a bag loaded with rocks? Like you're always fighting to keep from crying? Like you shouldn't smile at anything, even your best friend's stupid comments?

After school, Jason peered into Dad's home office and said hello. Dad muttered something about being busy and didn't even lift his eyes. Jason waited a moment, his mind searching for something to say, but nothing came.

Jason continued upstairs and passed Kyle's bedroom door—shut, as usual. Kyle had informed everyone about the invisible *DO NOT DISTURB* sign.

Jason poked his head into Della's room. A new picture of two baby horses playing in a field hung on her wall, adding to a growing collection of animal and ballerina posters. "Hey."

She was sitting on the floor, hunched over a board game. "Hey." Her voice was flat, Della-less.

"Can I come in?"

"Sure." She rolled the dice.

"You're playing Dog-Opoly?" Jason sat across from her. Their parents had bought the game to get the kids over wanting a dog. It didn't work.

"Yep." She moved the fire hydrant piece seven spaces.

"By yourself? Isn't it hard to play that way?"

"Not really. But it's not that much fun." She rolled the dice again and moved the mailman piece six spaces. "Mom used to play with me."

Jason swallowed a lump that had popped into his throat. "Can I play with you?"

Della looked up. "Okay. She scooted forward a little. "You're the mailman."

Jason scanned the board—the mailman was losing. "Okay." He picked up the dice and a spark shocked them out of his hand. He looked at his palm. It glowed bright blue. *What the . . .* He shoved his hand inside his sweatshirt.

"Now move your mailman."

"What?" Jason focused back on Della. "Oh right." He checked his left palm—normal. He noted the number on the dice and advanced his token.

Della rolled the dice and moved ten spaces. She raised her fist. "Yes. Good Dog." She took a card from the pile.

Jason peered down the neck of his sweatshirt. Nothing glowing.

"Best in Show. Collect one hundred buckeroos." Della added the money to her bank. "Your turn."

Jason eased his right hand out. Skin-colored. *Must be imagining things.* He shook the dice and rolled. "Lucky seven." He moved his piece, pressed his lips shut, then breathed in again. "So, you doing okay, Dell?"

She shrugged. "I guess." She moved three spaces. "But it's weird being the only girl in the house."

Jason hadn't thought about that. Della used to do girl stuff with Mom, like shopping, and toenails, and hair. "Yeah. That would be weird."

"It's your turn."

"Right." He rolled. "*Aaah,* Bad Dog card. Move back ten spaces." He clicked the piece backward on the board.

Della giggled. "Good one."

Jason stuck his tongue out at her and she giggled again.

"Dell, if you ever want to play games, or whatever, you let me know, okay?"

She rolled the dice. "What about dolls?"

"What about them?"

"Will you play dolls with me?"

Jason's head snapped up. Della's blue eyes, Mom's eyes, were fixed on him. He quickly turned his open mouth into a smile. "Well . . . if you promise never to tell Kyle, then you've got a deal."

"Pinky swear." Della held out her crooked little finger.

"Pinky swear." Jason sealed the doll deal with Della. Next stop— Googling *how to play with dolls* so he could sort of fill in for Mom.

✳ ✳ ✳

Mom had only been gone a couple of months when Kyle turned fifteen, and he made it clear he had no interest in celebrating. Not that anyone tried to talk him into it. When Della reached double digits a month later, she agreed to a party, but, "Just a little one with pizza. And cake. And a new Hot Wheels track set. But that's it," she said.

Jason turned fourteen in May. He grabbed a magnifying glass from his old bug kit and examined his face in the mirror—still no facial hair. He wasn't surprised. He didn't feel that different, except his brown hair was longer and shaggier and usually sticking out because of static electricity. That bugged him. That, and Mom wasn't there for his birthday. Or anyone's birthday. If she was alive, she'd be there, wouldn't she?

Grandma Lena arrived for Jason's party. Her wavy white hair hinted at the blonde shade it used to be, the same blonde that Jason's mom, brother, and sister all shared.

Grandma Lena was whispering with Dad when Jason came down the stairs. They broke off their conversation.

"There you are, birthday boy." She hugged Jason. "Happy birthday."

"Thanks, Grams." He pictured her house, her living room, her garden. Roses. That's how she smelled. Sweet. Nice.

The family visited her in Salton for a week every summer, but Jason didn't really like it there. Salton was a tiny town in the middle of nowhere. Unless you liked hanging out in cornfields or looking at cows, Salton rated high on the scale for boring.

After barbecued ribs and coleslaw, with chocolate cake and mint chip ice cream for dessert, it was time for presents.

"Here, bro." Kyle handed Jason an envelope.

Jason took out a card. It had a picture of a bulldog on the front and when Jason opened the card, it farted loud and long. Jason, Brandon and Kyle cracked up.

"Happy birthday to an old fart." Jason read it aloud. He leaned over, laughing more, and high-fived his brother.

"Grooooss." Della's lips curled.

"Okay, let's move it along," said Dad. "Della, your turn."

"Here, but it's not that funny." Della slid a card toward Jason.

The front had a bird holding a balloon that said *Happy Birthday*. He opened it. "For a brother you are pretty tweet. I hope you have a happy bird-day. Love, Della." Jason smiled at his little sister. "Thanks, Dell." He gave her a hug. "You're *pretty tweet* too."

"And here." Della whisked something from under the table and slid it to Jason. A jumbo-size package of Peanut M&Ms.

"My favorite. Thanks." Jason rubbed the top of her head.

"Don't mess my hair." She batted his hand away and pouted.

"Sorry, sorry. Just don't go getting all girlie or we won't let you play basketball with us anymore." Jason shook his head.

"Shut up." Della's lips shifted into a frown.

"It's true. We don't play with girlie-girls." Kyle shrugged.

"Don't listen to them, sweetie." Dad said. "I'll teach you a few moves and you'll be kicking their butts in no time."

Della grinned.

Brandon handed Jason a gift, a video game he'd been wanting. And Grandma Lena gave Jason a sweet card with an even sweeter wad of cash. Then Dad, smiling, put a large box in front of Jason. It was covered with three different kinds of wrapping paper.

"Sorry about the wrapping. Your mom would never . . . " Dad glanced away for a second, the smile slipped from his face. "Anyway, happy birthday. I hope you like it."

Jason shook off the reminder of his mom and focused on the gift. He tore off the ribbon and paper, and more paper, and lots of tape, and opened the box underneath. Inside was Dad's antique chess set, passed down through the Lex family for generations.

Jason sucked air in and held it for a second. "Seriously?"

"Yes, seriously." He smiled and nodded.

Jason eased the large set out of the box. Hand carved out of holly and cedar, the woodsy scent blended into the air.

"Dad, this is so cool." He examined one of the rooks. It was warm in his hand. He placed it on the board and grabbed another. That piece felt warm, too. Jason rolled it in his palm and the heat faded.

"I'm glad you like it." Dad helped him arrange the chessmen. "We haven't played in a while. Maybe you're game for a match after the party?"

"Yeah, definitely."

"Great. I'm looking forward to it." Dad placed the last piece on the board. "I know we've talked about the chess set and its history within our family. It's a treasure that I'm proud to be entrusting to you."

"I promise I'll take really good care of it, Dad. Really good."

"I know you will."

Jason looked at Kyle.

"It's cool, dude. I know you love that thing, and I totally don't. So, whatever."

"Thanks, bro." Jason ran his finger along the edge of the carved wood. He loved learning to play chess with his dad on this chess set. And now it was his.

All things considered, not the worst day for a first-one-without-your-mom-birthday.

✳ ✳ ✳

The school year was almost over and Jason looked forward to days without homework. He was ready to stay up late, sleep in later, and play chess with Dad—if he could make the time. Kyle said Dad was *going dark again*. But Dad was working on a new project. Jason had a new project of his own, one that would make the next school year the best one yet.

The family gathered at the table for dinner. Jason sat in his usual place.

Dad cleared his throat. "Kids, I have some news."

"Yeah, me too." Jason squirmed in his seat. "Coach asked me and Brandon to work on a conditioning program with him this summer, to help the basketball team get ready." He reached for a serving bowl loaded with spaghetti.

"Oh, that's nice."

"Nice? Try awesome." Jason grabbed a wad of noodles with the tongs.

Kyle half-nodded at Jason. "Totally cool, bro."

"Thanks. Yeah, Brandon and I are pumped. We've already gotten some ideas, and we're going to Google the top college programs, see what we can learn from them." He passed the bowl to Della.

"Well, I'm happy for you Jason, proud of you. But I have some news, too." Dad sounded nervous. Or angry. Maybe both?

"I've given this a lot of thought, I've talked to your grandmother about it and she thinks it's a good idea . . . we both do." Dad squared his shoulders. "We're moving to Salton."

Jason swung his arm and bumped the bowl out of Della's hands, knocking it into the pitcher. Water and noodles slopped into the bread and salad and meatballs.

"What?" Jason glared. Water ran over the edge of the table, into Jason's lap. He skidded his chair back and stood. Water dripped off his pants.

"What the hell?" Kyle's eyes locked on Dad's.

He stood. "I know this comes as a surprise, but Salton will be good for us." He brought the trash bin to the table, grabbed the platter of soggy bread and dumped it.

Jason grabbed paper towels. "I'm not moving." He wiped off his pants and dropped towels onto pools of water. "No way."

"We can't move." Kyle's fist lay resolute on the table.

Dad eased into his seat. "Listen, we've had a tough year. I've tried to help, but I know I haven't been good at it." He swallowed hard. "Because I've needed help, too."

The crack in Dad's voice triggered a flip in Jason's stomach. Dad wasn't going to cry, was he?

Parents don't cry.

Dad scrunched a damp napkin and threw it in the garbage. "I haven't been able to do it all and that's not good for you or for me. We need help."

"Then get therapy or something, Dad. I'm fine." Kyle shoved his plate away. He leaned forward. "You can't move us to another town just because you can't handle life."

Della lifted her glass of milk. "I don't want to move, I like it here." She took a gulp.

"This isn't a sudden decision, nor was it an easy decision. I've given this a great deal of thought. I know it will be a big adjustment, for all of us, but I think this is the right thing to do for the whole family."

"But it's not your decision." Jason jabbed his finger, pointing at Dad's face. "When Mom was here, we voted on big family decisions. She would never do this to us. She would never force us to do something we didn't want to do."

"Yeah, Mom would call a Family Vote." Kyle sat back in his chair.

"Yeah, Family Vote." Della echoed.

Dad bolted out of his chair. "In case you've forgotten, your mother is not here. Your mother left us. She's gone. There will be no Family Vote."

Della shrunk in her chair.

Dad leaned on the table and took several deep breaths. "I'm sorry. I didn't mean to . . . " He sighed. "Please understand, we don't need this much house, and the fact is we can't really afford this house on my salary. And, frankly, we don't need the bad memories. And we do need to be closer to family."

He stepped away from the table and turned his back to them. "I've discussed it with my partners at the firm. I'll work remotely. Your grandmother will be here in a few days to help us pack." He turned toward them. "We have a house ready and waiting for us in Salton."

Jason's gut wrenched tighter. "But I have basketball."

"They play basketball in Salton."

"But our friends—we don't have any friends there." Jason's mouth gaped.

"You'll make new friends. All of you will make new friends."

"Please Dad, don't do this." Jason offered more reasons and arguments and facts that proved things would not be better in Salton.

Kyle offered to get a job. Della said she'd sell her Barbies.

"Kids, I'm sorry." Dad shook his head. "Moving to Salton is our best option. We're leaving two days after the school year is finished." He left the room.

Jason stared at the spot where his dad had stood. Words screamed in his head and churned his stomach:

Moving sucks.

Salton sucks.

Life sucks.

THREE

Leaving Everything Behind

Brandon held the chess set while Jason made one last circuit of his room and checked his closet. Empty. Totally empty.

"Guess we're outta here."

"Bummer." Brandon handed the chess set to Jason. "Kyle still into the whole moving thing?"

"Totally. He's probably already in the car."

"What's his deal?"

Jason stepped into the hallway. "No idea. He just stopped complaining and started packing."

"Weird. Maybe he met some hottie?"

Jason shrugged. "He's been texting a lot more. Maybe someone online or something."

"Could happen." Brandon's phone dinged. He checked the text. "Mama bear calling. Gotta go, bro."

"Thanks for coming over, helping me pack." Jason led the way downstairs and outside.

"No problem. Keep in touch."

Jason fist-bumped Brandon. "Yep. You too." He waved as

Brandon rode his bike past the FOR SALE sign, and a moving truck parked in front of their house.

A moment later, the truck roared to life. Gears grinded, an air break released, and it rumbled away. It was an uncomfortable noise, too loud for their quiet neighborhood. *Their old neighborhood now*, thought Jason.

Dad locked the front door.

"Why do you have to lock it?" Jason rolled his eyes.

"Because you lock houses when you leave them."

"What's anyone going to steal?" Kyle pulled his earbuds out of his pocket and plugged them into his phone.

"Get in the car." Dad waved his hands toward Jason and his brother. "We have a long drive ahead."

They climbed into the minivan with the rest of their stuff. Jason tucked his chess set under the seat. Grandma Lena sat in the seat next to Dad, and Kyle took the third row for himself. He popped in his earbuds and tuned out. Jason and Della shared the middle bench.

"All right. We're off on our new adventure." Dad backed out of the driveway.

Jason's skin tingled, he turned toward the house. Why did he feel like he'd forgotten something? Then he saw movement.

"Stop!"

Dad slammed the brakes. The seatbelt seized and dug into Jason's shoulder.

Dad locked eyes with Jason in the rearview mirror. "What? What is it?"

"I saw something. There's someone in the house."

"What?"

Jason slid the door open and jumped out. "Mom. I think it's Mom," he yelled over his shoulder.

"Ja—"

Jason ran to the house, put his face to the window, cupped his hands around his eyes. Nothing. He knocked on the glass. A shadow? He balled his hands and pounded with the flesh of his fists.

"Mom? Hey—we're here." Jason glanced back at the van. Dad was still sitting in the driver's seat. Not unbuckling. Not moving.

"Come open the door." He pounded on the window again. "Mom?"

Dad and Della stared at Jason. Kyle's focus never left his phone. Grandma Lena got out.

"Grams, she's here. Did you see her? I saw her." Jason's pulse raced. He returned to the window. "Mom?" He squinted and tried to block the glare of the sun.

Grandma Lena put her arm around Jason's shoulders, clutching him close. "Honey, your mom isn't here."

He and his grandma were the same height but Jason felt like a little kid again. "But what if she is? Or even if she isn't, what if she comes home and we're gone?"

Grandma Lena stepped between him and the window. She held his face in her hands. "Then she would call us. She has my number, she has your number. She would find you."

Jason pulled away and pounded on the window again.

"Jason." Her calm voice flowed into him. "Your mom is always with you. Always. But she's not really here."

He swallowed.

Tendons twisted and grabbed in his throat, pulled at the plug that dammed his tears. He held onto it, tug-of-warring with the pain. He did not want to cry. He would not cry.

Grandma Lena wrapped him in her arms, hugged him hard. "She's gone."

Battle lost. Jason unplugged and undammed.

A few minutes later, Jason and Grandma Lena were back in the minivan. Dad pulled away. Jason locked his eyes on the house as they left it behind.

FOUR

Chased

Jason stared out the window and ignored Della, whose movie continued to run on the portable DVD player, but she wasn't watching it. She was looking at him. He was certain she'd get bored with the back of his head. He checked her reflection in the window. She still watched him. After a couple more minutes, she touched his arm.

"Are you okay?" Della whispered.

He turned toward her. "Yeah. Fine."

"What did you really see?"

Jason didn't know what he'd seen. Maybe he didn't see anything. Maybe it was just a shadow or a reflection or a wish. And even if he was sure he'd seen Mom, do you tell your little sister that you saw their missing mother?

"Nothing. It was just a reflection from the sun. Watch your movie."

Della put her hand in her lap. "Okay." She watched Jason for a few more seconds then switched her gaze to the screen.

They drove out of town and away from civilization, then over the Rocky Mountains and into Idaho. For hours they drove past endless fields of potatoes, fields of wheat, and fields and who-knows-what. A tractor pulled out in front of them onto the narrow road and rumbled along at a top speed of fifteen MPH. After a couple of miles, the tractor turned onto a farm road and Dad punched the gas. They passed an abandoned sugar beet mill. Grandma Lena said it used to provide a lot of jobs in Salton. Just past the mill was a blue and white sign that read, *Salton Pop. 2460.*

The crops stopped and familiar buildings appeared. There was the hardware store, a feed and pet supplier, a grocery store, and two gas stations. Downtown Salton was lined with old-fashioned street lamps and half-barrels of flowers. Dad continued on into the neighborhoods on the other side. The route was almost the same as the one to Grandma Lena's house except for a left turn instead of a right.

"There," said Grandma Lena, pointing at a two-story brick house. "The one with the red door." She took a clicker from her purse and opened the two-car garage.

Dad pulled into the driveway and they piled out. Jason stretched then grabbed his chess set. The house seemed okay. Big enough. But he didn't think Mom would like living in Salton.

"Which room is mine?" Jason asked.

"Upstairs, third door on the left," Grandma Lena said.

"After you drop off the chess set, come down and help us unload," Dad called after him. "Plus I want you to wipe out the kitchen cupboards before the moving truck arrives."

Jason inspected his new bedroom. It was bigger than his old one. And it had two windows—one with a view out the front of the house, the other on the side where a huge oak tree waved. Green leaves and big brown branches filled the frame.

He smelled fresh paint. Three walls were a sandy color, one navy blue. A second door led to the bathroom he'd share with Kyle. And he had a walk-in closet with built-in shelves. He put his chess set there.

He helped unload the minivan and finished cleaning the kitchen cupboards just as the moving truck arrived. The last things packed were the first things removed and they went straight into the garage: lawn mower, rakes, bikes.

"I'm going to do a quick ride around the block." Jason set a box in the garage and rolled his bike into the driveway.

"You can go out later. Right now we need your help." Dad stood on the front step.

"I won't be gone long, Dad." He pedaled into the road. "A few minutes, thirty max."

"Alright, fine . . . but don't go too far."

Jason crossed a bridge a short distance from their house. He turned left and rode on a path next to a canal flanked with willows and chokecherry bushes. He was heading in the direction of the new house, but along the backside now.

There weren't many people on the path. He passed someone on a bike, another person out for a stroll, and a man on a scooter who'd stopped to film something in the sky. Jason didn't see anything worth recording. He kept going.

On his right, he could see the yards of houses that backed to the path. They were large, like private parks with decks and swing sets and pools. The houses sat far away from the fence. A straw-hatted man rode on his mower, steering with one hand and holding a drink with the other.

The banks of the canal on his left smelled like the mud pies he used to make with Kyle. Water eased along the passage and swirled where rocks poked out. Thickets clustered close along the far bank and nothing was visible behind them. The new house was along here somewhere, hidden like every house on that side of the stream.

All in all, nothing that interesting. No surprise.

At least an hour had passed. *Better head home.*

An odd sensation ignited at the base of his neck and crawled down his spine. It burned like a flame held close. He reached around, touched his neck. A shock zapped from his hand and he jerked.

What the . . . ?

Noise crackled in his ears, in his head. He scanned for thunderclouds. But the sky was clear blue.

He refocused his gaze on the path. And he saw them.

Shiny, golden things, dozens of them, of different lengths, fluttered like dark-eyed ribbons on the wind. They flew at Jason.

Targeting him.

They waved, or flapped their wings, or flapped their . . . fins? Jason didn't know what he saw. But they were coming straight at him and they were coming fast. The crackling got louder.

He smashed his brakes and put his foot down to balance the skid as he U-turned. Unexpected power shot into his legs. He stood on the pedals and pumped, moving faster than ever.

He glanced back—only a few feet away.

How are they so close?

He jolted around. The bike pitched beneath him. He shifted his hips, regained his balance.

So many. Right there. Fast.

He begged his legs to pedal harder.

The creatures accelerated and closed in. They packed around him, above him, next to him.

Jason punched. Swatted.

Their fins and wings twitched and dodged.

A longer creature swooped toward his face. He swung. It dove. Missed.

An instant later he reached the bridge. At the last millisecond he hit the brakes, put his foot down, cranked the wheel.

Too fast.

His front wheel hit the bridge. The bike spun hard and slid out, flinging him down the bank, slick like a slide. His hand dug into the mud and he scraped against rocks and bike, stopping when his foot braced against a boulder, averting a water landing.

He twisted around and scrambled back on the path and scoured the sky, ready to defend himself.

Where? Where are they?

Jason stilled. A robin flew from the brush to a nearby tree. A daylight moon hung in the sky. A contrail cut through the blue.

The heat faded from his neck, the crackling receded. All he heard were his hammering heartbeats.

Mud coated him from his chin to his shoes. He stunk of sulfur and earthworms. His palms stung. Blood seeped through the sludge and a knot welled up on his arm.

The rim of his front wheel was bent. "Crap." Jason scanned the path. He didn't want to try and explain to some stranger how he ended up in the ditch.

All clear. He lifted the frame and dragged it, crossing the bridge toward home.

Dad was in the garage. He looked up and away then a double take snapped his gaze back. He rushed out.

"What happened? Are you okay?" He grabbed Jason's bike and leaned it against the garage wall.

"Yeah, I'm fine. I . . . hit some gravel. Got a few scrapes." He showed Dad his dirty, bloody hands.

"Did you hit your head?"

"No, only hurt my hands. And my arm." He angled it forward and pushed up his sleeve. A deep bruise was tattooing into his skin.

"That's going to be ugly. You're sure about your head?" Dad pawed through Jason's hair.

He leaned away. "Yes, Dad, totally sure. I haven't cracked my head open." But he wasn't so sure something wasn't wrong with him.

In the house, Jason washed off the muck, rinsed off his face. He stripped to his boxers and piled his stinky clothes on the floor.

"Here. These are clean." Dad pulled sweat pants and a T-shirt out of a moving box, and thrust them at Jason.

"Thanks." He dressed. "Um, Dad, on my ride I saw—"

Dad hugged him. Hard. Solid.

"That kinda hurts." Dad released him but Jason wished he'd hugged longer.

"Sorry about that. But I'm so glad you're all right."

"That's okay, I didn't mind. It's just—"

"I know, bruises. I wasn't thinking." He squeezed Jason's arm. "I worry about you. We've all been through a lot, and this move isn't easy for any of us." He put his arm around Jason's shoulder. "But I know you're a good kid. Strong. And becoming more of a man every day."

Strong. Becoming a man. Jason's shoulders dropped back, lifting him a little bit taller.

"I interrupted you. What did you see on your ride?" Dad asked.

"Huh? Oh, just . . . " Telling Dad about the flying things could wait. " . . . this cool path that runs behind the houses on our street. There's a canal and stuff. I'll show you sometime."

"Great. I'd like that." Dad smiled.

Jason pushed aside the idea he might be losing it, seeing things that aren't really there.

Strong men don't lose it.

FIVE
Hideout

Jason woke early the next morning when his room lit up as if all of the sun rose just outside his window. He kicked off his covers. Static sparks flashed, tiny flares against his skin.

"Jeez, annoying." Jason swung his feet to the floor.

A blaze zinged past his face.

"Aaaaah." He swung his arms wide and dove to the ground, making a bunker of his bed. Seconds later he poked his head up, searched for the invader, readied his sheets as a shield.

Nothing came at him. Nothing flew by.

Dad bolted into Jason's room. "What's wrong?"

Jason hoisted himself onto the mattress. "Nothing. I must still be half asleep."

Not seeing things.

Dad came closer and lifted Jason's arm, examining his injuries. "Yep, you're getting super-sized bruises this time, with all the colors of the bruise-rainbow. Falling out of bed probably doesn't help. How do you feel?"

"Sore." Jason flopped back on his pillows.

"I figured as much. Don't overdo it today, okay?"

"No problem."

"Get showered and I'll see you downstairs. Della and I are making waffles."

29

"I'll be there in five."

After breakfast, Jason felt better. Solid. Himself. He wanted to move, to be outside. And prove to himself he was fine.

With his bike out of commission, he set out on foot. At the bridge, he stopped short. He scanned the sky.

No flying streamers. No flapping fins. No unidentified-whatever-creatures.

He didn't cross the bridge. Instead, he turned left and searched the thicket between the backyards of the houses on his street and the canal, hoping to find a shortcut to his own backyard. He found a section not as thick as the rest. Jason ducked in and pushed past twigs and branches, adding scratches to those already carved into his skin by his wreck.

The willows became thicker and tighter, the branches too packed to move. He started to back out but something yanked at his foot—his shoelace was tangled in the brush. Jason tugged and pulled. And made it worse.

He hunched to unsnarl it, then moved to stand but halted. There was a low gap in the brush. A weedy tunnel unseen from any other angle.

Jason shifted onto his knees and crawled forward. Spiky tendrils pulled at his hair and poked at his eyes. He tucked tighter and pushed through. After a few feet, he emerged into a natural cove six feet high, enclosed by branches, and brambles, and leaves. The area was about twelve feet across, carpeted with dried leaves and broken stems. The space was cool, quiet, and light but not bright.

Jason could see people walking the path on the other side of the canal. But it seemed like they couldn't see him. He tested the theory.

A woman came by.

Jason meowed. He was good at it. He always fooled Della.

The woman stopped, searched, and said, "Here, kitty-kitty." Twice. No cat to be found, she moved on.

Jason tried it again. He meowed and whistled. No one saw him.

Jason tucked into a corner of the cove, stretched out his legs and soon fell asleep.

"Hey."

In his dream, something nudged the bottom of his shoe.

"Hey you."

A girl's voice, louder now, and the nudge morphed to a smack against his rubbery sole. Light flashed on his face. Jason hurtled from sleep and remembered where he was.

"Wha, huh? What?" He rose halfway, opened his eyes.

She loomed over him, hip jutted, arms crossed. A silver bracelet shimmered and dangled from her wrist. "What are you doing here?"

"Who are you?" Jason sat up and tried to defog his head.

"Don't answer a question with a question. What are you doing here?" She pushed up the sleeves of her red hoodie.

"Sleeping, in case you hadn't noticed."

"You can't sleep here. You can't be here. This is *my* place." She said *my* like she owned both the word and the property.

Jason stood and brushed bits of leaves off his pants. "Says who? Who are you? And I didn't answer a question with a question, so your turn."

"Whatever." She was about Jason's age and had shoulder-length, dark brown hair. She wore black-framed glasses. A green and brown book bag sat on the ground.

Jason sighed. "Hey, if this land belongs to your family, I'm sorry. I didn't know. I'm new around here, just trying to figure things out." He started toward the tunnel. "I'll get out of your way."

"No, wait." Her voice changed from cold and flinty to almost friendly.

Jason glanced back at her.

"I'm Sadie." She held out her hand.

He hesitated, checked her expression then turned toward her. "I'm Jason." He shook her hand.

31

"Jason Lex, right?"

"Yeah . . . how did you know?" His mind swirled.

"You said you were new here, so I guessed. And we've actually met before."

"We have?"

"Yeah, but don't feel bad—I don't remember it either. We were like three years old or something. Our grandmothers are friends, and you guys came to some party. Apparently you and I had a great time together. Mamo told me all about it after she found out you were moving here, like it would all come rushing back to me with a little prodding. Again though, three years old."

"Right." Jason half-laughed. "And 'Mamo?'"

"Irish for grandmother." Sadie sat and pulled a laptop out of her bag. "And hey, don't be shocked if a lot of people already know who you are. Mamo helped your grandmother get your house ready. And it's a small town."

"Great." Jason was not-in-a-cool-way famous.

"Sorry about kicking your foot. I'm kind of particular about this place. It is one of the few spots I've found where I can really get away."

"That's okay. I get particular about my stuff, too." Jason thought about his chess set.

"Since you've already discovered my secret hideout, you might as well stay. If you want. I'm going to hang out and do some stuff on my computer." She typed something and waited. "There's enough space for both of us."

"Thanks, but I should be getting home anyway. Maybe I'll run into you again."

"Yeah, maybe. I'm usually here in the afternoon."

"Okay. See ya' later, Sadie. What's your last name?"

"Callahan."

"Nice to meet you, Sadie Callahan."

"You too, Jason Lex."

Jason pushed his way out of the brush and headed home. He passed a few people but avoided eye contact. Did they know who he was? He focused on the street and picked up his pace.

SIX

A Family Secret

S adie was easy to hang out with. She liked riding bikes and promised to show Jason some trails after his bike was fixed. And she liked playing video games. And she didn't care if she got dirt on her clothes. Hanging out with Sadie was almost as good as hanging out with Brandon.

Sadie spent a lot of time on her computer. She always had it with her.

Jason looked up from his book. "What's with the laptop?" Jason asked one afternoon when they were lounging in the cove.

She lifted her gaze over the screen. Her fingers stopped typing but didn't leave the keyboard. "What do you mean?"

"You always have it with you."

"I like it."

"Yeah, I get that." Jason swiveled in the dirt to face her. "But why?"

Sadie half-shrugged. "There's a lot of cool things you can do on a computer." Her tone suggested she was stating the obvious.

"True. Totally agree. But what can you do without Internet access?"

"I have access. There's WiFi all over the place."

"Secure WiFi."

"Some're locked, some aren't." She smirked. "Doesn't matter."

Jason's head tilted forward. "No way. You're a hacker."

"I'd hardly call it hacking. No one around here picks strong passwords." She pointed at Jason. "And you are forever sworn to secrecy."

"No problem." He waved both hands. "I don't want HackerGrrl messing with me. Or Callahacker. Or what should I call you?"

"Aren't you soooo amusing." Her fingers clicked across the keyboard.

"Don't you have some secret handle or something?"

"Secret being the key word. Couldn't tell you even if I did." Sadie didn't look up, but she was grinning.

Jason turned to the path and watched people go by. Some rode bikes, some walked their dogs. Once in a while someone jogged by, though that didn't happen often. But the most unusual person was the man on the scooter.

Jason had seen him a few times. The man was always looking behind him, like he was checking to see if someone was following. Sometimes he'd stop and stare at the water in the canal, then continue down the path. And he always rode a scooter and carried a video camera.

Jason heard the scooter first.

There was the engine's hum.

And there was the man.

He stopped and stepped off the scooter. His brown wavy hair had been pushed back by wind. He wore khaki pants and a red button-down shirt with a brown belt. A brown leather messenger bag hung at his side, the strap across his chest.

He reached into the bag, retrieved a video camera and aimed it at the sky. "Week number one hundred twenty-eight, point fifty-two, starting at southern sky directional, twelve o'clock." He moved in a slow, clockwise circle, keeping the camera pointed skyward.

"Three o'clock.

"Six o'clock.

"Nine o'clock.

"Twelve o'clock and complete."

Jason studied the sky and wondered if those flying things were up there. They had to have been a weird swarm of bugs. Probably seemed bigger than they actually were. He hadn't seen them again. All Jason saw now was sun and clouds and the occasional bird, none of which seemed to be the man's target.

After he finished his circle, the man put the camera in his bag and got back on the scooter. He held his hand over his brow to block the light.

"Finn." The man called. "Finnea—let's go."

A big dog with a broad chest splashed through the canal and lurched up the bank. She trotted over to the man, her tongue dangling out the side of her mouth, her large teeth visible as she panted. Her short, wet, white coat sparkled in the sun and it seemed like she'd been chiseled out of marble. Every muscle, every tendon, every sinew was tight and solid and hard. She shook off the water.

"Ah, Finn, would it be too much to have done that before you walked over to me?" The man wiped water off his face with his sleeve. The dog wagged her tail and stretched with her head down, butt up. She followed that with a lean into her front legs and a stretch to each back leg.

"All set?"

She kept wagging her tail.

"Let's go then."

They set off down the path.

"I cannot figure out that guy." Jason listened to the fading hum of the scooter.

"Hah. You and everybody else in Salton." Sadie's gaze stayed locked on the screen.

Jason turned toward her. "What's his deal? Is he crazy?"

"Very funny."

"Why is that funny?"

Sadie blew a bug off her keyboard. "Well, I guess it's not funny-funny like joking funny." She typed while she talked. "It's just funny that you would ask that question."

Jason scrunched his brow. "I don't get it."

Sadie stopped typing and looked at him. "Are you serious?"

He jutted his chin. "Yes. I'm serious. Why is that funny?"

She closed her laptop. "Because," she said, her voice slow and even, "if anyone should know if that guy is crazy, it's you. He's your uncle."

Jason stared. A tingle traveled across his scalp. "What are you talking about? Are you messing with me?" The tingling zinged down his arms.

"No." Sadie moved and sat next to him. "His name is Alexander Fallon. He's your mom's twin brother."

Jason's mind zipped, spun, sprinted. He searched everything he knew, for anything that made sense. Something that proved it wasn't true. Something that proved he wasn't related to the town weirdo.

Blank.

He shot to his feet and spun around to face her. "My mom's brother doesn't live here. He lives . . . somewhere else."

"He just moved back here last summer."

Jason backhanded the air. "And now we live here. Don't you think someone in my family would have said, *Oh by the way, you now live near your uncle?'* There's no way, Sadie. No way. That guy is not my uncle." Jason's heartbeat pumped heat through his skin.

Sadie held both hands up. "Okay, Jason, okay. Whatever you say."

"I've got to go." Jason crashed out of the cove.

Moments later, Jason stormed Dad's office.

Dad was shutting off his computer. "Jason, hey. What do you think about going out for—"

"Does our uncle live here?" Jason yelled.

Dad's head tipped back like the words had hit him in the forehead. "What?"

"Our uncle. Does. Our. Uncle. Live. Here. In Salton?" Jason's palms were sticky and his face was hot.

Dad's upper body buckled and dropped deeper into the chair. "Jason, I'm sorry, yes. Let's get everyone together and go to your grandmother's house and—"

"And what, Dad? Announce that the brother mom didn't like, that she never wanted us to meet, now lives in Salton and is going to be part of the family? Or are we supposed to keep ignoring him?"

Jason wheeled out of the office and bolted upstairs, two steps at a time. "Kyle, where are you?" He knew Della was at dance class, but Kyle should be there.

Dad dashed after him, stopping at the foot of the stairs. "Jason. Would you please wait—Jason!"

Jason rushed into Kyle's bedroom, slammed the door, and gushed out everything he knew.

Kyle didn't respond.

Jason's fast breaths came harder. "What? Did you already know?"

"Dude, I have no idea what you even just said to me. Start over."

Jason rolled his eyes and plopped down, across from his brother. He told him about the times he'd seen the guy on the path. He told him about the sound and the video and the counting. And he told him he's their uncle.

"Are you making this up?"

"No." Jason gestured to the door. "Dad totally confirmed it."

Dad yelled from the bottom of the stairs. "Your grandmother will be here in forty-five minutes. I'm going to get your sister from dance class and we'll get pizza for dinner."

Neither Jason nor Kyle responded.

"See?" Jason mimicked Dad's words with a faux-deep voice. "He wants her to come over and explain everything."

A moment later the garage door opened. The van started and sped away.

SEVEN

Truths Told

Jason steamed like the pizzas on the table. He refused to eat, until wafts of pepperoni wrestled away his determination. He grabbed a slice and tore away a mouthful.

Kyle wanted the whole story. "So what's the deal with the uncle? Why haven't we ever met him?"

Dad wiped his fingers and mouth with his napkin and returned it to his lap. "He and your mom had some issues, a bit of a falling out."

"But now that Mom's gone, so are the issues?" Kyle frowned but not so much that he couldn't take a huge bite of pizza.

"It's complicated, and I'll let your grandmother explain it. It's really her story to tell."

Grandma Lena sat back in her chair. "First, I'm sorry we didn't tell you, and introduce you all earlier. I hope you'll understand." She fidgeted with the gold chain she wore around her neck. "It was your mom's decision. You see, even though Adrienne and Alexander are twins, they were always different from each other.

"Your grandpa and I had no idea we were having twins. We had to scramble when we brought two babies home to a nursery prepared for one. I thought we'd have to use a laundry basket until we got a second crib." She zeroed in on a pepper mill like it was transporting her back in time. "But they were so small they both fit in one crib. And

40

they seemed to like it that way. Even as they grew older, they were as healthy as can be. They were inseparable. They had all the same friends. And they walked together to and from school every day."

Della put her hands on her hips. "Hey, why haven't you been walking me to school every day?" She directed her question to Kyle.

"There's lots of reasons, Della. First, because you are—"

"Kyle." Dad side-eyed him.

"Because your school started later than mine. So lucky Jason got to walk you all by himself." Kyle fake smiled at Jason and Della. Jason fake smiled back.

"What about my new school?" Della asked.

"We'll see." Dad nodded to Grandma Lena.

She continued her story. "In high school, Adrienne and Alexander started drifting apart. Your mom was social and determined to succeed at everything she tried. Alexander was a bookworm and liked to dig into problems, ask lots of questions and investigate everything. He'd get lost in his research, miss activities, and even skip school. He was a challenge."

Grandma Lena took a sip of her water. "Your mom graduated from college, became a psychologist and married your dad. Alexander got degrees in biology and zoology, but wasn't successful when it came to pursuing a career. Adrienne helped him get *real* jobs but Alexander would show up late, or fall ill and miss too much time. He lost several jobs. Then he'd disappear for weeks, supposedly on some research excursion but we had no idea where he'd gone. And when he came back we'd find him out of it, sometimes not sure of his own name. Your mom and dad and I would get him cleaned up, and he'd be fine for a time—even thrive—then he would crash again. It got to be too much. His doctors finally said we weren't helping him, we were enabling him. So Adrienne cut him off, said some tough things, and told him not to contact any of us again." Grandma Lena removed her glasses and rubbed her eyes, wiping away glistening tears.

"That was easier said than done for me. I kept in touch with Alexander, but I didn't help him financially like I had before. It took some time but your uncle did figure out how to make things work. He writes and publishes articles, and he teaches online classes through a community college. He's not wealthy by any means but he's doing all right." She sighed. "He never called your mother again. He was pretty hurt by what she'd said to him. I think he regrets that now."

Grandma Lena stared at the center of the table where the pizzas sat. But it seemed like she didn't really see them.

"If he's been doing better, why didn't Mom call him?" Jason asked.

Grandma Lena refocused and tilted her head toward him. Her lips pressed together, and the bottom one pulled in for a second. "Your mom decided there was too much risk of Alexander having another crash. She didn't want any of you to get hurt by it. I disagreed with her, tried to change her mind over the years, but she wouldn't budge."

Jason raised his eyebrows and flashed an expression at Kyle that said, *I told you he's whacko.* His brother wasn't the only one who got the message.

"I want each of you to understand something right now," Grandma Lena said. "Alexander is focused, and maybe a bit eccentric, but he is most certainly not mentally ill. Your father knows him, and he agrees with me, or he would never have moved you to Salton."

"I'm sorry we didn't tell you about him living here before we moved," Dad said. "We thought it would be best to give you some time to get settled first. But I guess that wasn't a very good plan."

Jason's mouth stayed shut. *Why do adults get things wrong? How could they think it would be a good idea to keep this a secret?*

Or is Uncle Alexander really more whacked than they are saying? Why else would Mom want to keep them away from him?

Kyle swallowed another giant bite of pizza and washed it down with a slug of water. "So what's next? When do we get to meet the guy?"

Dad checked his watch. "In about fifteen minutes. He's coming over."

For a second, everyone sat frozen in their seats.

Kyle spoke first. "Cool." He and Della each took another bite of pizza. Della chewed fast and swallowed. "Can I show him my dance competition ribbons? And my softball trophy?"

"Maybe. Let's see how things go," Dad said.

Jason jumped up. "You guys do what you want, but count me out. If Mom didn't like him, neither do I. I'll be upstairs until he's gone."

EIGHT
Uncle Alexander

Jason plopped onto his bed and picked up a magazine. He flipped the pages but paid no attention to them. His palms tingled. He dropped the magazine and wiped his hands on his bedspread.

He had to be ready. Dad would come upstairs, knock on his door, try to talk him into meeting Uncle Alexander. Jason needed a good reason why he was right and Dad was wrong, but all he could think of was, *Mom didn't like him.*

A couple of minutes later, the knock came. Jason ignored it. The door opened anyway.

"Can I come in?" Grandma Lena poked her head inside.

Jason scrambled to a seated position. "Uh, sure."

She sat next to Jason and for a moment, didn't say anything. Jason picked at the mailing label on the magazine's cover. Was she waiting for him to say something? Explain himself? He opened his mouth, tried to find a word, any word, but Grandma Lena spoke first.

"Grown-ups are stupid."

"Huh?"

"You heard me. Grown-ups are stupid. It's not something we like our children to discover, but you need to know."

Jason searched her face for a sign of a joke, or a trick. "I—uh . . ."

44

"It was stupid of us to keep your uncle from you. We should have told you right away, before you moved. And we should have introduced you all as soon as you got here. We were stupid."

"Okay, but—"

"And your mom was stupid."

"No. She was not stupid." Jason pushed himself back against his headboard.

"Not always, no. But we make mistakes, Jason. All of us. Ideally you make fewer mistakes when you grow up but it doesn't always work that way. And some mistakes are bigger than others." Grandma Lena tucked a curl behind her ear. "One of your mom's mistakes was cutting Alexander out of her life. Yes, he's had his challenges. He's made mistakes. But he learned from them. And he changed. But your mom never got to see that."

"She didn't like him."

"Not true. She loved him. And she thought she was doing the right thing." Grandma Lena patted Jason's leg. "She was wrong."

"Maybe she wasn't."

"She's not here, Jason. You are. This is your decision, not hers. And I'll add this." She stood. "If it were Kyle or Della, would you give them another chance or shut them out forever?" She stepped into the hallway. "I hope I see you downstairs. He'll be here soon."

Jason watched the door shut behind her.

✳ ✳ ✳

The doorbell rang. Jason walked to the top of the stairs.

Uncle Alexander stood on the porch, pinching the bridge of his nose. His hair was wet and slick, like he'd combed it after a shower. He wore khaki pants and a button-down shirt, the same kind of shirt Jason saw him wearing earlier, but this one was green.

Dad reached out to shake Uncle Alexander's hand. "Thanks for coming over on such short notice."

"Oh, no problem, no problem. I'm glad I finally get to meet my niece and nephews."

"Please, come in." Dad stepped aside.

"Hi, Mom." Uncle Alexander hugged Grandma Lena.

"Hello, Alexander. I'm so glad you're here." She popped up on her toes and kissed his cheek.

Uncle Alexander looked at Kyle and Della. He put his hands on his hips.

"Well, aren't you a sight," Uncle Alexander said. "I've seen pictures of you but you're much more handsome and lovely in person." He approached Della and offered his hand. "Della, it's nice to meet you. I'm Alexander. Or Uncle Alexander. Whichever you'd like to use is fine with me."

"It's nice to meet you, too." Her hand disappeared inside his grown-up one.

"You're very pretty, like your mom."

Della brightened. "Thank you."

Uncle Alexander stopped and squeezed the bridge of his nose again, scrunching his eyes tight. "Sorry. I have a little . . . headache. The pressure helps." He released it after a few seconds. "But enough about me." He stepped to his left and offered his hand again. "You must be Kyle. You're going to be a tall one, huh? Taking after your dad, I suspect."

Kyle nodded. "Nice to meet you." He didn't smile. "Are you sure you're okay?"

"Oh, I'm fine. That's just a way for me to manage the—well, it's not important. You're important. This, right now, is important. Nice grip on that handshake by the way. Says you're a man who knows what he wants." Uncle Alexander winked at Kyle.

Kyle shrugged. "I guess."

Uncle Alexander craned his neck, looked around the room. "Are we missing someone?"

Dad spoke. "Sorry, but Jason—"

"I'm here." Jason sauntered down the stairs and stopped at the landing.

Uncle Alexander turned to him. Jason expected Uncle Alexander to pinch his nose again, but he didn't. He balled his left hand and tucked it behind him, extending his right one to Jason. "How nice it is to meet you. I see both your mom and your dad in you. And from what I hear, you have your dad's talents when it comes to sports and chess."

"Yes sir. I mean, Uncle Alexander." Jason shook his uncle's hand using the firmest grip he could muster.

"Being athletic with a little geek mixed in means you can do almost anything. That's good stuff, Jason, good stuff." He winked and nodded.

Uncle Alexander's grip felt hot. Jason pulled his hand back and glanced at it, half expecting to find it glowing. It wasn't.

At Grandma Lena's suggestion, the group moved into the family room where the conversations sputtered with strained small talk.

Between pauses for nose pinching, Uncle Alexander asked all of the usual questions grown-ups ask kids. Jason and his siblings reported how old they were, what grade they were in, what sports they liked. Boring.

Uncle Alexander told ancient stories about Salton High School. He yammered on about living in Salton and where to get ice cream, where to go swimming, and which pond was best for ice skating in the winter. Then he started talking about high school again.

Jason slumped deeper into the couch. "So, Grandma Lena told us you're a teacher. What do you teach?"

"I teach biology and zoology. But my personal focus is cryptozo-ology." Uncle Alexander's expression was like a little kid who'd won a shopping spree at a toy store.

"Crypto, cryptozo, what?" Jason asked.

"Cryptozoology. It's like zoology, with a little *crypto* sprinkled on top." He chuckled at the joke only he found amusing. "I can see by your faces that I've left you in the dust of knowledge, where it's all dust, no knowledge." Uncle Alexander waited for a response.

None came.

"Okay, let me explain. Cryptozoology is the study of creatures that may or may not exist. Like Bigfoot. Or the Loch Ness monster. You've heard of them, yes?"

They nodded.

"Well, there are hundreds more of these creatures that you've probably never heard of. There's the Ahool, Moas, and the Dover Demon." He flexed back each finger as he listed them. "And the New Jersey Devil, and Kappa, and Skyfish, and the Mongolian Death Worm."

"Mongolian Death Worm?" Jason arched his brow.

"Yes." Uncle Alexander jumped to standing and pointed at Jason. "They live in the Gobi Desert and they range from two to five feet long. Maybe even longer. They're dark red in color—though some believe they can change to match their environment—and they spit acid and are capable of throwing electricity."

Seems like he's getting a few jolts of electricity right now.

"You've seen these things?" Kyle leaned forward.

Uncle Alexander's gusto snuffed out like a lit match dunked in water. "Well, no, I have not seen them. Not the actual *them* them, anyway. But I've been to the Gobi Desert and I've seen signs of them. *I've seen signs.*" He emphasized the last three words as if that would assure them of his credibility.

"Okay, what have you seen? Have you seen Bigfoot?" Jason asked.

"I have seen irrefutable proof of Bigfoot's existence. Casts of tracks, impressions that could have been made by no other creature. And I have seen the scalp of a Yeti—a close cousin to Bigfoot—at a monastery in the Himalayas."

Jason tipped his head and rolled his eyes in one grand motion, landing the gesture on his dad. Dad's face stayed neutral.

"And let me tell you this." Uncle Alexander pressed his hands into his temples for a few seconds then continued. "There was a time when people spoke of seeing man-like, furry and fearsome creatures in Africa, but these claims were always dismissed. That is, until European explorers discovered the mountain gorillas." He nodded slowly.

"The same goes for tales about giant sea monsters that were two times the length of a bus." His arms swung wide. "These tales were laughed off, but now we know the giant squid exists. And another animal that was once considered a hoax was described as part camel, part leopard. But you know it today as the giraffe."

"What else, Uncle Alexander?" Della's eyes were fixed on him.

"Oh, there are so many, Della, I could go on and on. But I think I might be overstaying my welcome." Uncle Alexander cocked his head toward Dad.

"Not at all, Alexander," Dad said, "but we should probably let you get home. It is getting late."

Uncle Alexander glanced at his watch. "Indeed it is. I hope we can do this again soon. In fact, if it's all right with you, Zachary, the kids are welcome to drop by my home any time, any time at all. We can continue our conversation there and I can share pictures and details from my investigations."

"I'm sure they'd love that. We'll set something up."

I'm sure I would not love that. Jason wanted to blurt it out, but truth was he was kind of intrigued.

Uncle Alexander thanked Dad for inviting him over and kissed Grandma Lena again. Della offered Alexander a hug and he accepted.

Jason put forth a formal handshake. Uncle Alexander received it as politely as Jason offered it. And Kyle extended a handshake that morphed into a man hug—complete with two pats on the back before a quick release.

"I hope to see you again soon, Kyle," Uncle Alexander said. He stepped out and the front door closed behind him.

Better Kyle than me. Even if Jason was intrigued, probably best not to spend too much time hanging with the town crazy dude.

NINE
Happy Fourth of July

Dad invited Uncle Alexander to join them at the Fourth of July parade a few days later. He declined, said he had some work to do, but he'd see them at Grandma Lena's for the barbecue later that day.

The Lex family, including Grandma Lena, found a spot on Main Street. It was prime parade-watching real estate.

Things weren't as good when they attended a parade in New York City a few years ago. Mom and Dad took turns holding Della so she could see past an old lady wearing a giant Styrofoam cowboy hat. Jason tried to ignore an extra-large man stuffed into jeans that left his butt crack uncovered. Kyle kept pushing Jason closer. Before contact was made, Mom pulled Kyle back, and Dad yanked Jason next to him where Jason enjoyed a close up view of lemon yellow stretch pants on butt-crack's big wife.

Today there was nothing but a clear line of sight for everyone.

"Bummer. No butt crack for you today, bro." Kyle punched Jason in the arm.

"I'm looking at one right now." Jason darted to the other side of Dad before Kyle could punch him again.

"Knock it off, both of you. Kyle, go stand next to your grandmother." Kyle slinked over but eyed Jason with a look that would keep Jason on guard the rest of the day.

The parade started with kids on bikes and trikes, decked out in red, white and blue ribbons and streamers and flags. They peeled off as soon as they saw their parents along the route. The fire truck came next, lights flashing, firefighters waving, a blast from the siren startling the crowd. A Dalmatian wearing a blue and white star-print kerchief rode on top.

Behind them came clowns who tossed candy at the crowd. It wasn't the good stuff, though, just mints, and butterscotch, and cinnamon buttons. The kind Jason ate only if he was desperate. He loaded his pockets and popped a piece of butterscotch in his mouth.

Screeching trumpets announced the marching band's approach. Della covered her ears.

"I guess marching and playing instruments at the same time is something they're still working on, huh?" Dad smirked at Grandma Lena.

She chuckled. "It's summer. Maybe they're out of practice."

The kids trudged by, some skipping to try and get back in step. "Or never practiced," Dad said.

Jason joined Della and covered his ears until the band passed.

Next, a float from the 4H Club rolled by. It was a plain flatbed truck carrying calves and piglets and dried stalks of corn. Della went gaga and asked if she could get a baby pig. Jason knew the answer and tuned out their conversation.

A familiar face caught Jason's attention. Uncle Alexander, across the street, filming the sky. His dog sat near him.

A man standing near Jason saw Uncle Alexander, too. "There's that mad hatter Fallon guy." He spoke to the woman next to him. "What is he doing?"

"Maybe he's looking for Bigfoot-shaped clouds." They slanted their heads together and snickered.

Jason rolled his eyes and stepped to the other side of his dad.

A few seconds later, crackling started and heat zinged down Jason's spine. He looked up. Golden streamers, not bugs, coming in fast.

Can't be real. Can't be.

Jason ducked one that darted at his head then dashed around Dad to avoid the next. He stayed low for a second then sprung and swatted at one near Della. She shrieked and grabbed Grandma Lena, pressing her face into Grandma Lena's waist.

Jason swung at another and jabbed Kyle in the ribs.

Kyle elbowed him back. "What the fu—?"

Jason swiped left and clipped Della's head. He swung in front of Grandma Lena and she swayed back. Jason spun behind her then punched near Dad, and back at Kyle.

Dad grabbed Jason's shoulders. "What has gotten into you?"

Jason scanned the area. The creatures were gone. "Those things were trying to get us."

"What things?" Dad's nostrils flared.

"The . . . the gold things. You didn't see them?"

"Jason." Dad shook his head.

Dad didn't see the gold creatures. No one had. No one but Jason. "There were . . . wasps, Dad, seriously. There were a bunch of wasps. They were attacking. I was trying to get rid of them." Jason breathed hard. "They're gone now. We're good."

Della peered out from behind Grandma Lena. "Are you sure?"

"Yep. All gone." Jason's eyes darted from Della to Dad.

Dad released Jason's shoulders and stared at him an extra second before returning his attention to the parade. Grandma Lena acted like nothing had happened.

How did they not see those things?

Jason looked toward the parade but his eyes found Uncle Alexander. He wasn't filming anything. He was gazing at Jason, his head tilted to one side.

TEN

Barbecue and Flying Things

They went to Grandma Lena's after the parade. She lived in a brick house with a front porch where a two-person swing swayed in the breeze. Red, white and blue bunting hung from the railing and an American flag draped from its pole. Fragrance from her rose bushes, loaded with white blossoms, saturated the air along the walkway to her front door.

Grandma Lena's backyard was party central. Lots of her friends milled about, holding drinks. She'd invited them over to celebrate the holiday and meet her family.

Card tables covered with starred-and-striped cloths dotted the grass, ready for diners. A gazebo tent shaded two picnic tables loaded with buns and mustard, chips and veggies, salads and brownies. A glass decanter of lemonade sweated in the heat.

Jason saw Sadie and walked over to her. "Hey, Sadie. Happy Fourth, or whatever."

"Yeah, happy Fourth." Sadie shifted her weight from one foot to the other. Then back. She clutched a curl of her hair and twisted it around her fingers. "I gotta ask, Jason. Um, are you okay?"

"Yeah I'm okay. Why wouldn't I be okay?"

"Because—" Sadie stopped twisting. She grabbed Jason's arm and pulled him to a less busy part of the yard. Her voice quieted. "Because you were pretty upset the last time I saw you."

She released her grip but kept her hand on his arm for a moment.

"Oh yeah, that . . . " Jason shook his head. "I'm sorry about that. It was just, I mean, I . . . " He shook his head like he was trying to dislodge the right words from the rafters of his brain. "I was surprised, I guess. Really surprised. You were right about my uncle. Sorry I was such a jerk about it."

"That's okay. I get it."

Jason recounted the rest of that day and told her about meeting Uncle Alexander. "Grandma Lena and my dad say he's fine. Kyle and Della think he's cool or something but I'm just not sure. I mean, he seems kinda off, and my mom didn't want him around." Jason kicked at a dandelion and watched the seeds puff into the air.

"He doesn't seem that bad to me, just a little quirky. And you can't really avoid him, can you? You're going to run into him. I saw him at the parade and—"

"Yeah. The parade. Did you see him filming the sky again? He said he couldn't come to the parade with us because he was *working*. Working at being bonkers, if you ask me." Jason kicked at two more dandelion heads.

Sadie coiled her hair again. "Jason, I saw you at the parade, too."

He stopped. "You did?"

"Yeah." Sadie bit her lower lip. She'd done that when she told him about his uncle, too.

"You saw me swatting at the, the wasps and everything? You saw that?"

"Yeah."

"They were attacking Della. I was just trying to help. She's totally afraid of wasps." He laughed like a bad actor in a bad movie. "She's such a baby."

Sadie dropped her hair and grabbed Jason's arm again, pulling him further away from the growing crowd. She faced him, took a deep breath and *whooshed* it out. "I didn't see any wasps. What is up with you?"

Jason's shoulders slumped and he walked away. Not hearing her follow, he turned back and, with a small sway of his head, motioned for her to join him. She jogged to catch up and they sat down on the grass in the farthest corner of the big backyard.

"I totally get if you don't want to be friends with me anymore," Jason said.

"Don't even say that."

"Well, I wouldn't want to be friends with me if I were you."

"Jason, you're being ridiculous. Tell me what's going on."

Jason wasn't sure why, but he felt like he could tell Sadie everything. He told her about his mom's disappearance. He told her about seeing his missing mom in their empty house. He told her about the flying streamer-like things chasing him. And he told her he was sure he was going crazy.

"So get away while you can. Could be contagious. Better safe than loony," Jason said.

"I'll take my chances."

"Then maybe it's too late and you're already turning."

"Since we're not talking about zombies or werewolves or vampires, I'm going to take a giant leap and say I think I'm good." Sadie smiled. "I know we haven't known each other that long, but we're friends and that's important to me. Even if you are losing it, I want to help. Well, help you not lose it." Sadie smiled. "Okay?"

Jason scanned her face for some indication she was only being nice so she could get away unharmed, before calling the mental hospital.

But she was calm. Nice. Sadie.

"Okay. So what do we do now?" Jason asked.

"I think we go hang out with grown-ups. Mamo is waving at us."
Sadie raised her arm and waved. "C'mon, you need to meet her."

Jason rose to his feet and wiped his hands on his jeans. "And my
I see gold streamers stuff?"

"We'll figure it out."

Willene Callahan, Mamo, was about the same age as Grandma
Lena but her hair wasn't as white. Mamo's was a mix of shiny, silvery
grays. She wore cropped khaki pants with a pastel pink blouse and
flowery scarf. Her glasses were purple, rectangular, cool.

"Jason." Mamo opened her arms and scooped him into a hug.
She scrunched him tight and vigorously shifted him left and right,
then released him. "I'm so delighted to finally, more officially meet
you. Though we have met before."

"I heard. When I was three."

"So Sadie *was* listening to my story." Mamo smirked at Sadie
then returned her gaze to Jason. "Yes, but we also met another time.
A few years ago, you and your grandmother stopped by my booth at
the county fair. I won best zucchini that year. And best decorative
vegetable platter. It was a gorgeous vegetable platter, if I may say
so myself. But you seemed more interested in the kettle corn, and
wandered off in that direction. Didn't get much of a chance to chat
with you."

"Ah, sorry about that." Jason put one hand in his pocket. "Kettle
corn just smells so good. But I'm sure your vegetable platter was
great."

Mamo huffed. "Great nothing—it was spectacular, thank you very
much." She flourished her hand through the air and took a slight
bow. "And very tasty. In fact . . . " From the table behind her, Mamo
brought forth a plate loaded with chunks of raw, red bell pepper.
"You're probably getting hungry."

Jason waved both hands. "Oh, no thanks. I don't really like . . .
those."

"Peppers. Try one." She jutted the platter toward him.

Jason glanced at Sadie, hoping she'd step in to save him. He didn't want to eat raw bell pepper, or any pepper, or any vegetable unless it was covered with melted cheese. Lots of melted cheese. Here there was no cheese.

Sadie took a pepper and popped it in her mouth.

Abandoned by Sadie and trapped between gross food and being rude, Jason picked the smallest piece of pepper he could manage, put it in his mouth, held his breath and bit. He chewed like he was in a hot dog eating contest, wanting the thing to go down fast. But four or five chomps in, he stopped, and breathed, and bit again. Slower.

"Hah. Exactly as I suspected. Would you like some more?" Mamo's voice oozed in I-know-you-can't-resist-it-ness.

Jason nodded and grabbed a handful. "But I hate peppers. I hate vegetables."

"Oh, you've never had vegetables. This is real food, Jason." She waved her arm over the display of veggies. "I grew these myself. We have cauliflower, tomatoes, carrots, onions, cabbage, squash—lots of good stuff. Those things you get at the grocery store? They've been forced and faked and fabricated until there's not much left of the original plan. So they taste like crap." She crunched into a carrot.

Jason's head bobbed. He'd never heard anyone's grandmother say *crap*.

Mamo caught the look. "What can I say? I call it like I see it. Guess you're learning that about me right from the get-go. Good deal."

Jason kept his mouth shut, and chewed, and smiled.

She turned to Sadie. "You be sure to bring him by the house and we'll show him the whole garden. And the beehives."

Jason forced down his mouthful. "Beehives? You live with bees flying around everywhere?"

"Yeah, it's no big deal. It's fun," Sadie said.

"Fun? Living around millions of things that want to sting you is fun?"

Mamo snickered and gave Jason's arm a little squeeze. "I promise you will live through a visit to our garden. Now if you two will excuse me, I'll go help Lena with a few more things." She walked toward the back of the house. Jason heard her chuckling.

"Jason, bees don't *want* to sting you," Sadie said. "All they want to do is gather nectar, and pollen, and take care of the hive."

"Right. Except they also want to sting you."

"No. Not right. They only sting if they, or the hive, are threatened."

"What about the time my family and I were having a picnic and one kept landing on my hamburger? I'd wave it away and it'd come right back. And then it stung me. What about that?"

"That was probably a yellow jacket."

"Same thing."

"No. Not the same thing. Yellow jackets like people food; bees—with the exception of sugary drinks—don't. Yellow jackets can be aggressive. Bees aren't. Yellow jackets can sting over and over. Bees die after one sting."

Jason paused.

"What about killer bees?" Jason put his hands on his hips then removed one hand to take another pepper.

"Ah, forget it. I'm going to get a plate." Sadie left Jason standing there alone with his veggies.

Someone tapped his shoulder. "Jason?"

It was Uncle Alexander. He wore a pale yellow polo shirt, black shorts, and Birkenstock sandals.

He's dressed like a yellow jacket. "Hi, Uncle Alexander."

"Hi. Um, how are you?"

"Um, fine?" Jason snipped. *Why is everyone asking me that question? Unless . . .*

"I watched you at the parade today. What was going on?"

Jason's head tipped back and he talked at the clouds floating by. "Jeez. Doesn't anyone actually watch the parade?" He looked at Uncle Alexander. "There were wasps. Or, er, probably yellow jackets. Yellow jackets were going on. No big deal."

Jason trudged away.

Uncle Alexander caught up to him. When they reached an area with more privacy, Uncle Alexander leaned close to Jason's ear. "I don't believe you."

Jason turned to face Uncle Alexander. "I don't care what you believe."

"You saw something."

"I saw yellow jackets."

Jason moved to get away.

Uncle Alexander stayed with him. "You saw something else, Jason. I can help you. I can explain it." He stopped.

Jason walked faster.

"Skyfish." Uncle Alexander yelled.

The crowd quieted. Jason rushed to the back gate and escaped.

ELEVEN

Skyfish

Jason had been swinging on the front porch for about twenty minutes when Sadie found him. She sat down next to him.

"Soooo . . ." She pushed her feet off the porch floor, helping to keep the swing swinging. "Skyfish?"

Jason slapped both hands on his forehead and pulled them down his face, stretching his eyelids, his cheeks, his lips. Then he dropped his hands to his thighs.

"Yep. Skyfish." He stared at the other end of the porch. "Maybe it's a Batty Fallon Family tradition to see Skyfish. Woo hoo. Lucky me." He waved his hands in the air and kicked the ground harder.

"I Googled it." She scuffed her foot, slowed the swing and opened her laptop.

"You Googled *Batty Fallon Family?*"

"No, smartass. I Googled *Skyfish.*"

"Wow, you Callahans have quite the vocabulary."

"Shut up and listen. Or actually, look. There are pictures."

She slid the laptop to Jason. He scrolled down the page where images of streamer-like things were flying through the air. Some had fins, or wings that ran the length of their bodies. Others were shaped more like missiles. Some were bright gold in color, some were white, some appeared almost clear.

"Is this what you saw?"

Jason nodded. "Mine were gold."

"And check this out." She leaned over and clicked on the bookmark icon. Down dropped a list of websites, each dedicated to the study of Skyfish, or, as some named them, Air Rods. She clicked on the first one.

Qualities of Skyfish a.k.a. Air Rods
- *Size ranges from a few inches to 100 feet*
- *Cylindrical in shape with multiple sets of wings or a thick membrane of wings down its body*
- *Torso undulates as it travels*
- *Travels in both air and water*
- *There are 1000-year-old carvings in Argentina that resemble Skyfish*
- *Speed estimated from 150-1000 mph*
- *Generally cannot be seen by the human eye; have only been seen on film*
- *Speculated that they are made of electromagnetic fluxes or some other form of energy; would explain why they are visible on film but invisible to most humans; or, they are made from some undiscovered fifth phase of matter (something other than a solid, gas, liquid, and plasma)*

"So, they're real?" Jason asked.

"Well, maybe. Or, yes, because you saw them. But not really."

"You're not helping."

"Sorry, that's not what I meant." She shut the laptop. "I think you saw them. And lots of people believe they're real. But the scientific community doesn't believe they're real."

"But all of those photos and film footage?"

"Some of it's fake."

Jason planted his feet and stopped the swing.

"But not all of it, Jason. Some of it is *not explained*."

Jason left the swing and sat on the porch across from Sadie. "Oh, well then that's great. Some of the hoaxers are talented enough to create high-quality fake pictures. Or movies. Or whatever."

"But you saw them."

Jason twirled his finger next to his temple. "Sadie. I come from cuckoos. Fruitcakes. Loonies. Have you met my uncle?"

"Just go talk to him."

"Why? What is he going to tell me? He believes this stuff. He's a crypto . . . a cryptoz . . ."

"A cryptozoologist."

"Yeah. Crypto—crazyologist. He'll tell me what he believes and I already know what that is." Jason stepped back to the swing and dropped hard in the seat sending it cranking madly against its chains.

Sadie grabbed an armrest until the ride stabilized. "Well, I don't think it would hurt to go talk to him. Maybe he can prove they really do exist." She kicked off her sandals and folded her feet underneath her. "And I'd like to go talk to him."

Jason looked at her like she was the one who was nutso, but Sadie didn't cave.

Jason held up his hands. "Fine. We'll go tomorrow. But only because you want to."

"Fine."

"And we don't tell anyone. I don't want anyone to know I'm willingly visiting my out-to-lunch uncle."

"Done."

TWELVE
Attacked

Jason and Sadie arrived at Uncle Alexander's house the next afternoon. It was like many other houses in Salton except it sat by itself outside of town on a large lot. Jason rang the doorbell.

"This is exciting." Sadie rubbed her hands. Her laptop bag hung on her shoulder.

"Exciting isn't exactly the word I'd use, but okay." Jason pressed the bell again.

Woo woo woo woo woo. Wooo woo woo. Woo woo woo woo woo. Barks bellowed from inside the house.

"That must be Finn," Sadie said.

"You know Finn?"

"Jason. Small town, remember? I haven't actually met Finn. I just know of Finn."

Uncle Alexander opened the door. His eyes widened. "Jason. And Sadie, right? Willene Callahan's granddaughter?"

"Right. It's nice to meet you."

"You, too. Please, come in."

Sadie and Jason stepped inside. There sat Finn, grinning and panting at her visitors.

Jason eased away from the burly dog. His pulse thumped in his chest. "We thought you might not be home."

64

"Sorry about that. We were out in the workshop and I didn't hear the doorbell but Finn insisted we come back to the house and here we are." He shut the door. "I am surprised to see you."

"Yeah, well, Sadie wanted to come over."

Sadie punched Jason in the shoulder.

"And so did I. To see your workshop. And to talk or whatever." Jason glanced to his uncle and back to Finn. Her tail wagged rapidly.

"I'm glad you're here. Both of you." Alexander looked at Sadie. "But I've been rude. I should properly introduce you to my Finn." He turned toward the solid, white dog. "Finn, this is Jason."

Finn stepped up to Jason. He scrunched his eyes and backed into the wall. Finn ducked under his hand and tilted her head so Jason's fingers fit behind her ear.

"She won't hurt you. She wants you to give her a scratch."

Jason scratched while maintaining as much distance as he could manage. "But isn't she a pit bull?"

"Pit bull mix. And pit bulls are misunderstood. Dogs don't come preprogrammed to hurt anyone. People make them mean." Uncle Alexander waved his arm in Sadie's direction. "Finn, come meet Sadie."

Sadie gave Finn's back and chest a good scratching. "What a good girl you are, Finn. You're a sweetie."

Uncle Alexander crossed his arms. "Ah, success. It seems neither of you will die by Finn's hand, er, jaws."

"But you said—" Jason scooted away from Finn.

"I kid. You have nothing to fear. I do know a few Chihuahuas you should worry about. They're spoiled brats and would take your fingers off in a second. But not Finnea. She's all good."

Finn moved to Uncle Alexander and nuzzled his leg as if she understood every word.

He patted her shoulder. "Okay. You said you wanted to see the workshop. Let's go see the workshop."

Sadie and Jason followed him out the back door. They crossed the yard and entered another building, a smaller version of the main house.

"This was a carriage house, back in the day," Uncle Alexander said. "Now I use it for my files and reference materials, and I have a laboratory where I can examine samples and specimens. I also store all of my gear here, cameras, night scopes, motion detectors, sonar equipment, et cetera."

They stepped inside a musty room that would make a hoarder feel at home. Books were stuffed on shelves and piled on the floor. Filing cabinets—some metal, some wood, some tall, some short— overflowed with folders and papers and tabs. A large wooden dining table pushed against a wall was scattered with papers and pamphlets. Underneath it was a jumbo dog bed cradling a well-loved bone. Finn nosed the bone over and curled onto the bed.

Next was a kitchen that was equally messy, but not with books. Beakers, flasks and slides filled two sinks. One open cupboard door revealed old microscopes and Bunsen burners stained black and blue from fire. Another cupboard held graham crackers and dog treats.

They left the kitchen, walked down a hall and followed Uncle Alexander through a metal door with a coded lock. They stopped. And stared.

"Ta da." Uncle Alexander moved his arms like he was conducting an orchestra.

The room was a shiny, fancy laboratory. There were glass cupboards labeled and stocked with supplies, neatly stacked, carefully organized. A variety of machines and scopes sat on the counters. Fluids bubbled, spinners spun and printers printed out data. It smelled like a doctor's office.

"Wow." Jason and Sadie said in unison.

"I guess that means you approve."

66

Jason crossed to a Plexiglass container that covered the wall, floor to ceiling. It appeared empty, but every few seconds a spark popped inside, each a different color than the one before it, and never in the same spot. A purple spark flashed near Jason's face and he jumped.

"Apologies," Uncle Alexander said. "Energy monitor. Dangerous on the inside, but you're perfectly safe where you are."

Jason nodded and moved toward Sadie. She stood by bins containing samples of fur, scales, and skin. Or leather. Or something. Sadie nudged Jason and pointed to a label. *Bigfoot-382-1926.* She smiled. Jason rolled his eyes.

"Is that really—"

An alarm sounded and Uncle Alexander hurried to a bubbling beaker, its contents threatening an overflow. He adjusted a knob and the green concoction settled to a simmer. "Much better. Certainly don't need that on the loose in here." He wiped his hand on a towel.

On the counter next to him sat a plastic bin containing a four-fingered hand—three fingers with orange claws, and the fourth looking like the tip had been cut away. The label read *Kappa-413-2014.*

"Kappas have an ability to heal. I'm part of a team studying their biology, hoping to determine how their healing ability works so we can recreate it for the medical community. Could be a game changer."

"Awesome," Sadie said.

"Right . . .um, how did you do all this? Get all this stuff?" Jason asked.

"Things like the Kappa claw—often they're donated for research as part of an individual's last wishes, that sort of thing."

"So you're saying they're real, the Kappas."

"Of course."

"And you bought all this lab stuff?" Jason waved his arm over the room.

"There's an organization backing my work, and the work of others like me around the globe." Uncle Alexander showed them the rest of the lab, introducing them to each machine and scope, explaining their purpose and output. He shared facts, and data, and enthusiasm.

Jason's mind whirled. "So this is all part of your crypto . . . zoology stuff."

"Yes." Uncle Alexander nodded. "But there's more to it than cryptozoology. Let's go back to the house where we can be comfortable. We'll chat."

✳ ✳ ✳

Uncle Alexander went to the kitchen. Jason and Sadie waited in his living room. The walls were decorated with artwork—a painting of a landscape, African masks, a metal sculpture shaped like a tree growing both up and down, and another painting that seemed to be nothing more than a canvas covered with charcoal-colored paint.

"What is that supposed to be?" Jason pointed at the charcoal painting.

"Dirt?" Sadie tilted her head sideways.

"Does that make it any better?"

She tipped her head back to straight. "Nope."

In one corner of the room stood a totem pole, about ten feet high and three feet in diameter. In another corner stood a bronze sculpture of a woman reaching up from a pool of water, her fingers inches from the high ceiling.

Finn plopped onto a dog bed in front of a stone fireplace in the center of one wall. Two brown leather couches flanked the fireplace and faced each other, a wooden coffee table between them. Jason and Sadie sat on one of the couches. Uncle Alexander came in with a tray of red drinks, set it on the coffee table, and took a seat on the couch opposite them.

Jason picked up a glass. A vaguely cherry smell crept into his nostrils. He took a gulp. "Is this Kool-Aid?"

Sadie sipped and scrunched her face then smiled.

"Isn't this what kids drink these days?" Uncle Alexander took a big swig.

"Kids, maybe. Like five-year-olds." Jason set his glass on a coaster imprinted with *I Believe in Bigfoot.*

Sadie followed, setting her glass on a coaster that read *I Survived a Chupacabra.*

"You don't like it? I drink it every day. Makes me feel young." He twirled his hand in the air.

Crazy guy with a sugar rush. Excellent.

"It's just a little sweet for me." Sadie wiped her finger on a napkin leaving red splotches behind.

Finn snored. For a long moment, her snoring was the only sound in the room.

"So," Jason said, "nice artwork."

"Thank you. I've collected it during my travels."

"Where have you traveled?"

"All over."

"Like where?" Jason asked.

Sadie moved her gaze back and forth as if she were watching a slow match of ping pong.

"Almost everywhere," Uncle Alexander said.

"Nice, I guess."

Uncle Alexander broke the rhythm. "Do you really want to talk about my world travels? Or should we get to the Skyfish?"

Jason took a long draw of Kool-Aid and set it back down. "Skyfish it is, Alex." Jason used to watch Jeopardy with his mom.

"Skyfish are all around us." Uncle Alexander stood. He spoke to the whole room, like a professor giving a lecture. "They're also known as Rods or Air Rods, and there are stories of Skyfish from far back in history. As early as 747 AD, people in China described serpents flying through the air. We believe they were describing Skyfish. And there are thousand-year-old carvings in Argentina that appear to be Skyfish."

Just like the Internet said. Maybe he wrote it.

Uncle Alexander took a few more swallows of his drink and continued. "While some have reported seeing them with the naked eye, most humans are not capable of spotting Skyfish without the use of cameras. Images of Skyfish have been captured on film all around the world, both in the air and underwater. Additionally, there is some evidence that Skyfish are capable of moving through solid objects such as walls or even people."

Jason fought the urge to interrupt. To laugh. To leave. He crossed his arms.

"We believe that these are intelligent and even playful creatures. There is photographic evidence of them chasing each other around, likely for fun, and even interacting with birds. I have some pictures—" He reached for a folder on the lower shelf of the coffee table.

"Oh," said Sadie, raising her hand. "We saw some pictures already. I found them on the Internet."

"You did? Okay, then, I will skip the pictures . . ." Uncle Alexander fumbled with the folder.

"Jason, tell him," Sadie said.

"Tell him what?"

"Tell him what you saw."

"It wasn't really anything." Jason's voice tensed.

Sadie tsked.

"That's right. That's where we were going, isn't it?" Uncle Alexander's fumbling stilled. "You saw them at the parade."

"No I didn't."

"Yes, you did."

"I couldn't have. I didn't have a camera," Jason said.

"You saw Skyfish."

"No camera."

"Skyfish."

"No camera."

Sadie slapped her hands on the leather couch. "Knock it off."

They turned their heads like she'd smacked them instead.

Uncle Alexander took a deep breath and released it. "I know what you saw. You saw it with your own eyes." He removed a flash drive from his pocket. "And I have it recorded."

Jason uncrossed his arms and leaned forward, mouth open.

"Let's see," Sadie said, far too much excitement in her voice.

"Let me get my computer from the lab."

"I have my laptop," Sadie removed the computer from her bag and switched her seat, sitting next to Uncle Alexander. "C'mon," she said to Jason, snapping him out of his stupor. He moved to the other side of his uncle.

Uncle Alexander handed the flash drive to Sadie. She loaded the video. The picture showed blue sky above the parade, then fragments of the parade, then blue sky again.

"Apologies, no time to edit. It's coming," Uncle Alexander said.

Another minute in, the camera did a double take, streaked past the crowd and refocused on the Lex family. There was Jason swiping and swatting, ducking and dodging, swinging and taking Kyle's punch. There was Della squealing, Dad worrying, and Grandma Lena holding onto Della.

And there they were—Skyfish. Zooming, and zipping, and diving. About a dozen of them.

Attacking the Lex family.

THIRTEEN
The Order

O h . . . my . . . God," Sadie said. They watched the Skyfish streak around and then they were gone. The lens jerked through the air trying to find them again but failed. The screen went dark.

"For what it's worth," Uncle Alexander said, "I don't think they were attacking. I think they were playing. But I've never heard of this before. It's usually just one Skyfish, maybe two at the most."

Jason rolled his eyes but no one noticed because he was still focused on the laptop. "Again. Please."

Sadie hit the play button. And then again. And then a fourth time. And after every time they watched it, Sadie said, "Oh my God," like it was the first time she'd seen it.

"You really did see those things," she said.

"Yeah, I guess I did." Jason turned to Uncle Alexander. "Do you think other people recorded them at the parade, too?"

"It's possible," said Uncle Alexander. "But most cameras were aimed at the parade, not at your family. Even if people caught snippets of them, they'd explain them away as a trick of the light. I don't think we need to worry about that."

"No, it would be *good* if other people recorded the Skyfish. They'd have proof that Skyfish are real, and you have proof with this recording, and I can validate it since I witnessed it, right?" Jason stood and walked across the room. "I mean, this is great. We can show this to everyone, to the whole world. We'll put it on the Internet. And we'll prove to everyone that Uncle Alexander isn't mental—oh, sorry Uncle Alexander." Jason held his palms out toward his uncle. "No offense."

"None taken, none taken. I'm fully aware of my reputation in this town. But—"

"But now we can prove that you're not whacko. And you'll be famous." Jason's pace increased with the volume of his voice. "And maybe I'll be famous too. And—"

"And you can't tell anyone."

Jason stopped. "What?"

"You can't tell anyone," Uncle Alexander said.

"What are you talking about? Jeez. Maybe you are loco after all. We don't tell anyone—we tell *everyone*."

"Why can't we?" Sadie asked.

"Because, well, because it's not the right thing to do."

"Aw, c'mon. You're not making any sense. How can it not be 'the right thing to do'?" Jason mocked his uncle's words with air quotes. "I thought the whole point of cryptozoology was to prove the existence of mysterious creatures."

Uncle Alexander shut his eyes and squeezed the bridge of his nose. "There are things you don't know. And we can talk about those things. But not today." He waved one hand. "This has been enough for today."

"No way. You can't say something like that and bail. What things?"

"Another time." Uncle Alexander opened his eyes and picked up the folder. "I need to put this away and . . . and Finn needs her dinner." The dog's ears perked.

"Uncle Alexander, c'mon. I'm already here. Just tell me now." Jason sat and leaned toward his uncle. "Please."

"These topics would bore poor Sadie to death." He sort of smiled at her. "And so it makes more sense that you and I talk one-on-one *another time.*"

Uncle Alexander wanted to leave Sadie out of the discussion. "What's the big deal? You can tell me stuff in front of her."

Uncle Alexander's head jerked. "That's not a good idea." He put the folder down and picked up their glasses. "Are you finished with these?" He didn't wait for an answer and took them to the kitchen.

"Actually, I'd love some water." Jason called to Uncle Alexander. He glanced at Sadie and she nodded. "Same for Sadie."

"I think we're stressing him out," Sadie said.

"But he already told us about Skyfish, and Kappas. How much more can there be to tell?"

A long moment later, Uncle Alexander returned with ice water for everyone. He handed one to each of them and sat. His knee bounced. "This isn't how it's done." He muttered to himself and picked at lint on his pants.

"This isn't how what's done?" Jason kept his voice low.

"There are too many unknowns, too many anomalies. This isn't how it's supposed to be done." Uncle Alexander pinched the bridge of his nose and stared at the ceiling.

Jason glanced at Sadie.

Should I go? Sadie mouthed the words. Jason shook his head.

Uncle Alexander stood, downed his water, and took his glass to the kitchen. Another minute passed. He came back, glass full, and sat. "Things aren't like they're supposed to be but that seems to be the new standard, doesn't it, Finn. Everything's off. Or new. But mostly off."

Finn raised her head toward Uncle Alexander, twice *thwacked* the floor with her tail and relaxed.

Uncle Alexander drained his glass. He seemed to be pondering the ice cubes. Jason thought his uncle was about to make another break for the kitchen. He didn't.

"Skyfish are real."

"Yeah, we got that," Jason said.

"And so is everything else."

"Everything else?"

"Bigfoot, Loch Ness, Chupacabra, Ahool, Moas, Dover Demon—all of them. Well, a lot of them. There are still some we haven't confirmed so I don't want to exaggerate."

Sadie's eyes widened and she covered her mouth with both hands. Her eyes flicked from Uncle Alexander to Jason and back to Uncle Alexander. Then to Jason again with a *say something* look.

What do you say to a person who's been off the deep end for so long, there might not be any ladder out of that pool?

Jason started slowly. "Okay . . . every monster-thing is real—"

"They aren't monsters, Jason. That's the first thing you have to learn."

"Okay . . . every crypto-thing—"

"Cryptids."

"Cryptids. They have a name. I guess we're getting somewhere." Jason arched his eyebrows at Sadie. She shrugged.

"I know how this sounds. I thought the same thing when my dad told me and Adrienne about it."

"Please don't drag my mom into this—"

"Jason, stop." Uncle Alexander's eyes darkened. He lasered in on Jason. "Just listen. Sit there, mouth shut, and listen."

For a micro-second, Jason was ready to bolt. But he stilled, scooted back into the couch and gestured to Uncle Alexander that the floor was his. Sadie switched seats to sit next to Jason.

Uncle Alexander spoke. "Cryptids exist on this planet just as humans do. They live in the air, on land, and in water. Evidence shows that they have been on this planet at least as long as humans, and probably longer."

Jason raised his hand.

"Yes, Jason?" Alexander sighed.

"If they live here, and have always lived here, why is it that no one knows about them?" *Other than the fact that they don't exist.*

"There are many that do know about them and I'll get to that. In the meantime let me explain why they are unknown to most of the human population. First, you know that the human body operates with and generates electricity, yes?"

"Yes," Sadie said, "protons, neutrons and electrons send electrical signals through the body."

"Right. Cryptids generate electricity too, some at a much higher level. Humans produce between ten and one hundred millivolts. But some cryptids have generated as much as ten thousand times that amount."

"Seriously? As in you-seriously-expect-me-to-believe-this?" Jason shook his head, but remembered the crackling he'd heard when the Skyfish were near.

"Yes I do expect you to believe this. Even the non-cryptid electric eel—which by the way, isn't a true eel at all but is actually a member of the Knifefish family—can generate six hundred volts of electricity. That's six hundred thousand millivolts—one thousand times the human body."

Sadie's fingers flew across her keyboard. "Hmm." She nodded at her laptop.

"You're buying this?" Jason asked.

"What's not to buy? I Googled the electric eel—it's true."

Uncle Alexander continued. "Besides the amount of electricity generated, there is one other big difference. While our bodies *contain* the electricity—at least for the most part—many of the cryptids' systems actually *project* electricity either voluntarily or involuntarily. If a human came in close contact with such a cryptid, especially where the projection is involuntary, there would likely be disastrous results." He pushed his hand through his hair.

"In the simplest terms, it's like plugging a one hundred and ten volt appliance into a two hundred and twenty volt outlet. Lots of popping or burning or shock."

"So the Skyfish could have killed me?"

Uncle Alexander shook his head. "Only if they wanted to—their systems are voluntary. And of course the shield would have to be compromised."

"There's a shield? What shield?" Jason asked.

"I'm getting ahead of myself." He stood with his glass. "I'm going for a refill. Would you like more?"

They shook their heads. Uncle Alexander went into the kitchen.

"You don't think this is totally whacked?" Jason asked Sadie.

"Yeah, but . . . we saw the recording. You saw them in real life. Shouldn't we keep listening?"

"I guess . . . " *Mom might disagree.*

Uncle Alexander returned with a plate full of cheese and crackers and fresh veggies. "These are from Willene's garden. Mom—Grandma Lena—doesn't think I eat enough vegetables and apparently shared that with Willene, so she drops them off every so often. I thought you both might like some."

They munched for a moment and Jason spoke. "So you were going to tell us about a shield?"

"Right—the Rampart." Uncle Alexander stuffed a cheese-loaded cracker into his mouth.

Jason shrugged. "Huh?"

Uncle Alexander continued chewing, holding one finger in the air. He waved his other hand at his mouth and bobbed his head as if that would mush the food faster. He swigged his drink. "Sorry about that." He took one more swallow, set it down and slapped both hands on his legs.

"Okay, here's the bigger picture." Uncle Alexander walked to the totem pole. He fiddled with something on the side of it and triggered the lower jaw of the center face to spring out. He removed a thick book and brought it to the table. "Clear the food and drinks for me would you? Can't take any chances with this."

Jason moved the items to a stand behind the couch and Uncle Alexander sat down next to Sadie. He placed the book on the coffee table. Jason returned to the couch.

The brown leather cover was worn, and stringy pieces drooped around the edges. A gold medallion rose from the leather, an O surrounded by intricate design and black stones. The title on the cover was faded, the corners bent. Gold flecks of paint freckled the embossed letters.

Order of the Rampart Guards
Alexander Fallon

Jason ran his finger over the lettering. A spark snapped him through the cover and he jerked. An odd flutter skipped through his gut and he tucked his hand under his thigh. He glanced at Uncle Alexander and Sadie. Neither had noticed. "What is this?"

"This, my dear nephew, is what we are. Our family's legacy." Uncle Alexander opened the book. "Regions around the world are assigned Rampart Guards who are charged with sustainment of the Rampart—the shield I mentioned—to maintain the balance of energy between cryptids and humans, ensuring peace and safety for all." Inside the front cover was a chart that unfolded across the full length of the table, then unfolded down, and down, and down some more. Branches and names filled the paper. Sadie and Jason crowded closer.

Uncle Alexander pointed to a name. Tate Fallon. "This is my father, your grandfather." The name was written in gold ink, as were some of the others. But most were written in black.

He pointed to another name in gold. "This is my grandmother. Before her, it was her father, and before him, his mother." All of the names he touched were in gold.

His hand moved back toward Tate Fallon and then passed it to the next line down. There were two gold names. "And you know these two, of course," he said.

The names were Alexander Fallon and Adrienne Fallon. Jason paused with his mother's name, brushing it lightly.

"What does the gold mean?" Jason asked.

"The gold indicates those in the family who have been selected. They are the Rampart Guards." Uncle Alexander's chest puffed, his back straightened.

Jason pulled himself away from the chart. He searched his uncle's face for any sign that confirmed this was the truth and not some fairytale. Nothing clicked. "How did you guys get the assignment? Did you have to pull a sword out of a stone? Rescue a damsel in distress? Kill a dragon?"

"What?" Uncle Alexander sucked in a gasp. "No. We would never kill anyone. Besides, we're more maintenance workers than defenders. Guard is simply a title."

"So you don't wear a suit of armor to bed, just in case?" Jason mimed a sword slashing through the air.

"No." Uncle Alexander's jaw clenched.

"What about Jason?" Sadie asked, derailing Jason's questioning. "And his brother and sister? All of their names are in black."

"I'm not sure about that. Used to be that one Guard would be chosen from each generation. They were identified when their names were added to the chart shortly after birth. The specialized ink automatically changed to gold confirming their assignment. It meant they were born with special gifts, an ability to produce and channel energy, and survive even without the protection of the Rampart. Can't have a Guard go poof when they're implementing a repair." Uncle Alexander chuckled. "But things have been a bit out of kilter since Adrienne and I showed up."

He pointed to his and his sister's name, tapped twice on the paper.

"We surprised everyone, not only because there were two of us when our parents were only expecting one, but because both of our names turned gold." He seemed to sink into the ink, thinking about the past.

"What happened?" Sadie asked.

Uncle Alexander sat on the floor near the end of the couch, closer to Finn. She scooched herself over and put her head on his lap.

"It went to the League of Governors for review and they decided for the first time that there would be two Guards from one family in our region also from the same generation." He rubbed Finn's chest and she rolled onto her back. "They even summoned us to headquarters, gave us specialized training."

"The League of Governors? And you can channel energy?" Jason asked. *This was getting crazier by the minute.*

"Yes. The League of Governors is the ruling body, made up of world leaders and other representatives from every region, human and cryptid alike. They oversee the Rampart, the human and cryptid relationship, rules and regulations and so forth."

"World leaders, like the President of the United States."

"Yes, of course."

"Okay . . ." Jason tried to process the story. "Run through this again. You and my mom are—or, she was and you still are—Rampart Guards."

"Yes."

"Which means you can harness and use energy to repair and maintain this shield, the Rampart?"

"Yes."

"Do you use tools or something?"

"Just ourselves, our bodies."

Jason looked at his uncle. He pursed his lips. "And if the Rampart fails?"

Uncle Alexander gave Finn's chest one more scratch and then stood.

"If the Rampart fails, energy from the cryptids will destroy every human on earth."

FOURTEEN
Protect or Destroy

estroy every human on earth? What the . . . ? Jason slumped into the couch.

Uncle Alexander folded and tucked the chart back inside the musty book. "Oh don't worry—it would take a catastrophic failure for that to happen, and that's highly improbable. The Rampart is divided into regions, and we have regional Guards assigned worldwide. Each region operates separately, and there's never been a major incident. And even if one region did fail, it wouldn't impact the entire human population."

"Well, that's a relief," Sadie said. "So . . . what would be impacted?"

"Depends on the region. Populations vary between them." Uncle Alexander rubbed his temple. "If a region fails where there is more ocean than land, the impact would be less severe."

"What about our region?" Sadie asked.

"Oh, well, that's about a third of Canada, the US, and Mexico."

Sadie gasped.

This is real and *this is crazy* battled in Jason's brain. "Okay . . . then how does it, this Rampart, how does it work?" he asked.

"It's an energy field powered by the earth's core. It's attracted to the electricity projected by cryptids and attaches itself to them, keeping that electricity in check, like a damper. In essence, each cryptid has their own shield. It's not harmful in any way, and in fact they don't even notice it."

"Wait—they don't know this is being done to them?" Sadie's voice pitched up.

"That's not what I meant. They know about it. It's been agreed upon for centuries. The Rampart is benign and doesn't hinder them in any way."

Sadie's shoulders eased.

"So why do you need the Guards?" Jason asked.

"The Guards are the reason it's been working for centuries." Uncle Alexander flipped pages to a chapter titled *Symptoms and Signals*. "There are a number of things that indicate a breakdown in the Rampart." He pointed to a blurry picture of Bigfoot walking across a field. "This is one such indication."

"I've seen that photo before," Sadie said. Jason nodded his agreement.

"When all is working as it should, humans can't see cryptids. But if the shield is damaged or weakened somewhere, cryptid sightings spew forth." Uncle Alexander *whooshed* his hands high. "Some folks have been lucky enough to have a camera at the ready, even more so now that cell phones include cameras, but the remaining power in the shield keeps those photos blurry. That's what happened here." He tapped the photo of Bigfoot.

"A nearby Guard—and there are hundreds, multiple Guards in every region from a number of different families—is dispatched when signs demonstrate such a necessity."

Jason remembered his mom leaving on business trips. There were many conferences and meetings she was *invited to attend at the last minute.*

Uncle Alexander continued. "Sightings by humans aren't the only attestations." He flipped a few pages. "There are many. Sun dogs, for instance. And sun halos. Even some double rainbows depending on the intensity. And certain types of lightning strikes. And cloud formations. And wind." Uncle Alexander put his hand on the book.

"We also conduct regular maintenance on the Rampart. There are access points all over the world. You've heard of energy vortices?"

Jason and Sadie shook their heads.

"Vortices are high energy spots on the earth. Some have been identified and documented, but there are many more that are unknown to anyone but the League of Governors, and in turn the Guard. These vortices are access points to the heart of the Rampart. We check energy levels and efficiencies, slough off excess energy or boost energy levels, whatever is needed to keep the Rampart in peak operating condition. Guards use their bodies to interact with the Rampart."

"Your body, in the shield, like electrocuted?" Jason asked.

"That's oversimplifying it, but in laymen's terms, yes. Guards are not harmed. It would take that catastrophic event, a huge surge of power, for the Rampart to damage a Guard." Uncle Alexander ran one hand through his hair. "Of course being a Guard takes training and skill. As I mentioned, Guards are born with a certain level of ability. The ability is then developed and honed through apprenticeship with the Guard-in-service, learning to channel energy in a controlled, productive, efficient way."

"And for us, you're the Guard-in-service," Jason said.

"After the loss of your mother, yes."

"But I thought that the League of Governors approved both of you?"

"That's right. We trained with our father and worked well together. In fact, training as two gave us a power not before seen in a Guard and hopes were high that we would establish a new level of safety and security." Uncle Alexander closed the book and slid it slowly to the end of the coffee table.

"What happened?" Sadie's lips puckered as the words left her mouth. "Oh, sorry, I don't mean to push. Or pry. Or . . . "

83

Uncle Alexander's eyes were soft. "That's okay, Sadie. We've come this far." He leaned into the cushions and sighed. "Adrienne and I drifted apart. We still trained together with Dad, and at League headquarters, but she didn't want anything to do with the family, especially me. That continued through college. I thought she'd lost interest in the Guard, wanted to quit." He sighed.

"Then Dad died unexpectedly. It shocked our family. And it meant we would be made primary Guards. I wondered how she'd get out of it but that's not what she wanted. She wanted me out."

He removed a framed photo from a drawer in the coffee table. "This is the last happy picture I have of us." He handed the picture to Jason.

There was his mother, about sixteen years old. Her long, blond hair was pulled back in a ponytail, and she had an arm slung around Alexander's neck. They leaned into each other. Alexander's hair was long and wavy, and his eyes were shut. He was laughing hard. Adrienne was laughing too, but her eyes were open. She looked directly at the camera.

"She's beautiful," Sadie said. She nudged Jason's knee.

"Yeah," Jason and Uncle Alexander said in unison.

Uncle Alexander pinched the bridge of his nose for a moment and stood. He took the picture from Jason and placed it on the mantle. "Something changed her. I don't know what. Maybe it was Dad's death. But she wasn't the same Adrienne." He picked up the tray of food and drinks. "I'm going to take this to the kitchen." He left.

"If he comes back and tells me my mom was the problem, then we're going to have a big problem," Jason whispered to Sadie.

Sadie's mouth opened to respond but Uncle Alexander reentered the room.

"Anyway," he said, "I'd started having my own issues with migraines, illness, trouble staying focused, and it got worse. Adrienne said I was a liability. I didn't fight her. With the permission of the

League, I withdrew and she was appointed the primary Guard. I became something of an alternate."

Jason eased. "And when my mom disappeared . . . "

"I was moved to primary Guard."

"Just like that?"

"Just like that," he said. "I took over." He leaned back, hooked his hands behind his head and shut his eyes. "But I need to find my apprentice. Too much time has already been lost."

"Well, don't look at me." Jason held his hands like two stop signs. "My name isn't in gold."

Uncle Alexander opened his eyes. "And that disappoints me. After discovering you could see Skyfish, I was certain you were the one. But . . . " He unclasped his hands and leaned toward Jason. "Have you seen anything besides Skyfish?"

"What? Like Bigfoot or something?" Jason huffed. "No."

"Anything else? Anything you couldn't explain?"

"No."

"No blue sparks from your fingers? Your hands?"

"Blue sparks? Not really." Jason folded his arms across his chest and tucked his hands. "Well, maybe once when I was playing a game with Della. But I thought I imagined it."

"Maybe you imagined it, but it could be something more. Though nothing's definitive until we receive confirmation. Siblings of Guards often have negligible powers, useful for parlor tricks."

"Great. A career as a magician at kid's parties awaits me. Maybe Sadie can be my assistant."

Sadie rolled her eyes.

"What about the Skyfish, Jason? Did you sense they were coming? Did you hear anything or feel anything before you saw them?"

Jason pushed himself back into the couch but there was nowhere to go. He remembered the charge on his neck. He remembered the crackling and hissing in his ears. He remembered he didn't like it. "No. Nothing."

Uncle Alexander's head ticked two clicks clockwise. "Are you sure?"

"I swear." He held his hands up. "And look, no blue sparks."

"Hmm." Uncle Alexander's eyes were locked onto Jason's. "Well then, maybe it will be Kyle after all. It's often the first born."

"Yeah, Kyle. He's the oldest. Pick him."

"If only it were that easy." Uncle Alexander sat back and crossed one leg over the other. His foot bobbed. "Then again, maybe the chart will surprise us all and tell us it's Della. Stranger things have happened. Though I do wish it would get around to it. Too much time has already been lost."

"You said that before," Jason said. "What's the big deal?"

Uncle Alexander leaned forward again. "There are signs, but—well, it's probably nothing." He shifted away. His foot bounced harder.

"Is there a problem?" Sadie asked.

Uncle Alexander's eyes were on them but didn't see them. He'd retreated into his head. His eyes closed.

"Uncle Alexander." Jason snapped his fingers.

His uncle's eyelids sprung open, his pupils constricted.

"You've told us this much, you might as well give us the full scoop."

Uncle Alexander uncrossed his legs and put his elbows on his knees. He stared at Jason and Sadie for a second. "I don't have proof, but I think someone is trying to damage the Rampart. Trying to trigger a catastrophic failure."

"Why do you think that?" Jason surprised himself—he actually felt worried. He shoved the feeling aside.

"And why would anyone want to kill so many people?" Sadie asked.

Uncle Alexander shrugged. "I don't have proof. But there's too much happening, too many failures, too many anomalies in the Rampart."

"And signs, like the huge earthquakes? And the tsunamis?" Sadie asked.

Uncle Alexander nodded.

"There was a guy on the Internet who swears he saw Bigfoot in Montana, and another one in Canada—everyone thinks they planned their stories just to get attention."

"Yes," Uncle Alexander said. "And there's more."

Jason jumped up. "Oh come on. Suddenly the Rampart is going down. That's a bit over the top, isn't it?"

"I wish it was," Uncle Alexander said. "I reached out to the League to get assistance from other Guards because there are so many aberrations in our region. But there's no one to spare. Every region is equally or more challenged. There are even a few reports of Guards gone missing."

"But you said there are hundreds of Guards," said Jason

"Yes. And we're losing them. Much like your mom." He eyed Jason, his brows pulled together. Finn stood and walked over to Uncle Alexander. Her eyes were on Jason, too.

"Whatever. This is all a bunch of bull crap. I'm done." Jason's hands got hot and he balled them. He nodded to Sadie. "Let's get out of here."

She grabbed her laptop, stuffed it in her bag.

Uncle Alexander stood. "Jason, please—"

"Save it. It was stupid to come over here." He and Sadie turned toward the door.

"I need your help."

Jason kept walking. "I'm sure your magic book will come up with something. Keep watching those names. Maybe you'll discover gold." Jason waved his fists in the air, miming a cheering prospector who'd hit the big one. He turned the knob on the front door.

"Not as a Guard." Uncle Alexander called. "I need your help to find your mom."

Jason froze.

"I think she's alive. I think she's in hiding. And I think she's the only one who can help us."

Jason yanked the door open and bolted from the house.

FIFTEEN
The Decree

Hard steps jammed through his feet, jarring his knees, and his neck, and his jaw as he put distance between himself and his uncle.

I think she's alive. I think she's alive. I think she's alive. The words worked like a chisel into his brain. Sharp. Pointed. Painful.

Sadie hustled to keep up with him. "Jason."

He focused forward.

"Jason."

He didn't stop.

"Hey." Sadie reached out and grabbed his arm.

"What?" He swung her off.

Sadie skittered backward. "What is your problem?" Her voice was an icy mix of shock and concern.

Jason turned toward home, away from her, away from his uncle. "I—I'm sorry. I've gotta get out of here." Jason sprinted and built distance in record time.

Minutes later he was on the sidewalk in front of his grandmother's house. He hunched down to give his body a chance to catch up, to grab oxygen.

He wanted to go in and tell her everything, ask her if any of it was true. And he wanted to go in and tell her nothing, and talk about summer, and books, and whatever.

89

His pulse slowed. He stood. He ran.

Jason was spent and sweat-soaked when he got home. He smelled like wet dog and hot pavement. Dad didn't notice. He was focused on his work.

Jason showered and tried to ignore his thoughts but his mind wouldn't cooperate.

I think she's alive.

He surfed the Internet, played computer games, but nothing could beat back those words.

I think she's alive.

They were like an annoying song that gets stuck in your head then repeats, and repeats, and repeats.

He replayed everything his uncle said, questioned every word. It was stupid to believe she was alive. Impossible.

If she were alive, she'd be here. She'd be here with us.

His phone rang—Sadie. Jason didn't answer. This wasn't Sadie's problem. It was his. Only his.

✳ ✳ ✳

Two days went by. Sadie called, his uncle called, they left messages.

He didn't call them back.

Jason's stomach growled. He smelled Grandma Lena's roasted chicken and his mouth watered. But dinners these days were more frozen than fresh. He was imagining things.

Or was he? He followed the aroma to the kitchen.

"It took you long enough." She was chopping vegetables and putting them into a large salad bowl. "I was afraid I'd lost my touch." She wiped her hands on a towel and gave Jason a hug, kissed him on the cheek.

"Never, Grams. You make the best chicken in the world."

"You say all the right things. Now sit down and visit with me while I finish up." She gestured to one of the bar stools at the kitchen island. "How are you?"

Jason propped his head in his hands. "Fine."

"You don't seem fine. You seem tired."

"I haven't been sleeping that great."

She held out a wedge of avocado for him. Jason ate it in two bites.

"Why aren't you sleeping? Is there something on your mind?" Grandma Lena sliced a cucumber like a kitchen ninja.

"Um, no. I don't know." He watched her face for a moment, looking for some sign that she knew about Ramparts, and Guards, and cryptids. Or that Uncle Alexander had told her what happened. But she didn't push.

Three avocado wedges later, Jason spoke again. "I went to see Uncle Alexander."

"That's nice. I'm sure he enjoyed it." She minced an onion.

"Sadie went with me. He showed us his lab."

"He must like you." She smiled at Jason and chopped peppers, scooping them into the bowl. "Did he show you any of his projects?"

"Not really. He talked about stuff." *Did she know something or not?* "He talked a little bit about Grandpa Tate."

Grandma Lena stopped mixing the veggies. "It was tough on everyone when we lost him. So unexpected." She focused on the lip of the bowl. "Thank goodness the kids had as much time with him as they did. He was able to teach them so much. But it was too short."

Her voice quieted and Jason was sorry he'd mentioned it.

She raised her gaze to Jason. "One thing we learned from the loss of your grandfather—and your mother—is to value the time you have. Spend as much time with people as you can, ask all the questions you want to ask, learn as much as you can from people, and about people, while you have them in your life. You don't know when that time will be over." She stayed fixed on Jason for a moment then resumed tossing the vegetables.

"Okay, Grams." Jason cleared his throat to mask a hiccup of air.

She set the salad bowl on the table. "I think that does it. Tell everyone to wash up for dinner, would you?"

"Sure."

A few minutes later, they were having dinner. Jason decided he needed to talk to Grandma Lena. After dinner. As soon as they were alone again.

* * *

"Oh, look at the time." Grandma Lena stood and cleared her plate from the table. "I have an early appointment tomorrow."

"You go ahead, Lena. The kids will clean up." Dad stood.

"Maybe you could stay for just a few more minutes?" Jason scrambled to the sink with his dishes and hovered next to Grandma Lena.

"Nice try, son, but you're not getting out of clean-up duty that easily. Your grandmother needs to get going, and you three need to get busy." Dad pointed at Jason and his siblings. "I'll walk you out, Lena."

Jason thought about slipping out the back door and around the house to catch Grandma Lena at her car so he could talk to her. But he knew the routine—Dad would wait and watch until she was safely on the road. Jason's shoulders slumped and he carried another plate to the sink.

They finished loading the dishwasher and headed to the family room. Kyle popped in his headphones and started texting or emailing, or both. How could he have so many to send? A few of Jason's friends from the old neighborhood kept in touch. He and Brandon texted. But no way close to as many messages as Kyle was sending and receiving.

Della plopped onto the couch and clicked on the television. "Do you want to watch a movie with me?"

"Maybe later." Jason turned and followed Dad to his office. "Can I talk to you for a minute?"

Dad sat in his chair. "Can it wait? I'm very busy with this project."

"It's kind of important."

Dad pushed his reading glasses onto the top of his head and leaned back. "Okay." He gestured to a chair across from his desk.

"I went to Uncle Alexander's house last week . . . " Jason's thoughts skittered around, bounced through his brain. What was he going to say exactly?

"And? How was that?"

"Oh, well, he showed us—me and Sadie—his lab."

"Oh?" Dad's eyes widened for a split second.

"Yeah, it was really nice. Lots of cool equipment and stuff. And we talked about Uncle Alexander's work. About cryptids."

"What did you think?"

"I think it's a little bit out there. But . . . " Jason crossed one leg over the other and grabbed his ankle with both hands. "Well, I've seen some . . . some cryptids." He locked eyes with Dad.

Dad's mouth pulled tight. "Very funny." He pulled down his reading glasses, reached for his mouse and turned his attention to his computer screen.

"No, seriously, Dad. Uncle Alexander says they're Skyfish."

"Whatever your uncle showed you was fake. Don't let him fool you."

"No, Dad, *I* saw them. On my own. At the parade. And on the bike path when I crashed."

Dad turned from his screen and stared at Jason for a moment. "Son, you didn't see anything. Your uncle planted thoughts in your head and you're imagining things."

"I didn't know Uncle Alexander when I crashed, when they chased me."

Dad sighed. "You were tired after our long drive." He turned back to his computer. "Your grandmother, your uncle, there's things—" He shook his head and typed.

"What things?" Jason fought the urge to yell.

"Nothing. Just please don't get too invested in what your uncle tells you. I don't want you mixed up in his stuff."

"His stuff? I saw them, Dad. I'm not crazy."

"Of course you're not. But isn't it possible your imagination is getting the best of you?" Dad's fingers clicked the keyboard.

"But, Dad—"

"Please, Jason. I've got a lot of work to do. Go read or something. Relax."

Jason's grip constricted his ankle and strained the blood flow to his foot. "I'm telling you the truth."

Dad twisted in his chair. "Enough, son. I have to finalize these documents tonight and I still have a lot of work to do. I don't have time for this." It was the voice you didn't question.

For a nanosecond, Jason's mouth dropped open. Then heat fired in his face. "Fine. I'll go see Uncle Alexander. He says mom's still alive. We'll find her and *she'll* listen to me." He bulleted away and broke for the stairs.

"Stop right there." Dad's voice boomed.

Jason wanted to ignore him, to keep going, but steel in Dad's tone held him firm.

"You will not go see your uncle. Not tonight. Not tomorrow. Not until I tell you that you can. Understood?"

Jason kept his back to Dad and nodded.

"That goes for everyone in this house." Dad returned to his office and shut the door.

Jason glanced at Della, curled in the corner of the couch, her arms wrapped around her knees. Kyle sat nearby. Both stared at Jason. By the looks on their faces, they'd all heard Dad's decree.

SIXTEEN

Defiance

The next morning, Dad went straight to his office. He didn't mention Uncle Alexander. He didn't mention cryptids. He didn't mention his commandment from the night before.

Jason remembered it though, so he went out the back door.

It was early, but the summer heat combined with the overnight rain made the air feel like a sweaty palm.

Jason crossed the yard and clambered over the back fence, dropping into the bramble. He pushed through the branches and headed to Uncle Alexander's.

Jason was almost there when the crackling noise and the zing down his spine told him Skyfish were coming. He tried to ignore it. But the sensation deepened. The heat burned. He glanced back. They were coming fast behind him.

He sprinted.

The Skyfish zoomed over him.

Jason pushed harder. Sweat stung his eyes. The Skyfish hummed like power lines.

Uncle Alexander's yard was ahead. *Keep going? Lead them somewhere else? And then what?*

I think they were playing, Uncle Alexander said when they'd watched the footage from the parade.

Jason dashed into Uncle Alexander's front yard and skidded to stop. His momentum lurched him forward and threw him to the ground. He braced for the impact of Skyfish.

Nothing hit him.

But the hum and heat and crackle continued. Jason eased himself over and looked up.

Hovering above him, shimmering, were at least fifty Skyfish.

Jason gulped air. He inched to standing. The zing spread from his spine up to his scalp and his face.

He eyed the Skyfish. Their eelish forms ranged in length from two to eight feet. They were golden but almost see-through, and their bodies winked rainbows like a prism. They hung in the air, fins and wings undulating, watching Jason with dark, round eyes. Jason felt like a gunslinger in the old west, waiting for someone to draw.

He swallowed dusty air and his top lip pasted onto his teeth. He twitched it free. None of the Skyfish moved. They just . . . glistened.

This is how they play? A staring contest?

Jason blinked, relaxed his shoulders, forced a smile. The Skyfish didn't react. An artery throbbed in his throat. He kept the fake smile and took a deep breath. In slow motion, Jason lifted his left hand until it was just in front of the closest cryptid.

The group's glimmer flared. Adrenaline flushed his system but Jason didn't flinch.

The glimmer encircled his arm and held it, made it luminescent. Jason jerked but his arm didn't budge. He threw his weight backward, dug his heels into the turf. He couldn't escape.

"Uncle Alexander!" Jason hollered toward the house. "Help!" Jason pulled, and tugged, and fought. His arm remained fixed like it was anchored in concrete.

The closest Skyfish swam forward to the tip of Jason's finger. The heat intensified.

They connected.

Jason's muscles spasmed and locked. Fire surged into his veins. It burned his skin, his nails, his tongue. His bones. He tried to breathe but his lungs refused air. His eyes dried. His heart fought a vise.

Silver powder pushed out of Jason, filling the air like a fog. It swirled and swooshed into the Skyfish. Jason was turning to ash and they were taking it in.

Taking *him* in.

The radiance burst brighter and whiteness covered everything. He felt solid, like granite or marble or stone. A moment later the Skyfish released him and Jason crashed to the ground.

The white light receded. Jason struggled to make sense of the view. All color had faded. Only blacks and grays remained.

He couldn't breathe.

He couldn't move.

His heart stopped.

His eyes closed.

Dead.

SEVENTEEN
A Decision Made

Blades of grass prickled the back of Jason's neck. Birds sang in the distance.

Heaven has birds?

A second later, Jason's body seized. Stabs ripped into his chest. Air scraped like razor blades in his lungs. Pain crushed his skull. It dove down his legs. It arced through his arms. It punched, and avalanched, and swelled.

And then it receded, bit by bit, a tide flowing out. Heartbeat steadied. Breathing balanced.

Jason opened his eyes to blackness.

He waited, searched, and found light.

Then shapes. Then color.

Blue sky.

Green leaves.

Clouds.

Uncle Alexander's front yard.

He lifted his hands above his face and turned them over. No blackened skin. No silvery powder.

He moved his feet. He stretched his legs. He touched his neck, his chest and his hips.

Uncle Alexander ran out of the house, Finn on his heels. Her four legs outpaced Uncle Alexander and she reached Jason first. He pushed himself to sitting. Finn licked his face and investigated him, gathering scent from his hair, and his ears, and his face.

"What happened? Can you stand?" Uncle Alexander grabbed Jason under the arm.

Jason nodded. "Skyfish." He stretched his neck and rolled his shoulders, check-listing all was in working order.

"You were attacked?" Uncle Alexander guided Jason toward the house.

"Not exactly. They were chasing me and I got the wild idea to stop running. They stopped, too." Jason recounted what happened.

Uncle Alexander helped Jason into the living room.

He sat on the couch. "I thought I was dead."

"You should be dead. And maybe you actually were. But you should be permanently, really most sincerely dead."

"Ah, funny. But a house didn't fall on me." Jason checked his hands again. "My hands feel a little funny, kind of tingly."

Uncle Alexander took one of Jason's hands in his and examined it.

Finn sniffed Jason's leg. Some spots she flicked with her tongue and sniffed closer. "Is she always like this?" Jason scratched Finn behind the ears with his free hand.

"When she needs to be, yes." Uncle Alexander grabbed a magnifying glass and held it over the tips of Jason's fingers. "Curious."

"Me or Finn?"

"Both I suppose, but I'm mostly referring to you. Your hands are warm, yet the moons in your fingernails are tinged blue, as if you'd been chilled. Or . . . "

"Or what?" Jason pulled his hand away and eyed his fingernails.

"Wait here a minute." Uncle Alexander walked out of the room.

Finn continued her analysis of every thread, every bit of skin, every spot she could nose on Jason. He stopped petting her and picked up the magnifying glass. The metal handle sparked. "Jeez." He dropped it onto the couch.

Uncle Alexander walked in with a glass of ice water. "What? What is it?" He handed it to Jason.

"The handle, it shocked me when I touched it. I saw a bolt. It was blue."

"Are you certain?"

"I guess. I mean, maybe I imagined it." He picked it up again. No zap. "Or maybe it was static electricity."

"Hmm. Yes. Perhaps. Or perhaps not."

"What's that supposed to mean?" Jason drank some water and set down the glass.

"As I mentioned, Guards have an innate power, an ability to produce energy that's used to repair and defend the Rampart. Hmm . . . have you noticed any blue bolts before?"

"No."

"But you did notice a spark before. What about glowing blue?"

"Actually, yeah. My palms glowed blue a couple of times. I figured I was just seeing things."

Uncle Alexander turned Jason's hand palm up and scrutinized the skin.

"C'mon, ya gotta give me more than that, Uncle Alexander."

He released Jason's hand. "I don't know anything more than yesterday—the blue is likely an indication that some level of the Guards' power has been passed to you. We still need the final word from the book."

"So, same old, same old."

"For now, yes. But given what happened to you with the Skyfish today, I suspect the odds are on you."

Jason wasn't sure he wanted the odds on him.

Uncle Alexander took a stethoscope from around his neck and hooked in the ear tips. "I'm going to listen to your lungs and heart. Deep breath."

Jason filled his lungs and exhaled.

"Again."

Jason obeyed.

"One more time."

"Am I going to live, Doc?"

"I don't hear anything that says otherwise. But we should still take you to the hospital to be sure."

"No. I feel fine. And I don't want to deal with my dad. He'll kill me if he finds out I was here."

Uncle Alexander's brows furrowed.

"Uh, well, I had a fight with my dad. I told him you thought Mom was alive and he banned us from seeing you without his permission. And I don't have his permission." Jason lifted the glass of water to his lips.

"Aw, Jason . . . " Uncle Alexander ran his hand through his hair.

"I know. I'm sorry. It was stupid."

"If those are your father's wishes, why are you here?"

"Because I can't get what you said about my mom out of my head especially after I thought I saw her at our old house." He crossed his arms. "And I've gotta tell you, I don't believe she's alive because if she *was* alive, she'd be with us. But I can't not help you look."

"You thought you saw her?"

"Yeah. But why would she be there? And not with us?"

Finn finished her inspection and sat. She put her head on Jason's knee. Her brown eyes peered up at his face, prodding Jason to pet her again. She thumped her tail against the couch.

"All right." Uncle Alexander sat across from Jason. "So, let me see if I have this right, you might have seen your mom, but you decided you didn't, and you're here to prove me wrong about believing she's alive."

"Yeah, I guess so."

"Great. Your support is unmatched. But regardless, we should talk about the—" Uncle Alexander sunk his head into his palms and gasped air.

"What? Did you get zapped by Skyfish, too?" Jason teased, tried to lighten the mood.

Uncle Alexander rocked back and forth, gulping small mouths of air.

"Uncle Alexander?"

He moaned. "This isn't supposed to happen. This isn't supposed to happen. This isn't supposed to happen."

"Uncle Alexander."

Jason's uncle pitched faster. His fingers mashed into his scalp. Finn whined and rushed to him. She nudged his knee and head-butted his thigh.

Jason jumped up. The sudden movement felt like nails driving into his skull. He pushed through it, grabbed his uncle's shoulders, and shook. "Uncle Alexander." Jason yelled into his ear.

Uncle Alexander stopped rocking back and forth. Finn hopped on the couch and licked his face.

"What?" He answered like Jason had asked him to pronounce w-h-a-t. Calm. Even. Normal.

"You were rocking, and muttering, and definitely not here." Jason sat.

"I . . . I was? Oh . . . these blackouts. I swear they'll be the death of me." He shook his head. Finn pawed at him, wanting him to rub her belly.

"Do you need to see a doctor?"

"No, I'm fine. They're only migraines. They stealth attack me from time to time." He scratched Finn under the chin and took measured breaths in through his nose and out through his mouth.

"Then I guess we'll both not go to the doctor together." It seemed like more than a migraine.

"Fine. Yes. Very well, then." Uncle Alexander sighed. "You die in my front yard. I have some sort of fit in front of you. No wonder your dad doesn't want you around me." He cleared his throat. "But, since you're here, let's work on finding your mom, shall we? I'll make us some sandwiches, feed our brains."

Finn trotted into the kitchen behind them. Uncle Alexander made peanut butter and honey sandwiches, pausing at times to rub his temples. He served the sandwiches on plates that seemed more for decoration than for dining. Jason's was trimmed with gold and had pictures of a bagpiper, a Scotty dog, and the Loch Ness monster weaving through waves.

A sketch of Bigfoot's head filled Uncle Alexander's plate. *Welcome to Bigfoot Country* circled the rim. After a couple bites of his sandwich, Uncle Alexander took a drink of iced tea and wiped his mouth on his napkin.

"Your mom and I always had a connection, the ones you hear about with twins. How they know what the other is thinking, or if they're in pain or something. Have you heard of this?"

"Yeah." Jason took a bite of his sandwich.

"Well, it was even more pronounced with the power of the Guard. The connection was unimaginably strong, until your mom and I drifted apart." Uncle Alexander rose and pulled a bag of pretzels out of the pantry. "It faded. I thought it was lost for good."

Jason added pretzels to his plate.

"A few years ago, I sensed it again. Last summer the feeling became uncomfortable, unnerving. I had to find out if something was happening in Adrienne's life that correlated to these feelings, so I talked to Mom. Grandma Lena."

"Last summer? Everything was fine last summer."

"So I understood. But as time passed, the feeling increased in intensity, and by autumn the connection was overpowering, almost painful. I went to the doctor and had all manner of tests done to ensure that I didn't have a brain tumor or cancer or something equally ominous." Uncle Alexander returned to the pantry and got a package of chocolate chip cookies, taking one for himself. He set them on the table. "My bill of health came back crystal clear."

"What about the migraines? The blackouts?" Jason took a cookie from the bag.

"I thought they'd resolved themselves but lately they've returned with a vengeance. Part of my operating system, it seems."

Finn sat near the table, watching them, ready to clean up anything that might fall to the floor.

"Anyway, Grandma Lena worried about what was happening and talked more with your dad. She learned about the increase in Adrienne's solitary walks, that she seemed more distant." He took another cookie from the bag. "Grandma Lena thought we were indeed connected again."

Jason pushed away his empty plate. "So then what happened? What happened when my mom . . . when she . . . after she was gone?" He crossed his arms over his chest.

"That's just it—nothing happened. Nothing stopped. It's diminished a little in the past few months, but the connection is still there. And when I'm working on the Rampart, the connection is unmistakable." He tapped the table twice.

A buzz built in Jason's gut. He squashed it down. "So that's it? This feeling?"

"It's not just a feeling. It's a connection."

"Because you're both Guards?"

"And twins."

Jason's mind tried to process all that he had learned. *Crazy guy has a magic connection to Mom. But not if she's dead.*

Logic said go. Forget this. Leave.

But what if . . . ?

Jason stayed. "Okay, so now what?"

"The strongest connection happens when I'm working on the Rampart, so it's possible that she's nearby. I'd like you to come with me on the next operation. Maybe if Adrienne is close and sees you, she'll feel safe enough to reveal herself." Uncle Alexander gazed down at his hands and lightly clasped them together.

"Okay." Jason leaned forward to get an angle on his uncle's face.

Uncle Alexander rubbed his palms together.

"Is your headache bothering you again?" Jason asked.

Uncle Alexander raised his head. "Huh? Oh, no. I was lost in thought." He picked up their plates and carried them to the sink.

"Well, can I ask you a question?"

"Of course." Uncle Alexander returned to his seat.

"If she's alive, why hasn't she come back?"

Uncle Alexander sighed. "That's a tough one, Jason."

"Why?"

"Because I don't want to upset you."

Jason jutted his chin. "My mom disappeared. I thought she'd been eaten by mountain lions, and now you say she's alive. My dad moved us to this stupid town and I lost all my friends. I see things no one else sees, those same things supposedly killed me today, yet here I am. And if my dad finds out I've been here, I'll be grounded for life. I don't think anything you have to say will upset me." Jason felt the flush wash into his cheeks.

Uncle Alexander pushed away from the table and reached down to pet Finn who was lying next to his chair. "Fair enough." He took a deep breath. "I told you someone is trying to destroy the Rampart. Remember?"

Jason nodded.

"Well, I think your mom figured out who's behind it."

"So she should report them to the League thing or whatever and be done."

"If it were that simple, I suspect she would have done exactly that." Uncle Alexander stroked the bridge of Finn's nose. "This person, or cryptid—whoever it is that wants the Rampart destroyed—is powerful. If they figured out your mom discovered them, they would have moved to destroy her, you, maybe our whole family. I'm beginning to think Adrienne faked her death to protect us."

Jason sat taller. "Then we need to help her. We need to help her stop them."

"You're right. We have to stop them. We cannot let the Rampart be damaged, much less destroyed. You'd lose a lot more than your mom. We all would."

Jason popped up and stepped around his chair, gripping the top of it. "Okay, we'll find her. We'll find her and help her and fix everything. And then she can come home and everything can get back to normal."

"That's the basic plan, yes. But we must consider that I could be wrong. There was a lot of blood when she disappeared. I could be misreading the clues."

Jason's knuckles began to turn white. "In your gut, percentage-wise, how certain are you that my mom is alive?"

"I'd say . . . " Uncle Alexander canted his head side to side. " . . . ninety-two percent. But still—"

"Wow, ninety-two percent. That's like an A-minus. Good enough for me." Jason swung into the chair and grabbed a cookie, stuffing the whole thing in his mouth.

"I'm concerned about what happened to you today and I want to do some research. Why don't you head home and get some rest. I'll text you when a Rampart operation presents itself."

"Yeah, okay. I am kind of tired." Jason rose and took one more cookie from the package. "Thanks for the sandwich and cookies and, you know, everything."

"You're welcome. But wait, let's do one more thing before you leave."

Uncle Alexander rushed past Jason and into the living room. He triggered the drawer in the totem pole, removed *The Order of the Rampart Guards* and opened the cover. Jason stood next to him. Uncle Alexander unfolded the chart and scanned the names, running his finger along the paper until it came to the three Lex children.

All three names were still black.

"Damn." Uncle Alexander stared at the page as if willing it to change.

Jason stared too and his shoulders slumped. "Whatever." He headed toward the door. A blue glimmer shadowed his palms. He ignored it and stuffed his hands in his pockets.

❋ ❋ ❋

Jason braced himself. He'd been out without telling Dad. Jason pictured himself looking natural, tried to match the image, and opened the front door.

Dad was in his office, head down over a file. He didn't acknowledge Jason when he walked by. Did Dad even know Jason had been gone? He didn't want to push his luck. He headed upstairs taking the steps two at a time.

Della's bedroom door was open. She was sitting at her computer. Everything in her room seemed settled, like she'd always lived there. Two posters of horses hung on one wall, and a picture of some boy band hung on another. She had a corkboard above her desk. On it were movie stubs, a ribbon she'd won in dance, and a calendar that had a different baby animal on each month. This month was a baby giraffe.

"Hey, Della."

She minimized her screen and turned toward Jason. "Hi. Dad was looking for you earlier."

"Was he mad?"

"I don't think so." She shrugged. "He asked me if I knew where you were."

"What are you doing?" He nodded toward her computer.

"I'm chatting with . . . one of my friends from my old school. Dad said it was okay." She added the part about Dad too quickly.

"Don't worry, Dell. Chat all you want. I won't bust you with Dad."

Della's eyes flicked down and over to her computer screen, then back to Jason. "Thanks."

"Yeah, no problem. I'll talk to you later."

"Okay." Della returned her focus to the computer.

Jason walked into his room, stepped over boxes waiting to be unpacked, and collapsed on his bed.

EIGHTEEN

A couple of days went by but no call came from Uncle Alexander. Jason texted him. Uncle Alexander responded, saying he hadn't forgotten. There hadn't been any assignments. No issues with the Rampart.

Jason called Sadie. "Hey."

"Hey."

"About the other day, I was freaking out, and, I'm sorry I was freaking out."

"I get it—having your uncle say he thinks your mom is alive. That's . . . well, it's a lot of things. And wow. Have you talked to him since then?"

Jason told Sadie about the Skyfish and the sort-of-dying and the determination to see things through with his uncle. "Seriously, I'm still kind of freaking out about everything. I mean, I really start believing maybe my mom is alive. Maybe we can actually help her. Then I catch myself and think it's all so whacked, ya know?"

"Yeah, but Jason, look at what we've already learned. It makes sense to see how things play out. Can't hurt, right?"

"Yeah, can't hurt." Jason recalled how it felt when his mom disappeared. What if she really did come home?

✳ ✳ ✳

By day four, Jason twitched with nervous energy. He pulled out his chess set and tried to concentrate on a game. He placed the large pieces on the board—the tallest were about six inches high. He visualized moves and then played them out, both white and black. Or in this case, holly and cedar, the woods from which the set was carved.

He analyzed the positions of the pieces and searched for the next best move while fiddling with a rook he'd swiped off the board. He rolled the piece in his fingers and pressed the top of it. Rolled it and pressed, rolled it and pressed.

The base dropped off of the rook.

"Shit."

He covered his mouth and checked his doorway to see if anyone came to rebuke him. Or report him.

But no one heard him. Jason shut his door.

He returned to the rook, now in two pieces. How did he break it? Better yet, how could he fix it? Dad had trusted Jason with the chess set.

He examined the parts. He found a notch where they fit together. He matched the two pieces but they didn't stay together, no matter how hard he pressed or twisted or wished.

Glue. Jason had glue somewhere, leftover from his model airplane phase. He jumped off the bed and pulled open one of the cardboard boxes. He pawed through the stuff. Not here.

He moved to the next box. The kit had to be here somewhere. He found it in the third box.

Jason cracked off the cap and picked up the rook, carrying it to the window where there was more light. He squeezed the glue bottle carefully, then a little more. A stream of air wheezed out. He squeezed harder. Dried bits of glue dropped into the body of the rook.

He tapped the piece on his hand trying to shake out the bits. Something glinted. Jason set down the tube and turned the rook so the sun shined in. There was something inside.

Jason grabbed needle nose pliers from the model kit. He reached inside the rook and pulled. The item didn't budge. He wriggled it, pulled again, and wriggled it once more. It slipped free.

He dropped the item into his palm. It was round, a coin or a medal about the size of a quarter, the face dark and tarnished. Jason grabbed a shirt from his laundry basket and rubbed. Letters appeared.

L—E—X

The writing was old, different, almost unrecognizable. He turned it over and wiped the other side. A shield emerged, a cross on the front. Three points were rounded, the fourth, on the bottom, pointed. A helmet from a suit of armor was above. And the edges of the coin were embossed with rope or leaves. Jason kept rubbing to reveal the design.

His phone rang. Uncle Alexander.

"Hey." Jason held the shirt and coin in his hand.

"It's time, Jason. Get here as fast as you can and we'll head out to the site. We won't have to travel too far."

"Okay, I'll be right there."

Jason slid his phone into his pocket. He bunched the shirt around the coin and the pieces of rook, and stuffed them in his sock drawer. He ran out of his room, down the stairs and bolted out the back door.

He charged up the steps into his uncle's house and didn't bother to knock. "Uncle Alexander."

Jason hurried forward, peering into rooms. "Uncle Alexander, where are you?" He searched the living room, the kitchen, the office.

Vacant.

He continued outside to the carriage house and heard Finn barking. He went inside.

The front room was messier than before. Stacks of books were toppled, scattered files covered the floor.

He followed Finn's bark. "Uncle Alexander?"

Finn was inside the lab, behind the metal door. She scratched hard and fast, her bark frantic.

Jason rushed forward and pushed on the handle.

Locked.

"Hello?" He rose on his toes and looked through the window. A misty smoke crawled across the room toward Finn. He didn't see his uncle.

Jason's heartbeat vaulted. He had to get the door open. He had to get Finn out.

He raced back to the kitchen and spun round, checking every inch. A fire extinguisher hung on the wall. It was dusty and cobwebbed. Jason didn't know if it would put out a fire, but it was heavy and solid. Exactly what he needed.

He grabbed the extinguisher and scrambled back to Finn. She was whimpering. She'd stopped scratching. Jason hammered on the door handle, bending the lever. He powered down on it again then slammed it a third time. The lever broke free.

Jason opened the door and grabbed Finn's collar. She pawed her eyes and shook her head and pawed her eyes again. He dragged her out.

His eyes blurred and burned. He covered his mouth and nose with his shirt and rushed back into the lab, searching for Uncle Alexander. Jason blinked rapidly, trying to see, trying to focus. "Uncle Alexander!" Jason yelled. His throat seared. He searched under worktables and behind counters. His lungs craved oxygen. Uncle Alexander was nowhere. Jason fled and forced the door shut.

Finn was panting and gagging and swiping at her face. Drool dripped from her jowls.

Jason wiped his eyes with the inside of his shirt. "C'mon, girl." He coughed. "We've gotta get out of here." He took Finn's collar and led her out of the carriage house, into the fresh air. They crossed the yard and crumpled on the grass behind the main house.

Jason dialed 9-1-1.

Finn vomited.

The police, a fire truck and ambulance were there in minutes. Two EMTs dashed toward Jason and Finn.

"What's your name?" The EMT flicked a flashlight in Jason's eyes.

"Jason Lex. My uncle is missing."

The tech called out numbers to his partner and turned back to Jason. "I'm sure the police are looking for him. I'm going to wash out your eyes." He nodded to his colleague. "Get hers, too." He pointed at Finn.

Jason's eyes stung for a moment but soothed as the remains of the gas rinsed away. His vision cleared.

The tech handed Jason a towel and put an oxygen mask on his face.

Jason glanced at Finn. She'd stopped pawing her eyes. She still panted, but slower now. The second tech held an oxygen mask over her snout. Jason dialed his uncle—straight to voice mail. He texted, but no response.

A few minutes later, the rescuers gave Jason a bottle of water and filled a container for Finn. She slurped it and slopped it onto the lawn. Jason chugged some of his and dumped the rest down his back. He patted Finn's flank and called Uncle Alexander again. Voice mail.

A short man with dark hair and mirrored aviator sunglasses walked toward them. He wore a beige-colored uniform with a black belt and black boots. He had a gun strapped to his right hip, and a club strapped to his left. A gold badge gleamed against the bland color of his shirt. He had a pen and small notepad in his hand.

"I'm Sheriff Gunderson," he said. "And you are?"

Jason stood. He could see his reflection in the sheriff's sunglasses. "Jason Lex. This is my uncle's place."

"Jason Lex—you're new in Salton?" The sheriff opened his mouth and snapped his gum.

Stale mint wafted into Jason's face. "Yes. We just moved here."

The sheriff jotted notes.

"Sir, something's happened to my uncle. He asked me to meet him here but he was gone when I got here. I found Finn in the lab and got her out. But something's wrong. My uncle should've been here."

"I understand your concern, but Mr. Fallon does this sort of thing. Goes off on these expeditions and no one knows where he is and no one hears from him for long stretches."

"No, that's not what's happened. He called me, from here, in town, from this house."

"Then I'm sure he's just making a quick run to the store or some other errand, and he'll be back soon."

Jason clenched his teeth.

"I'm more worried about you," Sheriff Gunderson said. "Looks like tear gas back there in the lab. First thing I want to know is if you're okay—you feeling all right?"

Jason sighed. "Yeah, I'm good. I feel better."

"I'm glad to hear it. Glad you're safe, and the dog, too." Sheriff Gunderson patted Finn on the shoulder. She nuzzled his leg and the sheriff smiled.

"Now I'm not sure what happened in that lab, but tear gas and broken doors is quite a bit of excitement for Salton. This will be the most investigating I've had to do since someone swiped my granddaughter's tricycle. Spoiler alert. She rode it to her best friend's house and forgot it was there." The sheriff chuckled.

"Ah, hah." Jason faked a laugh. "But please, Sheriff, my uncle—"

"Right, right. Let's go over what happened, but I bet he'll be back before we finish." He flipped to a fresh page in his notebook.

Jason walked the sheriff through everything that happened, and the sheriff took notes. He closed with a question. "Tell me again, how much time has passed between that call from your uncle and now?"

"I guess about ninety minutes. And I keep calling him. He's not answering."

"Okay, here's what we're going to do. I truly think your uncle is fine. Maybe he got distracted with a project or something he's working on and forgot he was supposed to meet you. And airborne gases in his lab, well, let's just say it isn't the first time we've had to provide our assistance at this property."

"But—"

Sheriff Gunderson held up his hand like he was stopping traffic. "Jason, I know. I understand you're worried. But there's not a lot we can do right now anyway. In the eyes of the law, he hasn't been missing long enough for us to take action. So we need to wait this out a bit, see if he shows up on his own. Okay?"

"I guess." Jason wanted to argue but he knew the sheriff was right.

"We'll look for your uncle if circumstances warrant it. Right now, your dad is on his way to pick you up. I'll wait in my squad car in case he has any questions, and to make sure you two connect."

"Thanks, Sheriff," Jason said.

"You take care. And good job rescuing this beautiful dog. What's her name?"

"Finn."

"Miss Finn, you are a sweetheart." Finn licked the sheriff's hand and wagged her tail. "And quite a flirt, too. Girl after my own heart." Sheriff Gunderson pocketed his notepad and walked away.

A moment later, the back door slammed. Jason's dad stomped toward them.

"Hey." Jason offered a weak wave and shielded his eyes from the sun.

"What are you doing here? Are you okay?" Dad grabbed Jason's arm and pulled him close. He hugged Jason fast and pushed him back. "Let me see your eyes." Dad lifted Jason's eyelids and peered at his eyeballs.

"You do know you're not an eye doctor, right?" Jason tolerated his dad's prodding for a few seconds then turned his head away.

"They're red."

"Yeah, but they're fine. We're both fine."

Dad glanced at Finn then back to Jason. "What were you thinking?"

"I know, Dad, I know. Shouldn't have been here. I'm sorry." Jason hunched down next to Finn and draped his arm over her. "But Dad, Uncle Alexander is in trouble."

"Please don't start in on the Uncle Alexander stuff again. You're already in enough trouble. Let's go home." He gestured toward the car.

"No." Jason didn't budge. Finn stayed on his right side.

"Excuse me?"

"Please, just listen to me for a minute."

Dad took a long, slow breath. "Fine. I'm listening." He crossed his arms.

"Uncle Alexander called me. I was supposed to meet him here—"

Dad opened his mouth to speak.

"I know, against your wishes, and I said I'm sorry." Jason paused. Dad's mouth closed.

"But he wasn't here when I got here, and I found Finn locked in the lab."

"Yes, the sheriff filled me in on the phone."

"Okay, well Uncle Alexander should have been here. Something bad has happened to him."

Dad rolled his eyes and the corner of his mouth ticked up. "He's fine. He's off somewhere, working on one of his projects, researching a cryptid or something."

Jason stood. "He would have told me."

"No, he wouldn't have. He never tells anybody. He just goes."

"But he *called* me. He asked me to meet him."

"Jason, you know he's not known for being logical and organized. He forgot he called. He forgot he had another appointment." He put his hand on Jason's shoulder. "But I promise you, he's not in trouble."

"But the smoke, tear gas, in the lab—"

"An accident, that's all." Dad turned toward the car. "Now let's go."

Jason watched Dad walk away.

"Now, please," Dad said without looking back.

"C'mon, Finn." They both fell in step behind Dad.

"No dog."

Jason stopped again. "Then I'll stay here with her." Finn dropped to a sit next to him.

Dad turned back to them. Jason knew what he was thinking; that she'd need food, water, shelter. He was prepared to feed her, play with her, clean up after her, take her for walks.

"Fine. Bring her. Alexander will be back soon."

Jason dashed into the house and grabbed Finn's dog food. The three of them piled into the car. Finn licked Jason's ear.

Don't worry. We'll find him. And maybe Mom, too.

NINETEEN

An Impossible Note

Three days passed and Uncle Alexander didn't come home. Sheriff Gunderson opened an official missing person's report at Jason's prodding, and with Grandma Lena's support. But other than informing other agencies and keeping an eye out for him, it seemed the sheriff's office wasn't doing much to find Uncle Alexander.

Jason started each day feeding and walking Finn. Their route took them to Uncle Alexander's house, just to see if there was any sign that Uncle Alexander had been home. Four days passed and nothing.

Sadie joined them for their walk on day five. She'd helped get the word out about Uncle Alexander, putting up fliers and talking to business owners around town. After they'd walked around Uncle Alexander's house that morning, Jason, Sadie, and Finn headed to Grandma Lena's.

"Come in, come in," Grandma Lena said. "Any news?"

"No, nothing. His house seems as empty as ever." Jason grabbed a banana from the fruit bowl and peeled it. He gave a bite to Finn. "What should we do?"

Grandma Lena refilled her coffee cup. "I'm not sure, Jason. Honestly, I haven't been that worried about him, because your dad and the sheriff are right—it's not that unusual for him to just disappear for a while." She stirred in some cream. "But the fact that he left Finn alone, well, he's never left her like that before. I've come home surprised to find her in my house once or twice. But he's never left without making sure she's in good hands."

Jason tossed the banana peel in the garbage. "Well, this is stupid. There's got to be something we can do."

"Can't we get the sheriff to do more patrols or something?" Sadie asked.

"I believe they're doing all they can right now," Grandma Lena said. "There aren't any strong indications that something bad has happened to him. I'm not sure what further actions they can take." She held the coffee cup like she was using it to warm her hands.

"So we just keep doing what we're doing, which is basically nothing," Jason said.

"And we keep thinking positively, and we watch for any sign that may tell us what happened, and we have faith. That's more than nothing."

A short time later, they left Grandma Lena's and walked Sadie to her house then headed home.

Jason and Finn stopped at the door to Dad's office.

"Any word about Alexander?" Dad asked.

Jason was surprised by the question. "Nothing. Grandma Lena's stressing."

"I'm sorry to hear that. I know you're worried too. Is there anything I can do to help?"

"I dunno. Maybe just drive around and look for him? But I feel like we've looked everywhere."

"Well, let's do that—drive around. You have your morning walks, and we'll go out in the afternoons, cover more territory, okay?"

"Yeah, Dad, that'd be great."

Finn trotted into the office and sat next to Dad. She raised one paw. Dad held it in his hand.

"Good morning, Finnea. How are you today?" Dad dropped her paw. Finn rubbed the top of her head on his leg. He scratched her neck under her collar and she pushed into it, left side, right side, left side. "You're a good girl, Finn. Such a good girl."

"Um . . . what is going on?" Jason asked.

Finn's tongue lolled and her back leg bounced, transmitting "yes that spot yes that spot yes that spot" in dog-to-human code.

Dad grinned. "Finn and I have been getting to know each other. She's a great dog. Aren't you, Finn? Yes you are."

"What? When?" Jason was with Finn non-stop, twenty-four-seven.

"After you go to bed. The first night she was here, she came down to see me. I tried to shoo her out but she wouldn't have it. Then I tried to ignore her but that didn't work either." He shifted his gaze to Finn. "Did it, Finn? No it didn't. You are too smart for that."

"O . . . kay?" Jason slouched against the door frame.

"Yes, it was okay. Very okay."

Well, yeah, obviously. Dad was now a dog person, or at least a Finn person.

He stopped scratching Finn's neck. "Thank you for stopping by, Finn."

She licked the back of his hand, walked to the doorway and sat next to Jason.

"Jason, I'm proud of you for taking responsibility for Finn. You're doing a great job."

"Thanks."

"And hey, I know I've been distant when it comes to your uncle. I admit I've been a bit frustrated with him, with his stories and his antics, even before we moved here. Sometimes he and I are just on a different page. But I talked it over with your grandmother and I realize I was being unfair. I really do want to help find him."

"Great, Dad. Thanks."

120

"Well, I'd better get back to work. We'll make that drive this afternoon. And try not to worry too much, okay?" Dad turned to his computer.

"Okay. Talk to you later."

Jason and Finn walked into the family room and plopped onto the couch.

"What else can we do to find Uncle Alexander? Do you have an idea, Finn? Please share it with me. Preferably in English."

Finn kept wagging her tail.

"Not quite hearing you. Could you repeat that?"

Finn barked and turned around to face the foyer. The doorbell rang.

"Wha . . . ?" Jason stared at her for a split second. Finn jumped off the couch and he followed her to the door. Jason opened it.

Sadie stood on the porch. "My grandmother meant to give this to you this morning." She thrust a book at Jason. She kept her other hand behind her back.

Jason took the book, *Bees and Their Buzzness*. "Okay . . . what am I supposed to do with this?"

"You're supposed to read it." Those were her words but her tone said, *dork*.

"I really don't think this is my kind of story."

"Mamo figured you'd say something like that, so she sent a bribe." Sadie whisked her hand from behind her back. She held two vanilla ice cream bars with dark chocolate. "Plus she thinks you could use a distraction, something else to think about."

"Ice cream before lunch. It seems I can be bought." Jason stepped outside with Finn and accepted one of the bars from Sadie. They sat in a shady part of the front yard.

Jason unwrapped his ice cream bar and took a big bite. Finn scooched close watching every bite until Jason finished.

He picked up *Bees and Their Buzzness*. "So really, what's with the book?"

"Mamo said it would be good reading for you, so you'd 'understand more about this super-organism, and not be such a wimp.'"

"She called me a wimp? Maybe she's not so cool after all." He smirked and flipped the book over. The back cover had a picture of hundreds of bees clustered together. "See this?" He turned the picture toward Sadie. "I want to avoid that. Am I a wimp or am I smart?"

"Wimp."

"What?" Jason stared at Sadie.

"I've been around them forever. They're amazing." She pushed the book toward him. "Try learning something about them. You might be surprised. And if you're brave enough, you can help us collect some honey."

"I think that's best left to professionals."

"Well, I've been doing it since I was a little girl. But if you're not as brave as a little girl, then you should stay home. Preferably inside. Where you're safe from big, scary honeybees." Sadie clawed the air with her hands, her eyes crossed, her teeth bared.

"Jeez—were you absent when they did the no peer pressure program at school?" Jason teased.

"Hah." Sadie laughed. "I guess Mamo skipped that lesson."

"Your grandmother was a teacher?"

"My only teacher until I turned ten. I was home-schooled."

Jason cocked his head like Finn did when she didn't quite understand. "But you're so . . . "

"Normal? Please say normal."

"I was going to say nice, but, yeah, normal works." Jason leaned back in the grass. "Some home-schooled kids I've met are a bit different, or super-geeky, or something."

"I'm lucky I made it through, I guess." She smiled and fingered the charms on her bracelet. "Turning ten was a big deal for me. Double digits. Mamo gave me this bracelet. And she finally let me start public school."

"She wouldn't let you go to public school?"

"Not until I was ten. She said it was important I learn at home until then. Maybe she was lonely after losing so much of her family?"

"You always wear that bracelet."

"It was my mom's. Her parents gave it to her." She held out her arm. "She got this diploma charm when she graduated from college, and this heart was a gift from my dad." She moved the links around her wrist. "The sombrero is from Mexico, where my parents went on their honeymoon. And this one my dad gave to her when I was born." She shook a tiny rattle that hung on the chain. "It really rattles."

Tiny bits chimed inside the rattle's chamber.

"Nice." Jason didn't quite know what to say.

"I know, right? I love it." Sadie pulled the bracelet around her wrist. "Someday I'll add more charms but I haven't found any good ones yet. And I'd like to figure out what the other ones mean, if they mean anything."

"You must have been really young when you lost your parents." He rubbed his hands on his jeans. "What happened to them?"

"They were killed in a car accident when I was a baby. I was in the car but, obviously I survived. Good car seat, I guess." She gave Jason a sad smile. "And Mamo raised me." Sadie watched a honeybee working a nearby clump of lavender.

Jason eased away from it.

Sadie continued. "My grandfather passed away a few months before my parents. Because Mamo was going through so much loss, she says I took care of her as much as she took care of me."

"That sucks. The grandpa-parents part, I mean. Not your grandmother."

Sadie chuckled. "I knew what you meant."

"Are you okay?"

"Most of the time." Her face brightened. "And Mamo is awesome." Sadie untucked her hair where it had slipped inside her shirt collar. The charms on her bracelet jingled.

"That's cool. But I'm really sorry."

"Thanks." She adjusted her glasses. Her phone buzzed. "Ah, Mamo. She's waiting for me—we're doing the whole back-to-school shopping thing. Gotta go."

Jason stood. "Okay. Tell your grandmother thanks for the book. And the ice cream. I'll talk to you later." Finn popped up next to him.

"Yes. Talk later." She smiled. "Now go read about bees and find some courage."

Jason walked to the front door with Finn close behind until a neighbor's terrier raced past their house. Finn barked and took off after it.

"Finn! No! Come!" Jason hollered.

Finn didn't stop. Jason dropped the book on the stoop and sprinted after the dogs.

He caught up with them at a nearby park. They were chasing each other and tumbling in the grass. Jason scooped up the neighbor's escaped dog. She scrabbled against him, wanting to be down on the turf with Finn who was nipping at the little dog's feet. Jason tightened his hold.

"Finn, enough." He tried to sound serious but laughed at their antics. "Seriously, stop. Let's go."

Finn fell in step with Jason. He returned the runaway pup to her family then headed home with Finn. Jason grabbed the bee book as they entered the house.

Inside he found an envelope that had been dropped through the mail slot. He picked it up and his finger slicked through a glob of something slimy on the back.

"Gross." He wiped the goo on his shorts. The envelope had a typed label on it. *Jason Lex 9th Grade.* "Must be something for school." He walked to the kitchen and tossed the book and the envelope on the kitchen island. Finn stretched out on the floor and a heavy sigh blew out of her jowls. Jason stepped over her.

"Good spot, Finn. Do you have any idea how big you are?"

Thump thump. Her tail hit the floor.

Jason made a turkey, mustard and Swiss cheese sandwich, slicing an extra piece of cheese for Finn. He slid *Bees and Their Buzzness* closer to his plate and flipped the book open.

At least it has pictures. A color close up of a bee's eye stared out at him. He thumbed ahead. Bee larvae packed into honeycombs. Jason took a bite of his sandwich.

He flipped to a picture of a bee landing on a bright pink flower. "A single bee can visit as many as three thousand flowers in one day."

"No way." Jason bit into a pickle, then stacked three potato chips and stuffed them into his mouth. Reaching for his water, he misjudged the distance and tipped the glass over. Finn sprang to her feet. Jason snatched the book out of the way, but the envelope was soaked.

He snatched it up and opened it, pulled out the page inside and fanned it, dabbing at the writing with a paper towel. He smoothed out the paper on a dry area of the counter.

Dear Jason —

I'm sorry to be reaching out to you in this way. It's not safe. I want so much to keep you all safe. But I know Alexander is missing. I'm worried and want to help.

We need to meet. I will be behind the high school tomorrow evening, in the baseball dugout, eight PM. I am so excited to see you. But, please, it's important you tell no one about me. I know it's hard but right now there's no other way. We must protect everyone.

> *Love,*
> *Mom*

Mom was alive.

TWENTY
A Reunion

Jason's heartbeat throbbed through his head.

He took out his phone and tapped *Sadie* on his contacts list. "This is Sadie's cell. Can't talk right now but please leave a message. Thanks."

"Hey. I know you're shopping. But I—there's this note. I got this note. Call me back." He pressed *End Call*, dropped the phone on the floor and stared at the paper.

His gut was right, Uncle Alexander was in trouble.

Wait—what the hell am I thinking? This can't be real.

He picked up the phone and tapped *Sadie* again.

Her voice mail.

He hollered into the phone. "I need to talk to you. I'm freaking out and feel like a total ass-hat." *End Call.*

"What is with the yelling?" Dad stood at the edge of the kitchen.

Jason jumped up. "Oh—sorry." He stuffed the note into his back pocket. "I got an . . . email about registration, and the classes I have to take, and I got a little, uh, frustrated."

"A little frustrated?" Dad's expression said he wasn't buying it. "So when you're a little frustrated, you call someone an ass-hat?"

"Uh, yeah."

"And what is an ass-hat exactly?" Dad crossed his arms.

126

Jason kept a hand in the pocket with the note. "Um, I don't know."
He scuffed one foot back and forth on the floor.

"Watch the language, Jason." Dad went back to his office.

Finn followed Jason to his room. He shut the door and texted Sadie:
Can you please call me?

No response.

"How hard is it to stop shopping and check your phone?"

Music thumped through the wall. He tossed his phone on the bed
and walked through the bathroom that connected his room to Kyle's.

"Hey."

Kyle didn't look up from his magazine.

Jason picked a T-shirt off the floor and threw it. "Hey." The shirt
landed on Kyle's shoulder.

"Geez, ass-hat, you could've knocked." Kyle wadded the shirt and
threw it back.

"You're not supposed to say ass-hat." Jason kicked the T-shirt across
the floor into a larger pile of clothes. He sat on Kyle's bed.

"Can I help you with something, butt-hat?"

"No." Jason leaned back into the footboard. "I just felt like coming
in here."

Kyle eyed Jason like he'd spoken another language. "Well you came
in here. Now get out." He went back to his magazine, flipped the page.

"Can you turn the music down a little? For a minute?"

Kyle slapped the magazine down on his lap. "Dude—what is your
problem? Go hang out in your own room."

"I don't want to. I wanna . . . hang out here." Jason stretched his legs
out. Kyle smacked them off the bed and onto the floor.

"Not happening. Get out." Kyle cranked the music louder.

"Fine." Jason yelled above the noise. He stood. "Whatever. I
thought we could talk about Mom or something but whatever, effing
ass . . . hole." He darted back to his room. Kyle's bed creaked when
he leaped off it.

Jason tried to shut the door behind him, to lock it. Kyle banged through.

"What did you say?" He held the edge of the door where he'd pushed it open. Furrows trenched between his eyebrows.

Jason shifted into a fighting stance. "You're an effing—"

"Yeah, well you're a bigger one but that's not what I'm talking about. What about Mom?"

Jason's body eased. "I was wondering if, you know, you ever think about her."

Kyle's furrows dug deeper and he squeezed the edge of the door like he was trying to crush it. "Why are you asking about Mom?"

Jason's neck prickled. "Just curious."

"Why? She's been gone for months. Why are you curious?"

Why is he pissed? "Forget about it. You don't want to talk." Jason slid one foot back to better stabilize himself. "No problem." He shook his head.

"Fine." Kyle bounced the door off the stopper on the baseboard. He pointed at Jason. "Stay out of my room."

Jason watched the space where Kyle had stood, expecting him to come back in and tackle or punch or swing at him. But he didn't. Jason's muscles relaxed from rope to twine.

His phone rang and he dashed to it. "Hello?"

"It's me."

"I got this note right after you left and it's crazy. It can't be real." Jason raised his voice.

"What note? I have no—"

"A note from my mom."

"From your mom? How? What did it say? Oh my God."

"Yeah and I don't know what to do." He heard fumbling through the phone.

"Jason." Not Sadie. This voice was serious. Grown up. Mrs. Callahan.

Jason altered from wild to I'm-going-to-bed-without-any-supper.

"Jason Lex, are you there?"

"Yes."

"I'm not sure why you're upset, but you're upsetting Sadie."

"I'm sorry."

"Well, it's clear you have something that needs to be discussed, but this is not the right time. Such things should be handled face to face. We will be home at about five-thirty. You can come by then and discuss whatever this is like a mature young man. Do you understand me?"

"Yes, Mrs. Callahan."

"And you're staying for dinner."

"Okay. Thanks."

"Good-bye, Jason." Sadie's grandmother hung up.

✳ ✳ ✳

5:30 couldn't come soon enough. Jason reread the note what felt like a million times, looking for something—a sign, a signal, a feeling that told him the note was really from his mom. But nothing came.

Dad didn't question it when Jason said he'd been invited to have dinner at Sadie's. Jason figured Mrs. Callahan had called Dad.

Jason rang the doorbell. He bounced on his toes. He brushed his bangs out of his face. Sadie answered the door.

"Hey." Jason waved with his one free hand. His mouth dried up like dirt in the hot sun.

"Hey. Come in." Sadie stepped aside.

"Thanks." A vase of tall purple flowers sat in the foyer. Their sugary fragrance mixed with the savory smell of something baking in the kitchen, cheesy and tomatoey. "Those smell good." He nodded toward the flowers.

"Gladiolus. From the backyard."

"That's nice." Jason looked down at his feet and back up. "The food, too. It smells good."

"Lasagna."

"Ah. I like lasagna." Jason put his other hand in his pocket. "So, about the phone call . . . and your grandmother . . . "

"Yeah, she can be . . . direct."

"I find direct is the best way to get to where you're going." Mrs. Callahan walked in and handed each of them a glass of icy lemonade.

"Yes, ma'am. I'm sorry."

"Ma'am is not necessary or welcome in this house, Jason. Mrs. Callahan is fine, and if you're nice enough, I may let you call me Willene." Her firm smile softened. "Now, you two, out on the back porch and have this important conversation, whatever it is. I'm going to finish making dinner. I'll call you when it's ready."

A brown wicker couch flanked by two matching chairs sat under a covered porch. The furniture had white cushions with large, green leaf prints. Sadie sat on the couch, Jason on one of the chairs.

Hidden crickets chirped from flowerbeds lining the perimeter of the yard. Jason recognized gladiolus and snapdragons but not much else. When he was little, his mom showed him how to pinch a snapdragon blossom, making its dragon-jaws open and close.

Sadie clunked her lemonade on the tile-topped table. "Tell me about this note."

"After you left, Finn took off and I chased her. When I got back, I found the note. It's signed by my mom."

Sadie was shaking her head. "But that can't be . . . "

"I know. But here it is." Jason pulled the note out of his pocket and handed it to Sadie.

Her eyes tracked along the words and returned to the top. She read it at least three times. "Is this her handwriting?"

"I think so. I mean, it's been awhile since I've seen it, but I don't think I'd forget that."

"And it can't be an old note because it mentions your uncle."

"Right."

Sadie looked at the note again, turned it over, stroked the ripples left by the water. "So not only is your mom alive and well, she's in Salton."

Jason took the note and held it. "I guess so. If this is real. It's pretty weird."

"So, let's say it's fake. Does that mean you're not going to go meet whoever is going to be behind the high school tomorrow night?"

"Probably nobody."

"Okay. Probably nobody. You're not going to go meet probably nobody?"

Jason liked that Sadie was smart. Most of the time.

"You're right. I'm going to go meet probably nobody." He reached for his lemonade.

"I'm going with you."

"But the note says I'm not supposed to tell anyone."

"A little late for that. Besides, you don't believe anyone will show. Might as well have some company."

Before he could argue, not that he would have, Sadie's grandmother called them for dinner.

※ ※ ※

Jason, Sadie, and Finn climbed into the bleachers behind the dugout. The pungent smell of fresh fertilizer floated around them. Finn stretched and laid herself between two benches.

"We can watch from here and walk down to the dugout if anyone shows," Jason said.

"Okay." Sadie untied a sweatshirt from around her waist and pulled it over her head.

After a few more minutes, the lights in the school parking lot flickered, warming up and turning on as the sun lowered.

The meeting time passed. No one showed.

"Let's go." Jason pushed to stand.

Sadie grabbed his arm. "A couple more minutes. Maybe they're late?"

"I don't think nobody can be late."

A low growl churned inside Finn's chest and Jason dropped to his seat. Finn lifted her head and watched the back of the dugout, the growl deepening.

"That is giving me goosebumps," Sadie whispered.

Dark shadows wavered by the end of the dugout. Jason's neck prickled. He checked for Skyfish. All clear. "I'm going down there. You wait here."

Sadie nodded.

Jason stood and Finn popped up next to him, silent, her sight fixed on the dugout. Jason moved down the bleachers and Finn stayed in step, zeroed in on her target. Her feet patted noiselessly like they were walking on foam.

They reached the ground and moved to the opening. Jason peered around the doorway. A figure stood inside, facing away from Jason and Finn, wearing black pants and a black hooded jacket.

Finn growled. The figure spun around.

"I'd know that growl anywhere."

Finn quieted and dropped to a sit, a little wag flicking the tip of her tail.

"Hi, Jason."

Jason stood still but his heart rattled his ribcage. His mom, his missing mom, his not-dead mom, rushed over and enveloped him.

"Mom?" Jason's quivery arms moved around her.

"It's so good to see you." She squeezed him.

"Mom?"

"Yes, it's me. It's Mom."

Jason squeezed back hard, partly because it was her, and partly because the muscles in his legs felt mushy, watery, dissolved. He breathed in her Mom smell.

She tightened her hold. "I've missed you so much." She pushed back from him, held on to his shoulders. "Let me look at you."

She scanned Jason's face. He could almost feel her gaze brushing over his cheeks.

"You've grown so much. You must be a foot taller than the last time I saw you."

"Maybe a couple inches," Jason muttered. He stared at her. She was alive.

She pulled him close again. "I can't believe you're here, with me."

"Yeah, you too." Jason stepped back. "But where have you been?"

"It's a long story. There's so much—" She shoved Jason and stepped in front of him. "Get behind me."

His arm burned where she'd pushed him. He grabbed for the spot, applied pressure to the sting. He turned.

"Stay back." She wasn't talking to Jason. She faced the entry of the dugout, her hands up and open, like she was imitating a wild cat. A blue glow hovered around her palms, her fingers, her nails.

The person at the mouth of the dugout switched into a defensive stance, hands fisted. Next to them, Finn lowered her head and growled, the corner of her lip pulled up.

"No, Mom, it's okay." Jason grabbed her wrist and pulled one arm down but she kept her eyes fixed ahead. "That's Sadie."

Sadie slowly lowered her arms. She touched Finn's head, settling her.

"What?" Mom turned to Jason. "You told someone about me?"

"I didn't think it was real, that you were really, you . . . sorry?"

Mom walked to the back of the dugout, turned, and grabbed the chain link that protected players from stray bats and balls.

Sadie came over to Jason, leaned in and whispered. "Wow. That's really her?"

Jason nodded.

They watched Jason's mom gaze across the baseball diamond.

"Yeah. Really her." Jason rubbed the sore spot on his arm. "Mom? Are you okay? Are you mad at me?"

For a second she was distant again. Like the day she disappeared.

She took a deep breath, dropped her hands from the fence and turned toward them. Her mouth moved into a flat smile, pulling her lips thin.

"No, honey I'm not mad at you. Only . . . worried." She gestured toward the bench. "Why don't you two have a seat." Mom looked at Sadie. "Hi, Sadie. I'm sorry if I scared you."

"That's okay," Sadie said. "It is nice to meet you. I know Jason's happy you're here."

"That's sweet of you to say. But you might not think so if we can't fix things." She pushed the hood off her head, her blond hair framed her face. "We don't have a lot of time so I'm going to be frank with you. If you don't do everything I say, both of you, then we're all going to die."

TWENTY-ONE
A Plan Presented

It's all true then?" Jason watched his mom take another deep breath and release it.

"What has your uncle told you?"

Jason scooted forward on the bench. "Well, I know about cryptids, and the Rampart, that it protects everyone. And that someone is trying to destroy it. And you're a Rampart Guard, and so is he, and you've been hiding to protect us." He turned to Sadie. "Right?"

"Yeah. In a nutshell, anyway." Sadie tucked her hands into the pockets on the front of her sweatshirt.

Mom stared, her blue eyes locking with Jason's. They were bright blue, like the color Jason had seen around her hands.

He leaned back a couple of inches. "Mom?"

She broke her gaze, smiled at Jason.

"Are you coming home?"

Mom glanced away then back to Jason. "I really wish I could. But not yet. Not quite yet. I can't put you or Kyle or Della, or your dad at risk, and as long as they think I'm dead, then you're safe." She tucked her hair behind her ears. "In the meantime, there are some things that need to be done, and the first is to rescue your uncle."

Jason's back zipped straight. "You know where he is?"

"Not exactly, but I do know the general area. I can feel him through our connection, but the signal is weak. I'm hoping Finn can narrow it down."

Finn's ears perked at the mention of her name.

"Okay . . . so she finds him, then we call the sheriff," Jason said.

"No, I need you and Finn to find him then call me, and I'll figure out something."

"I dunno about that . . . " He glanced at Sadie. Her eyebrows arched.

"It sounds harder than it is. But you don't have to do anything more than that. If you find him, you call me and I'll do the rest," his mom said.

"But why not get the sheriff to help us? He knows Uncle Alexander is missing, they're looking for him."

"There are people we can't trust, Jason. I'm not saying the sheriff is one of them, but unless we know for certain, we can't trust anyone."

Jason gave a couple of small nods. *Maybe that's the real reason the sheriff wouldn't open a missing person case right away.*

Sadie twisted a chunk of her hair. "I have another question. Why don't you take Finn and find him yourself?"

Jason turned to face her. "Jeez, Sadie."

She stopped twisting her hair and sat on her hands. She looked at Jason and back to his mom.

"No, it's a fair question." Mom tipped her head toward Sadie. "I need to stay hidden, out of sight. It's too risky for me, but the two of you with Finn won't get a second look from anybody."

Sadie shifted in her seat. "Yeah, okay." She nodded at Jason.

"So who is it, Mom? Who's holding him?"

"I'm pretty sure it's the same person or organization that wants the Rampart destroyed. Guards are being attacked, even killed, in all parts of the globe." She clenched her fists.

"But I thought you knew who it was, and that's why you had to fake your death. And leave us." Jason's throat tightened.

Mom sat and put her arm around his shoulder, pulling him close. "Oh, I'm so sorry I had to do that." She kissed the top of his head. "I don't know exactly who's behind this, but I knew there was a problem and started investigating." She released Jason and stood again. "Apparently I stirred things up too much. I received death threats, against me and our family. This was the only way I could protect you, and keep searching for whoever is behind this."

"But you're going to figure it out? And everything will be okay again? You'll be safe? And come home?" Jason's breaths shortened.

His mom cupped his face in her hands. "We'll figure this out, and now we can do it together, okay?" She brushed his bangs off of his forehead.

"Okay, yeah, that sounds good." Jason exhaled and swallowed. "First, we see if Finn can find Uncle Alexander." He looked at Sadie. "You in?"

"Yeah, totally. It'll be a walk in the park. With a dog." She shrugged. "Right?"

Jason smiled and shook his head. "Or wherever."

"Speaking of which." Mom removed a map from her jacket pocket and unfolded it. "The signal is strongest in this general area." She pointed to a circle drawn on the map. It was just outside of town. "Let Finn run off leash. If Alexander is there somewhere, she'll find him. And then you call me." She wrote her cell phone number on the map and handed it to Jason.

"The connection between me and Alexander is getting weaker. He's alive, but he's been hurt or drugged or something. I don't think we have any time to lose."

"So, we have to go tonight . . . " Jason shifted in his seat. What would he tell Dad? "Finn and I will go. I don't want Sadie to get in trouble."

"No, I want to help." Sadie scooted forward on the bench. "I can't sit at home and do nothing."

"Then it's settled," Mom said. "Let's find Alexander and get him home before we lose him forever."

TWENTY-TWO
The Search

ose Uncle Alexander

Jason's gut climbed into his throat.

His cell phone rang. He stood and took it out of his pocket. "It's Dad." Jason looked at his mom.

She signaled it was okay to answer.

"Hey, Dad."

Jason listened.

"Yeah, we're about to head home." He shrugged at Mom who nodded her agreement.

"Okay, thanks. We'll meet you in the parking lot." He ended the call.

"Your father is coming to pick you up?"

"Yeah, he's on his way home from the grocery store, said he would swing by. I didn't know what else to say."

"It's good. You'll need your bikes to get to the search area." She stood and put her hands on Jason's shoulders. "Thank you for this. I'm so proud of you." She turned to Sadie. "Both of you."

She took his hand in hers. Her hand was hot. She offered the other to Sadie who stood and joined her.

"Please, please remember to keep our secret. I know it will be hard, but the best way to keep us all safe is to make sure no one knows I'm alive. No one." She squeezed their hands. "Okay?"

Jason nodded. He didn't want the knot in his throat to spring out and reveal he was more afraid than Mom knew.

"Okay," Sadie said.

Mom kissed Jason on the forehead. Then she hugged Sadie. "Thank you for being such a good friend to Jason."

"You're welcome." Sadie brushed back hair that breezed onto her cheek.

"You better get going. I'll watch from here until I see you've been picked up by your dad." Mom hugged Jason.

He hugged her back, as tightly as he could. "I'm so glad you're back, Mom."

"Me too." She released him. "Now go meet your dad or you'll have him worrying about you." She gave Finn a quick scratch behind the ears.

The trio left the dugout. Jason twice turned back to wave at his mom, and to confirm she was still there, watching over him, until she faded into the evening light and he couldn't see her anymore.

"Wow," Sadie said.

"Yeah, wow. Did we really just talk to my mom?"

"Yeah. You definitely did not meet nobody."

Jason chuckled and ran his hand through his hair. "No kidding. That was so awesome. This is all so totally awesome." He punched the air.

"There's your dad." Sadie waved at the car pulling into the lot.

✳ ✳ ✳

At home, Jason racked his brain but there was nothing he could say that Dad would approve of. A late night walk for Finn? No. A sleepover at a friend's house? The only person Jason knew was Sadie. So, no. Jason opted for plan C—don't tell Dad.

Jason slipped outside and leaned his bike, fresh from being repaired, against the side of the house. He put Finn in the backyard and told her to stay. Not long after that, when it didn't seem too unusual, he excused himself and said he was going to bed.

He messed up his blankets and arranged his pillows so it gave the impression that he was there, sound asleep. He threw on a sweatshirt, tucked a small flashlight in his pocket with his phone, and pushed open the window. His heart hammered as he looked at the tree that would carry him down. He'd never snuck out at night before.

But Uncle Alexander needs help. And Mom gave me permission, so I'm not really doing anything wrong.

He leaned out and swung onto a branch. It creaked with his weight but held. Jason shimmied to the ground.

He met Sadie and they rode their bikes toward the area circled on the map, far beyond town limits. Finn ran alongside them.

Jason didn't want to talk about where they were going, what they were doing. Didn't want to jinx it.

"Hey, what was with you and that action figure stance when you saw my mom?" Jason asked. "It was like you were really ready to fight."

"I was. I have a blue belt in Tae Kwon Do. I'm working toward my black belt."

"Seriously? Do you get in a lot of fights?"

Sadie laughed. "No, I don't get in a lot of fights. The whole point is to not get into fights, and to help build a more peaceful world. But I'm prepared if that doesn't work."

"So you weren't going to fight my mom?"

"First of all, I wasn't even sure it was your mom. Second, no, I wouldn't choose to fight her or anybody. I was just ready to defend myself, or help you."

They turned a corner and headed down the main road out of town.

"And given all that's going on at the moment, my blue belt isn't that big of a deal. What about your mom's blue hands?"

"I know. Freaky, right? It's a Guard thing. Uncle Alexander told me about it." Jason rubbed the spot on his arm. "I think she burned me when she shoved me out of the way."

"Burned you?"

"Yeah. It's red and it stings. Totally weird."

"That pretty much sums up all of this stuff. Totally weird."

A few minutes later they passed the *Thanks for visiting Salton!* sign. Dew flashed on the nearby crops whenever they pedaled under a streetlight. Giant sprinklers that rolled like robots across the field sat still in the darkness. It smelled like wet dirt.

Sadie clutched her stomach.

"Are you okay?"

"My stomach is bugging me. And my head hurts." She kneaded the back of her neck.

"Do you want to go back?" They were close to where their search would begin. "I can go with Finn. You head back."

"No, it's not that much farther. Maybe I'll feel better after we get off the bikes."

They turned down a farming road that ran between fields of corn. Large cottonwood trees loomed along the back of the fields. Jason and Sadie stopped and dismounted. Jason switched on his flashlight and scanned the area.

Sadie sat and tucked her head into her knees. She breathed out slowly, took a short breath in and held it, released it, and breathed in again.

"Better?"

She shook her head. "Worse." She sprang from her spot, scuttled to the left and vomited.

Finn whimpered. Sadie moved away from the mess and lay down. Finn snuggled in next to her.

"That's it," Jason said. "I'll call my dad and have him come get us."

"No, I'm okay here. You go with Finn, look for your uncle. Besides, your dad will kill you and I definitely don't want the wrath of Mamo. Just go."

"I can't leave you alone. You're sick."

"No, it's okay. I'm sorry I can't help. But I'm fine here. Really."
Sadie folded one arm over her eyes.

"If you're sure."

"Yes. Go."

Jason called to Finn. She sat up but didn't leave Sadie.

"C'mon girl. We're going to look for Uncle Alexander."

Finn's head cocked to the side.

"Uncle Alexander. Let's go." Jason slapped his leg. Finn lurched forward and bounded past Jason. "We'll hurry." He jogged to catch up with Finn.

She bounded into a row of cornstalks. Jason followed and watched the back of her head bob between sniffing the ground and sniffing the air. The stalks in the light were bright green, but the shadows looked like arms reaching out of the blackness. Jason tried to ignore it. His hands felt clammy.

After a few more minutes, Finn slowed her pace, gathered up the scents around her, then darted right, crashing through the corn. She sped up and Jason lost sight of her.

"Finn! Wait up!" He smashed against the plants and they scraped his skin. Finn yelped in the distance. "Finn!" He surged forward, fighting against the stalks. He reached the edge of the crops and stumbled into a field of wild grasses and scrub oak. He hunched down.

Thirty yards ahead was the abandoned sugar mill, the one Grandma Lena had told them about when they'd driven into town that first day. It sat empty and ugly, a victim of vandals and bad graffiti. Finn was at a back door, whining and scratching hard. A fluorescent light shone overhead. Moths flung themselves into it over and over.

Jason called her but she didn't hear him, didn't stop. He pocketed the flashlight and loped forward. He ducked behind a clump of scrub oak. A camera hung near the door, sweeping left and right.

Seems it's not so abandoned after all.

"Finn." Jason whispered more than yelled, but she heard him. "Come, Finn." She trotted over and lay down in the grass, panting. Her tongue bounced up and down. "Good job, girl." Jason scratched under her collar.

He pulled out the map and dialed Mom's number. The call connected after only half of a ring.

"The person at this number is unavailable. Please leave a message."

"What the?" Jason hung up and double-checked the number. He dialed again. Same message. He waited for the beep. "Mom, I think Finn found something. We're at the old sugar mill, the one way out of town. It's supposed to be abandoned but I don't think it is. Call me back." He ended the call.

He waited a couple minutes for her to call him, but she didn't. He pressed redial. The call went straight to voice mail. He pressed *End Call.* "This totally sucks."

Jason studied the area around the mill. No cars, no movement, no sign of life except for that camera. He thought about calling the sheriff or his dad, but he didn't know for certain that Uncle Alexander was in there. What was he going to say? *Uncle Alexander's dog scratched on the door so would you please go in the abandoned mill and look for him? Oh, and sorry I snuck out?* Yeah, that would work.

Maybe he should make his way back to Sadie and get her home, then try calling Mom again. But if Uncle Alexander was hurt or drugged, how much time did he have left?

Jason dialed Mom's number one more time. No go.

Maybe I could just take a look inside. Jason sat on his haunches. Finn popped up next to him, wagging her tail.

"No, you stay." He pointed to the ground. "Lie down."

Finn dropped to her belly but kept her ears perked.

Jason considered the windows. They were too high off the ground, above Jason's sightline. He'd have to try the door.

He studied the path of the camera and waited for it to point away. When it did, Jason stepped into the open and ran. He rushed to the building and pushed on the handle. Unlocked. He gave Finn one more signal to stay, and slinked inside.

Bare bulbs hung on cords, and concrete walls surrounded a large open space. Fat metal pipes snaked across the high ceiling. It smelled musty and sweet, like cooked broccoli and burned marshmallows.

Footprints marked the dusty floor, leading to the right. Rigid, Jason listened for voices, movement, anything that told him he wasn't alone. He heard nothing. He inched ahead, hugging tight to the wall. The cavern of space seemed to magnify the sound of his quick breaths. He fought to slow them but the struggle made him breathe harder.

The path ended at a smaller room set off from the main space. Jason leaned into the open doorway and peered around the edge. The room was clear. Sweat trickled into his eyes. He wiped it with the back of his hand and stepped inside.

The stench of rotten meat triggered a gag. Jason swallowed it. A trash can in the corner overflowed with take-out food cartons. They were flocked with flies. A rickety green recliner sat nearby, its stuffing oozing out from the seat and back. Next to it was a small wooden table. A wave of fresh air swept in through a broken window, but not enough to wash away the stink.

A waist-high wall cut through the end of the room. Jason crossed to it and the funk morphed to outhouse in summer. He could almost taste the rot when he breathed through his mouth alone.

He pulled the collar of his shirt over his nose and crept around the wall. A body lay on a small, smashed mattress. Jason froze. He waited for the person to move, to notice him. They didn't. Jason eased closer.

The body was a man with a short scraggly beard and ratty brown hair. He wore khaki pants, wet and stained, and a torn shirt that may once have been white. One of his arms was flung wide, off the mattress and onto the floor. His eyes were shut, his mouth hung open, and a fly sipped on drool that ran down his cheek.

It was Uncle Alexander.

TWENTY-THREE
A Fight For Family

Jason dropped and grabbed his uncle's shoulders. "Uncle Alexander." He shook him. The reek of urine and feces forced their way into Jason's head, gagging him again. He gulped it back. "Uncle Alexander."

No response.

Jason took out his cell phone and dialed *9-1-1*. A moment later the honking sound of an unconnected call squawked from the phone. He redialed—same result. "Dammit." He shoved the phone back in his pocket.

He snatched up Uncle Alexander's arm and tried to find a pulse. Blood crusted in a dry stream from his uncle's elbow down to the floor. His skin was clammy and cool.

Jason pressed his fingers into his uncle's neck. "C'mon, Uncle A . . . " A beat. Or was it? Jason wasn't sure if he felt his uncle's heartbeat or his own.

He pried open Uncle Alexander's eyelids. "Wake up, wake up." No reaction. Jason released and the eyelids sprung shut.

He slapped his uncle's cheeks. "C'mon, I need you to wake up. C'mon." He shook his uncle's shoulders again. Hard.

Nothing. *Mom knew they'd done something to him. But this is bad.*

He seized Uncle Alexander's lifeless arms and heaved him to sitting. Jason tucked himself under one arm and wrapped his own arm around his uncle's back. He lifted but Uncle Alexander's dead weight held them fast.

Jason leaned forward, set one foot behind and lifted again. He got them both up but Uncle Alexander's body swung back and they fell to the mattress. Jason's chin planted in brown gooey something.

His stomach lurched. He shoved himself up and wiped his face with the front of his shirt.

Don't think about it. Just don't think about it.

Maybe he could drag the mattress like a sled and get Uncle Alexander out to the fresh air.

Jason repositioned his uncle in the center. He pulled at the foot. The mattress moved easier than he expected. This was going to work.

Jason's spine heated and sounds around him burst from quiet to crackling. He dropped the mattress and swung around. He didn't see Skyfish. But he knew they were coming.

Glass shattered and Skyfish zoomed through the window. Different ones. Silver. Sleeker. Shaped like bullets.

Jason held his ground and raised his arms. Heat shot through him and into his palms. Blue light surrounded his hands.

What the? No time to think. Jason lunged.

Zags of electricity shot out and into the Skyfish, disintegrating them. Others dashed and regrouped, speeding in from the side. Jason ducked. Three skimmed his arm and his skin sizzled. He fired overhead. Skyfish sparked and popped and zapped to nothingness. More came and Jason rolled to face them, fired. They dodged and he blasted holes in the wall behind them. They redirected. He connected and incinerated five as they hurled toward him. A haze coated the air.

More Skyfish attacked. Jason's vision clouded. He jumped but one burned a gash in his thigh. Jason staggered, tried to maintain his balance. The flash, his power, weakened. He lowered one hand to the wall behind him, holding on, still fighting.

But he knew he was going to fail.

He dropped to his knees. He couldn't move fast enough. His arms ached. His head hurt. His vision darkened.

A new band of Skyfish careened in from the hallway.

Finished.

This group of Skyfish, golden like those he'd seen before, slammed into the silver ones and exploded. Other goldens circled behind Jason and melded together, shifted forward and enveloped him.

New power bolted him upright. He raised both arms. Blue energy erupted.

He zeroed in on the silver Skyfish. Fire engulfed them. Jason's strength surged. The silvers sizzled and dissolved and fled.

The goldens released him and Jason's strength eased. Every silver Skyfish was gone. Golden Skyfish hovered above. Except one. It floated in front of Jason's face. He reached out and it moved forward, connecting to Jason's finger.

A shock shot through him but there was no pain. This was solid, strong, secure, like high-fiving his teammates after a big game. The golden Skyfish released and joined the others.

Jason kneeled next to Uncle Alexander and slapped his cheeks. "Uncle Alexander?" Still no response. "Seriously? After all that?" Jason sighed. *Not good.*

He moved to the end of the mattress, lifted it and took two backward steps toward the door.

"I don't think so."

Jason dropped the mattress and spun around. Two men stood inside the doorway, one shorter than the other, but neither of them could be considered tall. Jason's height exceeded theirs by at least three inches.

They both wore brown trench coats and brown pants. The coats were buttoned high under their chins. The shorter man was bald and he had his hands in his pockets. The taller man was bald on top with black stringy hair, long enough to reach his shoulders, ringing his head like greasy worms. His eyes were as dark as his hair, his skin tight, tinged yellow, shiny. His face was sharp with a pointed nose, pointed chin, and a mouth that pointed out almost like a beak.

"Oh, I've startled you. My apologies." The taller one grinned and stepped closer to Jason. "Allow me to introduce myself. My name is Mizu."

The odor of maggoty fish engulfed the room.

"Okay, Mizu." Jason's muscles twitched. He glanced at the Skyfish. They were bunched together, like a large ball, an indoor sun.

"Proper etiquette dictates that you now introduce yourself to me." Mizu waved a gloved hand. "But no matter. I already know who you are, Jason Lex."

Jason stared at Mizu. Had he met him somewhere?

"I see I've surprised you." Mizu's eyes narrowed and his grin flattened.

"I don't like surprises." Jason kept his eyes on Mizu but concentrated on his hands, flexed them, summoned the blue light.

There was not even a tingle. *Not really a Guard.*

"That's too bad. You've already surprised us." Mizu nodded toward his companion. "Me and Haru."

Haru didn't move, didn't gesture, didn't smile.

"Haru doesn't speak much or he would have introduced himself properly." Mizu shrugged. "Instead we all have to tolerate his rude behavior."

Haru looked at Mizu, then back to Jason.

"As I was saying, you have surprised us." He walked to the ratty recliner and sat. "Defeating our Skyfish like that. Really, no one expected anything like that from you."

"*Your* Skyfish?" Jason watched Mizu but kept Haru in his peripheral vision.

"Yes, they're on our side. They want the Rampart destroyed. I want the Rampart destroyed." He leaned forward. "Anyone who's anybody wants the Rampart destroyed."

"So it's you. You're behind it." Jason noticed a surge in the glow of the Skyfish above him.

"Hah. Yes. I'm behind it." He leaned back in the chair and the footrest kicked out. "But I'm one of many, Jason Lex. One of many cryptids who are tired of humans and their wastefulness, their destruction, their pollution. We eliminate the humans, the planet thrives. And there will be no need for the Rampart."

"You can't just kill everyone, every human."

"I think of it more as a regeneration project, like we're eradicating an invasive species of plant that's doing more harm than good. Humans are noxious weeds. We will eliminate all of you."

"No. You won't." *Mom will stop them.*

"Your pseudo-courage is charming. Or is ridiculous the word I'm searching for? Regardless, it's going to take a lot more than pretending to be brave to stop us." He waved at the golden Skyfish. "And your shiny friends aren't going to be much help."

Mizu sprang from the chair and landed ten feet in front of Jason. Jason raised his hands and begged for the power he'd found earlier. Small sparks spit and faded from his fingers.

"Adorable." Mizu pulled off the gloves and threw off the overcoat. His arms were long and scaly and slimy. He had four bony fingers, two long and two short, each one finished with a sharp orange claw, just like the one Jason had seen in Uncle Alexander's lab—a Kappa.

Mizu screeched and charged.

Jason dove behind the wall where his uncle had been.

Mizu crashed into it and howled. "Enough, Jason Lex. I'm tired of you." He leaped high, clearing the wall.

Jason dashed under him. He clenched his hands, prayed for them to heat, load, anything.

Still nothing.

Mizu chased.

Jason grabbed the end table. He swung it, hitting Mizu's arm. Slime smeared off Mizu and onto the tabletop. Mizu jumped sideways. Jason jabbed, blocked, swung again, and wished he had a baseball bat.

Haru moved toward the fight. Jason's grip slipped on the slimy table. He swung hard and connected with Mizu's chin, throwing him to the ground, the table slinging past him.

Jason ran to the garbage can and kicked it, dumping the contents. Haru moved away and Mizu charged again. Jason grabbed the metal handles on the can and shielded himself, bracing for impact.

Intense light erupted from the Skyfish above. Jason shielded his eyes, saw only shades of gray around him, white above. The ball of light sank onto Uncle Alexander and shot from the room.

Jason's eyes adjusted. Uncle Alexander was gone.

"Go after them." Mizu yelled at Haru. Haru ran out. Mizu attacked.

Jason blocked with the garbage can. It dented where Mizu's arm connected. Jason pulled back and swung, hitting Mizu's other arm. Mizu whirled around and kicked the can into Jason's gut.

His breath gushed out. He stumbled, found his footing, held firm to the can, and searched for another weapon.

Nothing.

Mizu charged. Jason ducked Mizu's swing and pushed him backward. Jason ran forward and slammed the bottom of the can into Mizu's chest. He reeled.

Jason yelled and plowed the metal can into Mizu, pinning him against the wall.

"Nice try." Mizu unwedged an arm and swiped a claw across Jason's forehead.

He stumbled back. Blood poured into his eyes.

Mizu punched the can and ripped it from Jason's hand, popping Jason's fingers from their sockets. He wailed and ran for the door. Mizu leaped in front. He spun and swung his leg into Jason's thigh. Bone crunched. Jason screamed and dropped and writhed on the floor.

Mizu hunched next to Jason. "Oh, dear, the little boy is hurt. I bet you want your mommy, don't you?" He was grinning again, this time with open lips showing a mouth full of pointed, yellow teeth. "But there's no mommy for you. Only me."

He drew a claw through the blood running down Jason's face and licked it off with his green tongue. His swamp-water breath crept into Jason's mouth and nose.

"Hmmm. That's tasty enough, but I prefer my drinks direct from the tap." Mizu pressed a claw into Jason's neck.

Jason grabbed Mizu's arm, tried to push him back. "No." He forced the word out between throbs of pain and gasps for air.

"Fighting to the last possible moment? Admirable. But ridiculous. You're finished."

The claw pierced Jason's skin. New agony shot into his neck and shoulders and forced his eyes shut. He shoved at the slippery arm, but it was no use. The claw went deeper then withdrew fast. Something suctioned onto the wound.

He opened his eyes. Mizu's tongue stretched to Jason's neck. The puce green tissue was spackled with spots of gray, like mold on bread. It was framed by Mizu's fangy teeth. Jason willed himself to fight, to push Mizu one more time.

Mizu's tongue popped free and Jason stared into the ropes of slithery hair on the back of Mizu's head. A second later a flash like white marble crashed into Mizu and sent him flying.

He scrambled, tried to get to his feet, but Finn had him by the leg. She shook Mizu and pounded his head into the wall. She hurled him, sailing him to the other side of the room. Mizu landed on one arm. Claws snapped off and pus oozed out. He tucked his arm and rolled to his knees.

Like a sideways bolt of lightning Finn lunged, grabbed the top of Mizu's head and whipped him around again. With the third thrash, Mizu's scalp ripped off. His body slid across the floor, green liquid from his head trailing behind him. Mizu did not move.

Finn dropped the flesh and trotted over to Jason.

Jason kept one hand pressed against the gash in his neck. He pushed himself to sitting, cringing at the pain that sliced through his leg. "Oh my God, Finn, you are the coolest dog ever." Finn licked Jason's face. He sucked in a breath. "I don't suppose you can carry me out of here?" She wagged her tail and sat. "Yeah, I figured that would be too much to ask."

Jason dragged himself a few inches toward the door then collapsed when the pain swelled through him, threatening to send him to unconsciousness. He rested, let it pass then lifted himself again to make another push toward the exit.

Haru entered.

Fresh adrenaline shot through Jason. "Finn. Get him." Jason yelled, pointing at Haru. Finn didn't move.

Haru came over and pressed on Jason's broken leg.

"No. Get away." Jason tried to shove Haru but Haru might as well be made of stone. Or straw. Jason had nothing left and Haru didn't budge.

"It's okay. I'm a friend of your uncle's. Not all cryptids want the Rampart destroyed." Haru used one claw to cut open Jason's pant leg. He ran his scaly hands along Jason's femur and stopped. "This is going to hurt."

"Yeah, well, it already—aaaahhhh." Jason jolted and fell back, blackness covering his eyes.

"Sorry about that. But it will feel better in a minute." Haru applied pressure to Jason's thigh.

"I don't know how it could feel anything but better after that." Jason kept his eyes scrunched shut, taking short, shallow pants of air.

Haru moved to Jason's dislocated fingers. "Once more."

The pain whipped Jason's eyes open. "Fu—what is your problem?" The pain in his hand flowed out fast. Jason flexed his fingers. "Huh?"

"That's good. You should be able to stand on your leg now, too. Don't run on it right away, but it should be fully healed in a day or two. Your other wounds are healed as well." Haru stood and reached down to Jason. His clawed hand morphed into one that appeared human.

Jason clasped Haru's arm and stood.

"I have to go before they figure out I helped you. You have a clear path back to Sadie. She's with Alexander. You need to get him to a hospital." Haru headed for the window.

"But wait. What? How—?"

"Kappa. We have a talent for medicine." He smiled. "Good luck, Jason Lex." He jumped to the ledge and was gone.

* * *

Finn rushed to Uncle Alexander and lay down. She licked his ear and sniffed.

Sadie jumped up. "Jason, are you okay? What happened to your head?"

Jason touched dried blood where the gash had been. "I'm okay. Way better than I was a few minutes ago."

"What happened?" She sat back down.

Jason told her everything. "I think my leg was broken, and my fingers were dislocated—"

"But you're walking."

"Thanks to my new friend, Haru. Nice bruises, huh?" Jason's leg was mottled red and purple and black. "Like I said, I'm way better now."

155

"Haru fixed you?"

"Yeah. Crazy. Nothing but crazy in there." He thumbed in the direction of the mill then squatted and put his fingers on Uncle Alexander's neck. Definitely a pulse this time. "What about you? You're feeling better?"

"Yeah. Haru. I didn't even know he was here. I felt a hand on my forehead then I was better. I opened my eyes and there he was, next to your uncle. I guess the Skyfish brought him here." She gestured to Uncle Alexander. "I've already called an ambulance."

The sound of sirens grew. Blue and red lights flashed above headlights in the distance.

"Right on cue." Jason walked into the clearing and waved his flashlight. The vehicles hammered up the road. Two sheriff's cars and an ambulance. And close behind them, Jason's dad.

"What are we going to tell them?" Sadie pulled a piece of meadow grass out of her hair.

"I dunno. I guess I'm winging it."

Before Sadie had a chance to respond, the doors opened and people rushed toward them.

The medical team reached them first and went straight to Uncle Alexander. Finn stood watch as one tech called out vital signs, the other logged them. They asked how Uncle Alexander got this way, if he'd taken anything, how long he'd been like this. "I don't know," Jason answered to every question.

Dad ran to Jason's side. "What are you doing here? You are supposed to be—my God, what happened to you?" He examined Jason's forehead. "Where did all this blood come from?"

"A small cut. It's stopped bleeding already. I'm okay."

"And your leg? What happened?"

"Uh, these guys had Uncle Alexander—"

"What? You were attacked? Where are they?" The tendons in Dad's neck seized like metal cables.

"They're gone. Finn chased them off."

Finn walked over and leaned into Dad. She nosed his clenched hand. He relaxed it and petted the top of her head. "Unlimited dog bones for you, girl." Finn's tail swished.

"Sadie. Oh, Sadie." Sadie's grandmother hurried from her car and scooped Sadie into her arms. "What are you doing here? Are you all right?"

"Yes, I'm fine." Sadie's voice was muffled by her grandmother's tight squeeze. Sadie twisted her head an inch. "Except you're smothering me."

Willene released her grip and pressed Sadie's cheeks between her hands. "How many times have I told you, you can't leave town? And sneaking out on top of it. What were you thinking?"

"We're not exactly in Paris or anything." Sadie pulled away.

Willene bit her bottom lip and released it. She took Sadie's hand in hers. "Right. You're right. I was just so worried when the sheriff called. But you're okay? Not hurt? Are you feeling sick?"

Sadie tilted her head. "I was sick but . . . I'm better now."

"Oh, good." Willene patted Sadie's wrist and her bracelet jingled. "That's really good."

One paramedic examined Jason and Sadie while the other finalized Uncle Alexander's prep for the trip to the emergency room. Aside from Jason's bruises, both he and Sadie checked out fine though the paramedic suggested a visit to the hospital, just to be safe.

"Can they answer a few questions first?" Sheriff Gunderson walked up, his hand on his holstered gun.

Dad and Willene nodded. Jason felt a headache mounting.

The sheriff took out his notepad. "First of all, nice work finding your uncle." He nodded at Jason.

"Thanks, but, it wasn't just me." He gestured to Sadie and Finn. "It was all three of us."

"Well, it seems you make a good team." He smiled. "But what brought you way out here, especially at this time of night?"

Jason glanced at Sadie. "Uh, it was my idea. I couldn't sleep, and I've been thinking it would be cool to come out to the cornfields at night, ya know, 'cause they're kinda creepy."

Sadie spoke up. "Yeah, and he called me, and I thought it would be fun, too."

"Right. But we knew we'd never get permission to go, so we had to sneak out."

Dad crossed his arms.

Jason continued. "So, we came out here on our bikes, and then we stopped to rest for a minute. But Finn took off through the fields all of a sudden and I had to chase after her."

"I stayed with the bikes," Sadie said. Her grandmother shifted her weight and clasped her hands behind her back.

"All right," Sheriff Gunderson said. "So Miss Finn here catches some sort of scent or something, Jason races off after her, and I'm guessing she led you to the mill?"

"Right." Jason thrust his hands forward. "Exactly."

"And you decided to go in there by yourself?" Dad asked. His eyebrows arched.

"No. No, I didn't. First I called—" Jason swallowed. "First I called 9-1-1. It didn't go through. And I tried a couple of times, but I guess I had a bad connection, or something." He shoved his hands in his pockets then took them back out. "And I still wasn't going to go in. I wanted to look through a window or whatever, but that didn't really work because they are high up, and then I heard a noise."

"What kind of noise?" Sheriff Gunderson asked.

"Like, yelling. Like someone yelling for help. Finn heard it, too." Jason pointed to Finn and she cocked her head. "I had to do something and the door was unlocked . . . " Jason shoved his hands back in his pockets.

Dad ran his hands through his hair. "You could have been seriously hurt, or killed. That was a very poor decision."

"But I wasn't . . . " Jason tuned into the soreness in his leg. "And we helped Uncle Alexander . . . Finn chased the bad guys away."

Dad sighed and looked upward.

"How did you manage to get your uncle all the way out here, all by yourself?" The sheriff asked.

"Yeah . . . he was awake enough to walk while he leaned on me, and then he passed out."

"Hmm. Okay." Sheriff Gunderson closed his notepad. "We'll continue the investigation here, track down the owners of the property, see what we can find out from those security cameras and such. But you can all head home now, get some rest."

The group turned toward the cars.

Sheriff Gunderson spoke. "Oh, and one more thing, Jason?" Everyone stopped and looked back at him. "That was very brave, what you did today. Please don't ever do something like that again."

"No problem, Sheriff," Jason said. He stole a look at his not-blue hands.

Now that Uncle Alexander is back, I'll just let the real Guards handle this stuff.

❋ ❋ ❋

At home after a hot shower, Jason tried his mom's number again. The call still didn't connect. He wiped his palms on his pants and pushed out the thought that she might be in trouble. A moment later, his cell phone rang.

"Hey, Sadie."

"Is your dad mad?"

"Strangely, no. Said something about being a kid once, and he understands why we did what we did."

"Wow. Seriously?"

"Yeah, totally serious. Though he did make me promise never to sneak out again. What about your grandmother?" Jason plopped down on his bed.

"She's a little freaked out."

"Because you left town by, like, twenty-seven feet or whatever?"

"I know, right? That was so bizarre. I mean she's always told me we should wait until I'm older before we travel anywhere so I can appreciate it more, but I thought she meant Europe or Asia or even Disneyland. Not the next town over or whatever." Sadie cleared her throat. "But hey—I've been thinking about the Skyfish. If they could move your uncle, why didn't they do it before today?"

"Good question. And I also wonder why I could zap with the blue light one minute and have nothing the next. I didn't even know I could do it in the first place."

"Maybe you need each other."

"Huh?"

"Maybe you're connected to them, the golden Skyfish anyway. Maybe it has something to do with when they killed you, or sort of killed you. Whatever they did to you," Sadie said.

"I didn't feel all that different when I woke up. Not stronger or faster. No intense desire to leap tall buildings in a single bound."

Sadie chuckled. "Well, seems kinda logical to me."

The idea bounced around Jason's brain.

"Have you been able to reach your mom?" Sadie asked.

"No, the number still won't go through."

"That's weird. You'd think she'd have called by now since she hasn't heard from you."

"Yeah, well, she must be really busy with something else. Or she needs to be radio silent for some reason. There's gotta be a good explanation." Jason rubbed the soreness in his thigh. "I'm sure she'll call when she can, when it's safe."

"Yeah," she said and paused. "How's Uncle Alexander?"

"He's still unconscious, but stable. The docs aren't sure what's wrong with him. They're running a ton of tests."

"Keep me posted on what you find out, okay?"

"I will."

"Thanks. I'm gonna go." Sadie yawned into the phone. "I'm super tired."

"Okay. And thanks for going with me tonight."

"No problem. Talk to you tomorrow."

Jason disconnected the call and put the phone on his nightstand. Finn jumped on the bed and laid her head on his chest. He scratched under her chin.

"Big day, huh?"

Finn licked him once on his wrist.

Jason rubbed Finn's ears.

Mom will be proud. Mom will come home.

TWENTY-FOUR
A Question of Trust

Dad woke Jason late the next morning and they headed to the hospital to see Uncle Alexander. Jason smiled to himself. He saved Uncle Alexander. Mom's alive. They know Mizu, a Kappa, is part of the group behind everything. Uncle Alexander would get better, he and Mom would save the Rampart, and everything would be normal again, or as normal as they could be with Skyfish and Kappas and whatever else hanging around.

Yep. Things were good. And weird. But good. Weird good.

A doctor met with the family in the hallway outside Uncle Alexander's room. "He was heavily drugged." He flipped open the chart. "He has track marks on both arms and we're still waiting for the toxicology report. He's dehydrated and malnourished, he wasn't bathed, and he was left in his own feces and urine which resulted in infected bed sores."

Jason could almost taste the memory of the stench. He swallowed hard. Twice.

The doctor snapped the chart shut. "Needless to say, he's going to feel poorly for a while. But I'm confident the worst is over. We have him on IV fluids and antibiotics. He needs some time, but I expect him to make a full recovery."

"That's good news," Dad said. "Thank you, doctor."

"Can we see him now?" Jason bobbed on his toes.

"Yes," the doctor said. "But he's in and out of consciousness, and when he's awake he's not exactly lucid. He's been hallucinating. If he wakes while you're here, don't expect too much."

Dad nodded and Jason practically ran into his uncle's room. Kyle and Della followed.

Uncle Alexander was asleep. He wore a white hospital gown with a blue diamond design, and he still had the scraggly beard. An IV needle was stuck in a vein on the back of his hand, a clip pinched one finger, and monitors around him beeped and buzzed. He looked a lot better than the last time Jason saw him. Smelled better, too. Like rubbing alcohol and soap.

Jason sat in a chair next to the bed and tapped his foot on the floor. Kyle leaned against the windowsill behind him. Dad and Della stood at the foot.

"He doesn't look so bad." Della pushed aside the tray table and hopped up.

"Yeah. I expected more zombie than human after hearing the doc," Kyle said.

"He wasn't even as good as zombie yesterday." Jason stretched the tight muscles in his leg.

Uncle Alexander's eyes fluttered and opened.

"Hey, Uncle Alexander." Jason pressed his uncle's arm.

"Jason?" Uncle Alexander squinted. "Jason. You have to get out of here." He tried to push himself higher, and swatted at the tubing that ran from IVs. "They'll catch you. Go."

Jason held onto Uncle Alexander's wrist. "It's okay, Uncle Alexander. It's okay." Jason zeroed in on his uncle's face. "You're in the hospital."

Dad stepped to the other side and guided Uncle Alexander back down into the pillows. "You need to stay calm, Alexander. You've been through a lot."

163

Uncle Alexander stopped squirming. "I'm in the hospital?" His eyes locked onto Jason's. "It's safe?"

"Yeah, you're safe. You're okay."

Uncle Alexander relaxed. "Safe." He regarded everyone again. "And you're all here. Well, we should go then." He pushed off the covers and moved his legs toward the floor.

"You're not going anywhere." Dad again eased him back and replaced the blankets. "You're staying right here until you're better. The doctors need some more time with you yet."

"Doctors?"

"Uncle Alexander, you're in the hospital." Della giggled.

"How? But your mom . . . "

Jason shook his head. "She's not here, Uncle Alexander. Only us." He squeezed his uncle's forearm. "Okay? Just us."

"Alexander." Grandma Lena rushed through the doorway. She hugged Uncle Alexander, kissed his cheek, and put the back of her hand on his forehead. "I'm so glad you're awake. And your fever is down, too." She took Uncle Alexander's hand in hers.

"Mom, have you seen Adrienne?"

"No, honey, I haven't seen your sister." Her eyes flicked to Jason and back. She palmed Uncle Alexander's forehead. "Maybe you do still have a fever."

"She was there. I saw her. And I felt her until they stuck me with needles. They wouldn't stop sticking me with those needles." He grabbed at the bend in his arm.

"Why is he talking about Mom?" Della asked.

"He just imagined some things. He's not feeling so good," Dad said.

Kyle whistled. "They drugged him up solid."

Dad opened the door to the hallway. "Kids, let's give your grandmother some time with Alexander." Dad waved them toward the door. Della slid off the bed and Kyle walked to her. Jason didn't budge.

"You've been through quite a lot, Alexander." Grandma Lena patted his hand.

"They hurt me. They want to hurt all of us."

"I know they hurt you, honey, I know." She pushed Uncle Alexander's hair off his face.

Dad spoke. "C'mon Jason."

Jason took two small steps and stopped.

Uncle Alexander continued. "We have to stop them, Mom. They're going to ruin everything. She's going to kill everyone."

"Jason." Dad's do-not-question-me voice.

Jason trudged around the bed, fixated on his uncle and grandmother.

"You don't have to worry about anything like that right now. You need to rest." Grandma Lena picked up a cool compress and put it on Uncle Alexander's forehead.

"We have to find Adrienne." The heart monitor beeped faster.

"Relax, honey, please. You have to get well."

Jason stepped into the hallway, the slow hinge of the door inched it closer to closed.

"But Mom—Adrienne's the one. Adrienne is destroying the Rampart."

A moment later, alarms sounded and people in scrubs rushed into Uncle Alexander's room. Jason glimpsed inside. Uncle Alexander's eyes were scrunched shut and he struggled to breathe. Someone put an oxygen mask on face.

Grandma Lena exited the room and put her hands on Jason's shoulders, directing him to the waiting area with the rest of the family.

"Your uncle is going to be okay. They're giving him a sedative." She sat next to Jason.

"He's crazy." Jason slumped and crossed his arms.

"Just give him a little bit of time. Who knows what they did to him?"

"I don't care what they did to him. Mom would never do any of the things he said."

Grandma Lena turned to Dad. "Zachary, if you don't mind making a run to the cafeteria, I'll treat everyone to a snack. Would that be okay with you? And you kids?" She nodded at Kyle and Della. "Jason and I will wait here."

Della jumped out of her chair. "Yeah. French fries and root beer."

"Thanks, Lena, that's a great idea." He stood. "C'mon you two, let's go spend Grandma Lena's money." He winked at her.

"Herbal iced tea for me, if they have it." Grandma Lena called after them.

"You got it," Dad said. "What do you want, Jason?"

"Nothing."

"Cool. More fries for me and Della." Kyle high-fived his little sister and the trio headed for the elevator.

Grandma Lena turned back to Jason. "All right. It's you and me now. What's going on?"

"Uncle Alexander's sick. That's what's going on."

"And he's going to be okay, thanks to you and Sadie."

"Yeah. Great."

"You're upset about what he said."

Jason spun in the chair to face Grandma Lena. "She's how we found him. She's his sister. She's *good*."

Grandma Lena raised her eyebrows. "She's how you found him?"

"Yes, she's . . . she's . . . " Jason shook his head and shoved his hands in his pockets.

Mom said tell no one. Too dangerous.

"I just mean she's the one that told me . . . about how she used to play in the cornfields. At night. She told me that a long time ago."

Grandma Lena didn't say anything.

"What?" Jason shrugged.

She sighed. "Give your uncle a couple of days to get better, to get the junk flushed out of his system and some real food in his belly. Then talk to him. Okay?"

Jason rolled his eyes and turned away.

"Jason. Do not jump to judgment right now. It's not fair to either of you."

"Fine."

"Promise me."

"Fine. I promise." He crossed his arms again.

After the rest of the family returned from the cafeteria, the doctor said it was best to let Uncle Alexander rest for the remainder of the day. He'd call if there were any changes.

On the way home, Jason texted Sadie. *Can u meet at cove 30mins?*

Y. CU there.

A few minutes later, Dad pulled into the garage.

"I'm going for a run." Jason dashed down the driveway.

"In those clothes? Dinner's at six," Dad yelled after him.

Jason waved his hand and bolted.

※ ※ ※

Sadie was already at the cove, with her computer. "Hey." She shut the lid on her laptop. "How's your uncle?"

"Fine. Or not fine. I dunno." Jason dropped to the ground. Leaves crunched beneath him. "He's saying crazy crap." He flicked a twig off his knee.

"That's not new."

"Fine, crazier crap, then. You won't believe it." Jason pushed his hair off his face. "He said that *my mom* is the one trying to destroy the Rampart."

"He did?"

"I know, right? I mean, we wouldn't have even found him if it wasn't for her." He picked up a stick and broke it in pieces, tossing each segment aside.

"Yeah . . . I guess . . . "

Jason stopped tossing and eyed Sadie.

She lifted her hand. "Walk through this with me for a minute to make sure I understand everything correctly."

"Okay . . . "

"In fact, don't say anything. Just listen."

Jason nodded.

"We know that someone is trying to destroy the Rampart, and that would be very bad."

Jason stayed quiet.

"We know your mom is alive and she has the power to protect the Rampart, along with your uncle, and your uncle and mom have a connection. They know where the other one is, or what they're feeling."

"Mmmhmm." Jason waved her along and dropped his hands in his lap.

"Okay. Your mom has some sort of blue light power that helps her protect and repair the Rampart. It stands to reason that your uncle does, too. And maybe you do too, but we're not one-hundred-percent sure about that. And she basically knew the area where your uncle was being held. Yes? All true so far?"

"Yep."

Sadie swallowed. "Well, here's where it gets a bit tricky. Remember, just listen, okay?"

"I'm listening." Jason's stomach tensed.

Sadie took a deep breath. "Your mom sent us, with Finn, to find your uncle. And, kind of amazingly, you did."

"But—" Jason leaned forward.

"No. Listen."

He closed his mouth tight and settled back.

"The number she gave you doesn't reach her, doesn't reach anyone. And she hasn't called you. I know you think it's because something more urgent came up. But what's more urgent than you and her brother?"

Jason breathed through his nose, slow and deep.

"I'm done. You talk now."

"What if something's happened to her, Sadie? Or are you saying you believe my uncle?" He tightened his throat to keep from raising his voice.

"I'm saying we should examine everything."

"Everything like my mom is trying to kill us all?" The vise loosened.

"Please don't get angry." She pushed her laptop aside and leaned toward him. "I'm worried that we're missing something. I'm worried that we're being naive. I'm worried that you might get hurt, that we all might get hurt, if we're not careful."

Jason's brain spun like helicopter blades. He couldn't grasp anything that confirmed she was wrong. And he didn't dare believe she was right. "But Sadie, that could mean . . . "

"Jason, I'm sorry." Sadie's voice broke.

"I've gotta go." He forced his way out of the bramble.

TWENTY-FIVE
A Guard Revealed

Jason ran until his throbbing leg forced him to stop. He limped into the kitchen. Dad was slicing onions and adding them to a tray that already held tomatoes, pickles and lettuce. A plate of hamburger patties were ready for the grill.

"Hey, are you okay?" Dad asked.

"Yeah, fine. My leg's sore from . . . everything. But I'm fine." Jason washed his hands and soaked his head under the running faucet. The water trickled down his back.

Dad handed Jason a wad of paper towels. "Don't get water all over the floor."

Jason pressed the towels into his hair and took an apple.

"And don't eat too much. Dinner's almost ready."

"Okay." Jason stalked past Dad.

"You're sure you're okay?"

"Fine, Dad. I just need a shower." *And to talk to Mom.*

✳ ✳ ✳

Jason put on his boxers and walked out of the bathroom. He stopped short. Kyle was sitting on Jason's bed.

"This is weird." Jason rubbed the towel on his head.

"What is?"

170

"You. In my room. Waiting for me. I think that's happened probably, oh . . . never." Jason pushed his fingers through his wet hair. "What's the deal?"

"No deal. A question."

"What question?" He hung the towel.

"Have you seen Mom?"

Jason's hands faltered and the towel dropped from the hook on his door. He rehung it. "Um, not since she did the whole disappeared-in-the-woods thing." He pretended to pick at a snag in the cloth, keeping his back to his brother.

"Since then, Jason. Have you seen Mom since then?"

Jason's stomach fluttered. He walked to his dresser. "Hah. Very funny. Like I see dead people." He pulled a pair of shorts over his boxers, a T-shirt over his head.

Kyle shifted toward Jason. "Dude, I'm serious."

Jason cheeks warmed. "Why are you asking me this?"

"Because I want to know if you know."

"Know what?" Jason wanted to yell but kept his voice low enough that it wouldn't be heard outside the room.

"That Mom's alive." Kyle's voice sounded strangled.

Jason stared, his mouth open, trying to form words. But what words? Keep the secret or not? Kyle knows? If he knows, why did she say to tell no one? With a fluster of air, one word eased out. "Yeah."

Kyle fell back onto Jason's bed, covering his face with his hands. "Goddammit." He shouted but the sound stopped at his fingers.

"You know too, apparently." Jason crossed his arms over his chest.

Kyle sat up and smacked the bed. "Hell yeah, I know. She started texting me months ago, before we moved. Told me we were all in danger, told me she needed my help, told me not to tell anyone she was alive until she figured things out."

That's why he's been texting so much. "Figured things out . . . about the Rampart?" Jason's breath hitched in his throat.

Kyle cocked his head. "Wow—she told you the same thing, huh? Did she tell you about the Guards?"

"No, not exactly . . . " Jason pictured the book at his uncle's house. "She didn't tell me anything about the Rampart. Or the Guards. Uncle Alexander told me."

"Of course Uncle Loco would spill his guts. Did he tell you that you're chosen?"

"By chosen, do you mean chosen to be a Rampart Guard?"

"Yep. That's what Mom told me. That I'm chosen."

Disappointment slugged Jason in the gut. "Not me. That's all you." *Why wasn't Kyle's name in gold?*

"But something's off." Kyle fell back on the bed again.

"Like what?" Jason straddled his desk chair.

"Like everything." Kyle squinted at the ceiling. "Why couldn't I tell anyone about her, especially you, since you know she's alive? And why couldn't I go to the sugar mill since I'm the one who figured out Uncle Alexander was there?"

"You did?"

"Yeah." Kyle popped up. "I saw a map on her desk when I was with her last week."

Jason's chest squeezed. *Kyle's been spending time with her.* Jason forced a neutral expression, forced himself to keep listening.

"And I remembered some things shc'd mentioned during training."

"Training?"

"Yeah, Rampart Guard training. Anyway, I put two and two together, and told her Uncle Alexander might be at the mill. She said she'd check it out." Kyle stood. "I wanted to go with her but she said it was too dangerous, that since I was chosen, I couldn't be seen by whoever was holding him."

But not too dangerous for me. Jason scrunched his eyes and rubbed the bridge of his nose.

"And when I heard you'd been there, and gotten Uncle Alexander out, I was like what the hell? If it's too dangerous for me, then it's definitely too dangerous for you. And why were you even there? I knew she had to have told you. There wasn't any other way."

Jason's stomach dropped.

"Bro, she told you, right?" Kyle asked.

"Yeah, basically, she told me."

"See? That's just wrong."

"Wrong. Yeah, it's wrong." Jason stood and walked toward the bathroom, his hands clammy.

"Wait. We gotta figure things out."

"Yeah. Sounds good." Jason held one finger in the air and continued to the bathroom. "Give me a minute."

He went in, shut the door, and vomited.

TWENTY-SIX
Punished

Bro, you okay?" Kyle spoke through the door.

Jason flushed and pushed himself up to the sink. "Yeah. Something I ate, I guess." He swished his mouth with berry flavored dental rinse, the same one his mom had insisted all the kids use. The berry-puke combo made him gag.

"You sure?"

"Yeah. No worries." Jason tossed the bottle in the trash and brushed his teeth and tongue with toothpaste. He took a deep breath and went back into his bedroom.

He and Kyle sat on Jason's bed. Kyle told him the texts from Mom started a couple weeks before Jason's birthday.

"No way I believed it at first. I thought it was some creep playing a sick joke. But she texted about stuff only Mom could know, like how I was afraid of kittens when I was little. I'm not anymore, obviously." Kyle quickly added. "Later we talked on the phone. It was bizarre, but cool." Kyle lay back on the bed.

Jason remembered how he felt when he saw Mom in the dugout. Amazed. And confused. And uncertain. But happy. Kyle had been feeling that for months.

"She told me she was in Salton, and we'd start my training as soon as we got here. She's hiding out at her place in the boonies, way out of town, and I've been meeting her there two or three days a week. Dad's working, so he never missed me."

"What do you do to train?"

"Mostly strength stuff, self-defense skills, learning the different types of cryptids—things like that. But when my power comes in, that will be when the cool training begins."

"Your power?"

"Yeah, Mom has this power with her hands. She can shoot freakin' bolts of electricity. It's used to repair the Rampart."

Jason glanced at his hands and shoved them into his lap. "And you can do that too?"

"Not yet. But soon. All Guards can do that."

Jason eyed Kyle's hands. No hint of blue. "So Uncle Alexander has the power too, since they are both Guards and twin-connected and everything."

Kyle rose up on one elbow. "Connected?"

Jason explained what Uncle Alexander had told him.

"Dude, I had no idea. All Mom said was Uncle Alexander was loony. Told me to stay away from him. She thinks he may be the one trying to bring down the Rampart."

"I don't think he could do it even if he wanted to. He gets weird headaches and can barely deal. Not the best skill set for being the big bad."

Kyle thought for a moment. "Yeah. Plus the whole kidnapping and getting drugged thing." He jumped up and pulled open Jason's desk drawer.

"Hello. My room, my desk." Jason leaned over and pushed the drawer shut.

"Relax, bro. I'm just looking for paper. I wanna write some things down before we call Mom."

Jason handed him a notepad and pen. "Why don't we just call her and talk to her now?"

"Can't. I only call at predetermined times, when her phone is encrypted or decrypted or something." Kyle plopped back down on the bed.

Jason felt nauseous. He swallowed a few times and ignored it. They made a list of questions.

"And write down other suspects," Jason said. "That Kappa, Mizu, said he was one of many, so it's not just him. And the silver Skyfish. I think there are other cryptids too."

Kyle scratched the pen across the paper. "Mom already knows who it is."

"Who is it?"

"She wouldn't tell me, said it was too dangerous for me to know."

"She told me she didn't know."

"Probably just protecting you, bro."

"Well, whatever. But we need to make sure she knows it's not just Kappas." Jason's voice ticked higher in volume.

"Fine dude, I'm writing it down. You don't have to get pissy about it."

Jason shook his head. "Yeah. Sorry."

Kyle finished writing. "What else? Anything?"

"No. But . . . " Jason dug his fingernails into his palms. *Stop thinking it. Don't say it.*

"But what?"

Jason had to ask. "Kyle, what if it's her?"

"If what's her?"

"If she's the one trying to destroy the Rampart."

After a long moment, Kyle spoke. "It's not." He switched his gaze to the paper and drew tiny triangles in the margins.

"Are you sure?"

"Yeah. Mostly." His voice was little, like a kid answering a too hard question.

"Yeah, I'm only mostly sure, too." Jason watched his brother scribble on the paper. "We gotta be more than mostly sure."

Kyle dropped the pencil and rubbed his eyes. "I know, I know." He stood walked to the window. "But I really don't want to ask that question."

"Me neither."

"And besides, how would we even ask it? *Mom, you're great and all, but are you the one trying to kill everybody?*"

"Probably not like that."

Kyle raised his arms. "Okay, dude, think about it. She's our mom. We've known her forever. No way it's her. We'd totally know for sure if it was her. She's our *mom*. We'll just talk to her and help her catch the bad guy."

Jason didn't have a better idea. "Okay."

✳ ✳ ✳

The next morning at the predetermined time, Kyle dialed his phone and put it on speaker. The call went straight to an automated voice mail.

"The person you are calling is not available. Please leave a message after the tone." Beep.

Not her, but Kyle got further than I did.

"Mom, it's Kyle. And Jason."

"Hi, Mom." Jason waved, though no one saw the gesture except Kyle.

"Jason and I talked. Now we can work together on everything. We want to figure out what's next so call us, okay? Bye."

Hours passed and Mom didn't call back.

Late Sunday evening, a text arrived. *I'll be in touch.*

"That's it?" Jason stood in Kyle's room and stared at the message.

"I guess so." Kyle set the phone on his desk. "At least we know she's okay."

"Not good enough. We need to talk to her. Call her again." Jason grabbed for the phone.

Kyle beat him to it. "Knock it off. We're not calling her. She made me promise not to call unless I had to, and I don't have to."

"Yes, we do." Jason reached for the phone but Kyle whipped it away.

"No, we don't." Kyle shoved Jason hard and he fell onto Kyle's bed. "She's probably already mad that I called her. Now get out."

Jason glared at his brother. "Fine." He pushed off the bed. "Some brave Rampart Guard you are, afraid of your own mommy. Let me know when she gives you permission to talk to her again." Jason walked through the adjoining bathroom and slammed the door.

Jason tried reaching Mom on his own phone but he received the same message he'd gotten before. No voice mail for him.

Jason didn't see Kyle the next morning. He left for school before Jason came downstairs. He fed Finn, grabbed a banana and headed toward the door. He passed Della in the hall and rubbed the top of her head. "Have fun at your new school, Dell."

"Don't mess with my hair." She ran to the stairs. "Now I have to go fix it."

Jason rolled his eyes.

"Bye, Dad." Dad was in his office, Finn sitting next to him. "Don't forget Finn's walk."

"I'm sure Finn will remind me." He scratched her chin. "Have a good day and I'll see you this afternoon."

"Okay. I'm going to the football team meeting after school with Kyle." Though probably not exactly *with* Kyle. "I'll be home after that." Football was more Kyle's sport, but Jason liked to play and figured it couldn't hurt to try out.

He swung by Sadie's house and they headed to school in silence.

After a few minutes, Sadie spoke. "I didn't mean to upset you, talking about your mom."

For a second Jason thought Sadie was reading his mind. "Huh? Oh, yeah, it's okay or whatever. Besides, Kyle's got you beat."

"What do you mean?"

Jason relayed everything Kyle had told him.

"No way," Sadie said. "You had no idea he was meeting with her?"

"Zero. Zilch. Nada. Score one for my not-so-brilliant powers of observation."

During lunch period, Jason scanned the crowded cafeteria for Sadie and Kyle, but didn't see either of them. He sat at an empty table. Salton High seemed okay so far. His geometry teacher was a doofus—she'd slammed her fingers in her now-locked car door that morning—but everyone else seemed normal enough.

He was about to take another bite of his PB&J when icy wetness gushed down his back. Jason popped out of his seat and spun around.

"Oops. My bad." A kid with spiky blond hair stood there, shrugging into his mock apology.

"What's your problem?" Jason grabbed napkins and mopped his face and his neck. He sopped soda from his hair. Stares came from all sides.

"No problem." The kid sneered. "It was an accident. Seems to happen a lot to new kids. They're clumsy, I guess." He held out a napkin. "Here. Take mine. You need it more than I do."

Jason didn't take it.

"Suit yourself." The boy retracted the napkin. "But try to be a bit more . . . careful." He walked off, whooping to the crowd.

"Ass. Hole." Jason wiped off the bench. He slid everything to the other end of the table.

"Derek Goodman, actually, but same thing." Sadie sat down across from him.

Jason jumped. "Jeez, were you there the whole time?"

"No. Only the end of the conversation. But I can guess what I missed." She took a lemon-scented wet wipe out of her bag and handed it to Jason.

"Wow. You're prepared."

"It's a wet wipe. It's not like I pulled out bath towels and a shower."

"Well, thanks." Jason cleaned his face and hands, and the back of his neck. "Ugh. My hair's getting crunchy. And my shirt's sticking to me."

"It's nice to see you're making friends." She bit into an apple.

"I'm a social butterfly." He threw the wet wipe on the table and examined his lunch, soggy with soda. "I guess lunch is a bust."

"Here." She put a second apple on the table in front of him. "And you might want to rinse off the rest of the soda in the locker room. If you want a clean shirt you can buy a Salton High School T-shirt in the office." She smirked and took another bite.

"That would make me the coolest kid for sure, wearing one of those on my first day." He took the apple. "Thanks for this, but I think I'll pass on the T-shirt."

"Right. Because wearing a sticky, stained shirt the rest of the day will definitely up your cool factor."

"My ultimate goal." Jason collected the mess of his lunch and soggy napkins and tossed them in a trashcan. "Off to the showers."

✳ ✳ ✳

Jason spent the rest of the day enduring giggles and whispers and gapes. He was relieved when the final bell rang. He headed outside.

Kyle was out on the field, tossing a football with a couple of guys. Jason waved and Kyle waved back but didn't come over.

Jason sat on the sideline bench.

"Tough first day?" A man wearing a Salton High School baseball cap approached from Jason's side.

Jason turned his head, wondering who the man was talking to.

The man held his hand out to shake Jason's. "Coach Martel." He gestured to Jason's stained shirt. "Looks like you had a, shall we say, challenging day."

"Oh, yeah. Hi, Coach." Jason stood. "I had a . . . an accident in the cafeteria."

"Hmmm. I sense a disturbance in the force."

Jason stared at the coach, unsure what to say.

Coach Martel smiled. "You're trying out for the team?"

"Yeah, me and my brother, Kyle. He's really good. I'm Jason."

"Well, I hope you're both really good, Jason. We can use all the good we can get. Hang tight, and we'll get started in a few minutes." Coach Martel made a note on his clipboard and walked a few steps away to talk to another student.

Jason pulled at the back hem of his shirt and peeled the sticky fabric from his skin.

A moment later, he saw her. She was across the field near the end zone.

Mom.

She was watching Kyle, waving her hand in the air. Kyle didn't see her. He was walking in to join the meeting. Jason stood and waved at him, pointing to the end of the field where she was standing, but Kyle didn't notice Jason either.

Jason looked back at his mom. She was still waving. No, not waving . . .

A silver cloud gathered above her and hovered. She raised her arms into them. The Skyfish vibrated and pulled into a tight knot. She dropped her arms like she was starting a drag race and the Skyfish bulleted toward Kyle.

Jason bolted from the sideline and raced toward his brother. "Kyle, watch out!" he hollered across the field.

Kyle noticed Jason sprinting toward him. He stopped.

Jason signaled toward the Skyfish. "Run!"

Kyle ran, away from the Skyfish, away from Jason. But he was too slow.

The Skyfish reached Kyle just as Jason did. Jason tackled his brother, tried to shield him, but several Skyfish streaked into Kyle.

Kyle wailed. The Skyfish ripped through him. Jason held tight. His brother's back arched and his body convulsed.

Jason burned when more Skyfish slammed in and through him, but he didn't let go.

Then almost as quickly as it started, it stopped.

The Skyfish were gone.

Kyle stopped moving.

Jason scrambled and rolled his brother onto his back. "Kyle?" He patted his face. "Kyle? Wake up." Kyle's head lolled to the side. "Wake up."

"Get back." Coach Martel yanked Jason away and knelt next to Kyle. He checked for a pulse. He tilted Kyle's head. He blew into Kyle's lungs. He pumped Kyle's chest.

Kyle didn't open his eyes.

Students crowded around, some covering their mouths, their eyes wide. "Call 9-1-1," the coach yelled and kept pumping. Jason's heart beat harder.

Mom was gone.

Paramedics arrived and took over.

"What the hell were you thinking, tackling him like that?" Coach Martel spun Jason to face him.

"What? No, I—I was trying to help him."

Jason saw the paramedics rushing Kyle into the ambulance. Jason moved to follow them but Coach Martel grabbed his shoulder.

"Not so fast."

"He's my brother." Jason tried to push the coach off him, to get into the ambulance. The doors shut.

"Let them do their work. We'll call your parents, and I'll drive you to the hospital."

The ambulance sped away. Jason shook off the coach and back-stepped. "No parents. Just—" Jason's lungs spasmed and sucked in a gush of air. "Just my dad."

Two deputies crossed the field toward them, the lights of their squad car flashing in the distance. "What happened here?" One of the deputies asked.

"I'm not sure." Coach Martel took his cap off and ran one hand through his hair. "You should talk to Jason here. It looked to me like he tackled his brother hard, like he was trying to hurt him."

"No, that's not what happened." Jason's breath quickened.

"Did you have a fight with your brother?" The same deputy asked the question.

"No, I—" Jason's eyes flicked from Coach to the deputy.

"What's your name?" The officer had a pencil poised, ready to take notes.

"Jason Lex. But I—"

"Did you attack your brother, Jason?"

"No. No, I—" How was he going to explain this?

The students came closer. Coach Martel waved them back but they barely moved. Derek Goodman smirked from the front row.

The officer put his hand on Jason's shoulder. "Son?"

"I've gotta go. I've got to get to the hospital."

"Just a few more questions."

But Jason's adrenaline spiked. He ran. He ran away from the police, away from the school, away from everyone.

He had no choice.

He had to get away.

※ ※ ※

Jason huddled in the cove. He sat with his knees pulled into his chest, his arms strapped around, his head tucked. He rocked back and forth. His gut, and his lungs, and his eyes wanted to puke, and collapse, and cry, but nothing came.

Only pain.

Kyle is hurt and Mom did it. She's doing everything.

Jason breathed deep and blew it out, breathed deep and blew it out, breathed deep a third time, blew it out.

How did I let this happen? I never should have talked to Kyle.

Kyle would be fine now, if it wasn't for me.

Jason buried his face. Sobs rocketed through him.

TWENTY-SEVEN

Trust and Betrayal

Jason smelled dirt and dried leaves. His mind fogged between images of Kyle and flashes of the school cafeteria, Skyfish, football. Exhaustion yanked on him like a weight, dragging him toward darkness until Kyle's face pulled him back into semi-consciousness.

Footsteps crunched outside the cove. Jason huddled into the farthest corner.

"Jason?" Sadie whispered. "Are you here?"

He cringed. He wished he could sink into the soil and be gone forever. He didn't want to face her, to face anyone.

Sadie appeared at the entrance. "You are here."

Jason shook his head and wiped crust from his eyes.

"You heard about Kyle?" Jason asked.

She nodded and hunched down next to him.

"Is he okay?"

"I don't know."

Jason sat up and put his head in his hands. His throat tightened.

"What happened?" Sadie asked.

"My mom happened. You were right." He ripped off a leaf. "Happy?"

"No, I'm not happy. I never wanted to be right."

"I know. I'm sorry. I'm . . . God, I am so stupid!" He punched his fist into the ground.

"Jason."

He stood. "What? Are you going to tell me to look at the bright side or something? Because where I'm standing, there is no bright side. There's not even a dull side. Just black. Black that I caused. Me." He grabbed a branch, wrenched it from the bush and hurled it.

"You are not the bad guy here."

"No, that's right. My mom is the bad guy. My mom, who was training Kyle to be a Rampart Guard. My mom, who hurt Kyle, why? Because he talked to me?" His phone vibrated in his pocket. Jason ignored it.

"If that's why she hurt him, then that makes her a million times worse than stupid. And a few other words I won't say." Sadie threw a twig and hit Jason in the chest. "But not you."

Jason waved his hand in the air. "Whatever."

"What are you going to do now?"

"Go to jail? Do not pass Go? Do not collect $200?"

"Seriously."

"I'm pretty sure jail is serious."

"Shut up and focus. No one is blaming you."

"The coach thinks I tackled Kyle because I was trying to hurt him."

"Just explain that's not what happened." Sadie tucked a section of hair behind her ear.

"Oh, okay. I'll tell everyone my missing-and-presumed-dead mother sent evil Skyfish to attack my brother and, well, I tried to stop them by tackling him, like that would even work, but I'm a huge loser so I wasn't able help him." He staggered to the side of the cove where he could see the path. No one was on it.

"God, Jason. Maybe you are a loser if that's your best answer. Game over." She slapped her hands on her thighs.

"Sadie, I caused this. Me."

"Get over yourself, Jason. Your mom caused this. All of it. She left you guys, she hurt you all when she did that, and she's still hurting you. And you're letting her."

"What? What am I supposed to do about her? I'm fourteen. She's my mom."

"So you just give up? You don't even try to stop her?"

Jason ran his hands through his hair. "She's my mom . . . "

"She's not going to stop, Jason, and a whole lot of other people are going to get hurt next, including your dad and Della, and me and Mamo." Sadie sighed. "And just because she's your mom by birth doesn't mean she's a good mom. Or a good person."

"I . . . " Jason sank to the ground. He grabbed a fistful of leaves and crushed them. He watched the crumbles fall from his hand, grabbed another fistful and crushed them, too. "You're right." He swallowed hard. "I can't just do nothing."

"Correction—we can't do nothing." Sadie wiped her hands on her shorts and stood.

"Okay, but I have no idea what to do next."

"Maybe we talk to your dad?"

Jason pulled himself up to standing. "Yeah, we can try. And maybe Grandma Lena." Jason sucked in a breath. "But wait—Della."

"You want to talk to her about all of this?"

"No, I mean, what if Mom wants to hurt her? Dad won't know she's in danger. And maybe he is, too. I've got to get to them." He hurried to the cove entrance and Sadie followed.

They worked their way to the spot behind the Lex house and prepared to climb over the fence. The plan was to first check the house and make sure no one was there then grab bikes from the garage to ride to the hospital. But a deputy stood in the front yard, just on the other side of the backyard gate. Jason and Sadie crouched in the thick tangle of bushes and grass.

"Why is he here? Do you think they're looking for me or something?" Jason kept his voice low.

"Probably just want to ask you questions." Sadie pushed at a branch that poked her ear.

"Not good timing. And what would I say anyway? I need to get to my dad and Della." Jason shifted his position to see more of the front yard but the path alongside the house didn't reveal much. "I think I can climb the tree to my bedroom, but I wish I knew if anyone else was around." His phone vibrated in his pocket again, and again Jason ignored it.

"I'll go to the house and see what's going on. I'll text you if it's clear."

"Okay." Jason nodded once.

Sadie made her way out and was gone. Jason waited for what seemed like forever. It was too long. He needed to get in there.

Another moment passed. Still no signal from Sadie. Jason decided not to wait any longer. He'd make a run to the house. He was about to go when his phone vibrated. A text had arrived. *Not yet.*

He held firm. *How long can this take?*

The back door opened and Jason hunched deep in the thicket. Two officers came into the yard. One was Sheriff Gunderson. Jason didn't recognize the second man.

"Scared kids hide. You check that storage shed over there." The sheriff pointed across the yard. "I'll do a perimeter sweep."

The other officer nodded and moved away. The sheriff placed his right hand on his hip and started walking the fence between Jason's yard and the neighbor's. Jason pushed himself as low as he could and prayed it was enough.

Sheriff Gunderson walked slowly, peering behind lilac and evergreen bushes, roses and snapdragons.

Seriously? He thinks I can hide behind snapdragons? Jason rolled his eyes and stilled his lungs.

The sheriff turned the corner and walked along the back fence, approaching Jason's cover. He inched closer.

Jason's heart hard-knocked on the inside of his chest. Air forced its way through his nose, fluttering leaves in front of him.

Sheriff Gunderson stopped.

Seven feet separated them, seven feet filled with thick bushes on Jason's side, a pine tree on the sheriff's side, and a chain link fence in between. The sheriff took out his flashlight and ducked his head under the low branches of the tree. He scanned the ground around it and the thinnest edge of the light skimmed the front of Jason's shoe. The sheriff shined his light into the pine branches above, weaving the beam back and forth, working to see every spot. He switched it off and stood.

"Adam-one, come in." The radio's sudden noise whipped a shot of adrenaline into Jason's system.

"Go ahead." Sheriff Gunderson answered.

"The girl says she doesn't know where the boy is. She came here looking for him."

"Alright. She's free to go."

"Roger that."

Sadie.

The sheriff dropped his hand from the radio mic and continued his sweep. Soon he was ten feet away from Jason, then twenty, then forty, until he finally went back into the house.

The door shut and two big breaths forced their way into Jason, releasing the tight muscles, and tendons, and ligaments. His jaw cracked when he relaxed his bite.

Another text message arrived. *Everyone out front.*

Jason didn't hesitate. He pushed out of the cover and leaped the fence. He sprinted to the tree by his window and monkeyed up it as if he'd climbed it a thousand times before. He leaned over, opened the window, and pulled himself through.

Finn tackled him on the other side. She pinned him and gave him three big licks, covering every spot on his face.

Jason hugged her hard, pressing his face into her shoulder. "You have no idea how much I needed that, Finn." He pulled back and stood. He winced at the sight of the room where he'd seen Kyle yesterday.

Both doors, one to the hallway, the other the adjoining bathroom, were shut. "They locked you in?" Jason asked Finn.

She walked to the door and scratched. She pressed her nose to the crack between the door and the frame and took a deep sniff. She looked at Jason and scratched again.

He rubbed behind her ears. "I'll get you out of here, Finn, but I can't let you out now or they'll know something's up."

Finn sat.

Sadie texted again. *Where are you?*

My room.

Coming up.

A few seconds later the door to the hallway opened and Sadie slipped inside.

Finn tried to push past her but Jason grabbed her collar. "Not yet, Finn." She gave a little whine and sat again.

"Did you see Della?" Jason asked.

"No, she's not here. Neither is your dad. He's at the hospital and he gave the sheriff a key to come look for you, and meet Della when her carpool drops her off after dance class."

"That's good. She'll be safe with a deputy." He swallowed. "But they are looking for me."

"Yeah, but mostly just to ask you some questions about what happened, and make sure you're okay. Everyone's worried about you."

Jason thought about his bolt from the football field. "Running away probably wasn't my best move."

"No, but understandable." Sadie sat on the floor next to Finn and stroked her neck. "And Finn's in here because she's been acting weird and trying to get out the front door. She wouldn't stop barking at one of the deputies."

Jason laughed and sat down next to both of them. "Well if you don't like him, neither do I, Finn." She licked Jason's face.

"So now what?" Sadie asked.

"I don't know. Maybe I'll call my dad. Not sure we can get the bikes out with a deputy sitting out front." He looked at his phone. "Dad's already called me six times."

"He's probably freaking out."

Jason stood and walked over to the window.

"It would help if he knew you were okay." Sadie grabbed a tissue from a nearby box and dabbed her eyes.

"What do I even say? It was Mom? And don't let Mom, who's actually alive and well and living in Salton, hurt you or Della?" He turned back into the room, his fists clenched. He raised them to punch the wall, to punch the dresser, to punch something then threw them to his sides.

He dropped to the floor and held his face in his hands. "I wish I had listened to you. I wish she wasn't my mother." He looked at Sadie. "And I know it's horrible but I really, really wish she'd stayed missing."

Sadie put her arm over Finn's back and leaned into her.

Jason's phone vibrated in his pocket. "God, it's probably my dad again." He glanced at the screen. "Not Dad. It's my uncle." Jason answered his phone. "Uncle Alexander?"

"Where are you?" Uncle Alexander was panting.

"At home."

"Get out of there. They'll look for you there."

"The police? They didn't find me."

"Not the police." His voice was high and his words rapid. "Them. Your mother. The Kappas. Get out of there."

Jason jumped to his feet. "Okay. Right." He scooped at the air signaling Sadie to her feet. "We'll go. Somewhere."

"Where?" Sadie mouthed the word.

Jason shrugged, shook his head.

"Go to my house," Uncle Alexander said.

"But they know—"

"Do you have Finn?"

"Yes."

"She'll lead you to a safe place," he wheezed. "We'll talk . . ." He hissed ". . . later." The call ended.

Jason slipped the phone back in his pocket. "Go outside with Finn. Tell the deputy you're taking her for a walk." He scanned the sky outside his window. "I'll meet you at the bridge."

"Okay." She grabbed her bag and hung it across her body. "And then where? Your Uncle's house?"

"Yeah. But you should go home."

"No." She dropped her phone into a pocket.

"It's not safe."

Sadie planted herself and put her hands on her hips. "It's not safe because maybe she's trying to kill you. It's not safe because she *is* trying to destroy the Rampart." She opened the door and Finn bolted. She stepped into the hall. "I'll see you at the bridge."

Jason climbed down the tree and arrived at the bridge a moment before Sadie and Finn. Finn was pulling Sadie along as fast as Sadie could go, like a sled dog dragging a loaded sleigh. They stopped next to Jason.

"She's in a hurry." Sadie bent forward, gulping air.

A familiar crackle rose in his ears. "And I think I know why. We gotta move." He unclipped Finn's leash, grabbed Sadie's arm and they ran.

They were clear on each side. He didn't dare check behind them. They had to keep moving.

The crackle engulfed him, the heat on his neck mounted. "Keep running. Skyfish. Not sure which ones."

They were almost at Uncle Alexander's when Jason spotted the Skyfish, a golden mass flying a short distance above. The good guys. Never in his life had Jason liked something sparkly as much as he did right now.

Finn, Sadie and Jason rounded the corner of the lonely street that led to Uncle Alexander's house. They pushed hard and sped into the yard when an ear-splitting boom forced them to the ground. Jason rolled on his back, hands up and ready. They were hot. Blue. Fiery.

Above him, the golden Skyfish were battling silvers, cracking the sky, burning into each other. "Get inside," he yelled to Sadie.

She scrambled onto the porch. A silver Skyfish zoomed toward her.

"Duck!" Jason swung his arm and zapped Sadie's assailant. She sprung up, opened the unlocked door and rushed inside. Finn waited outside, rigid, watching Jason.

Jason jumped, a silver Skyfish lasered toward him. He thrust out his right hand and blue bolts incinerated the attacker. He used both hands, aimed, and one Skyfish after another sizzled to ash. Three headed for Finn on Jason's left. He fired, stopped them, but wailed when one hit his forearm. Another buckled his leg and five more headed for Jason from his right.

Jason fought until the goldens outnumbered silvers. He raced inside, Finn tightly in step.

"Wow." Sadie's eyes were wide.

"You saw them?" Jason shook his hands.

Sadie nodded, her mouth gaping.

Finn ran down the hall to a door. Using both front paws, she scratched hard and fast. Jason opened it.

It was a walk-in closet. One side was lined with a variety of coats, the other was shelves holding board games and vacuum bags and bottles of water. Finn trotted in, turned around and sat in front of the back wall. They followed her inside and stood, glancing at each other.

"We're supposed to be hiding in a closet?" Sadie wiped the sweat off her forehead with her sleeve.

Finn barked once. They waited.

Nothing happened.

"Great. That must have been the deranged and drugged uncle on the phone instead of the I-have-a-clue uncle."

Finn nudged the door shut. She sat again and barked once.

The floor dropped and Sadie grabbed at a coat to steady herself. But the coats were staying. Finn and Sadie and Jason were descending. Rails rose and surrounded them on three sides. As soon as they'd cleared the bottom of the closet, a new floor closed above their heads.

They dropped about thirty feet and the platform stopped. They followed Finn into a tunnel and through strips of heavy plastic hanging from the ceiling, separating the tunnel from the next space. They found themselves in a huge, high-tech lab, almost identical to the one Uncle Alexander showed them before. They moved through the lab to a second set of plastic partitions and stepped through.

They entered a living room. A plush couch sat in the center, a red leather recliner next to it. In the recliner, hooked to oxygen, was Uncle Alexander.

Finn trotted to him and put her front legs on the arm of the chair. She licked him and sniffed him and licked him some more, her tail wagging in a blur.

"Good girl, good girl, Finn." Uncle Alexander's arms were around her neck and he ducked his head into her scruff, trying to avoid some of her kisses. "Oh yes, I've missed you, too. You're such a good girl."

Finn moved to climb onto the chair with him. "No, no. Off please. Not quite ready for you as a lap dog, my dear." She stopped and licked his face again. He laughed. "Okay, that's enough. All the way off, please." Finn dropped to a sit next to the chair, her head resting on the arm.

"Uncle Alexander." Jason bent down and hugged him. Finn's dog-breath lingered on Uncle Alexander's skin. "How are you? You didn't sound so good on the phone."

"Oh, I'll be fine. I was a little taxed from the move. The doc wasn't too happy about the early release, but it needed to be done. It's good to see you." He looked at Sadie. "And you too, young lady."

"Thanks." She gave a little wave. "I'm so glad you're okay."

"All thanks to you three, according to Grandma Lena." He scratched Finn behind the ears then gestured toward the couch. "Have a seat. We're safe here." He noticed the burn on Jason's arm. "Sadie, there's a first aid kit in the closet over there, top shelf."

Sadie grabbed the kit and bandaged Jason's arm. After she was finished, Jason and Sadie sat on the couch. Sadie slipped off her shoes and crossed her legs underneath her.

"So, your mom . . . "

"She hurt Kyle . . . " A hiccup of air hung on the end of Kyle's name. Jason held his breath for a second then relayed the story of the Skyfish attack.

Uncle Alexander shook his head, clenching and unclenching his jaw. "I heard about Kyle at the hospital. I never thought . . . I never thought she was this far gone. But once I heard that, I knew you were in danger, too."

"You knew she was behind this?" Jason asked.

"I didn't know for certain. I didn't want to believe it. I searched for every other possible explanation. And then they took me."

"Why did they do that?" Sadie asked.

He sighed. "Lots of reasons, apparently. That arrogant-piece-of-disgrace-to-all-Kappas Mizu was happy to fill me in on the details. Perhaps he thought I wouldn't remember any of it. Or that I'd never get out of there . . . " He pinched the bridge of his nose for a moment. "But apparently we were getting too close."

"Too close? How?" Jason leaned forward.

"Because you, and your brother and sister, are like booster stations for the connection between your mom and me. While I noticed some additional connection to Adrienne, she must have felt a lot more, especially when you and I started spending more time together." He took a deep draw on his oxygen.

"Why didn't you notice it?" Jason asked.

"Ah, well, it seems your mother has become quite the pharmacologist. She's been dosing me with Jimsonweed. Started in high school."

"Oh my God." Sadie picked up a throw pillow and clutched it.

"Well, she did stop for a while, after I bowed out of the Guards. But she started again after she disappeared so I'd be less able to connect with her."

"How did she . . . " Sadie pressed her fingertips to her lips.

"She planted it in my drinks—my Kool-Aid, my tea. It gave me hallucinations, headaches, dizziness—all things that affected my behavior, made me seem crazy. Hell, it made me feel crazy." He sucked in oxygen through the tubes in his nose.

"Why would she do that? Why do any of this?" Jason slapped the couch cushion.

"I don't know, Jason. It may be that everyone had the wrong sibling pegged for mental illness." He breathed deep.

"But . . . so . . . so she was mental, or whatever, even when she seemed like herself? When she was home with us?"

"I'm not sure. Maybe she was better for a while. Maybe she'll get better again. But right now she sees you as a threat."

"I'm fourteen, and I'm her *son*. How am I a threat?"

Sadie shifted toward them. "Because Jason is a Guard."

"It's not entirely certain yet, but yes," Uncle Alexander nodded.

"No, Kyle is the . . . she was training him. Not me. Him."

"She couldn't have known that for certain. You saw the book—none of your names were in gold. I think she was just making an educated guess." He gestured to Jason's hands. "But then you surprised her at the sugar mill and things changed."

"Mom was there?"

Sadie put her hand on Jason's arm and squeezed.

"My memory is not the best from that day, but I'd bet she was there, somewhere. Watching."

Finn walked to Jason and put her head on his knee. He scratched behind her ears and rubbed her cheeks with his thumbs.

He stayed in that moment with Finn. He wanted to wipe it all away. Wash the slate. Purge the data. But it was permanent, like words chiseled into stone.

Jason raised his head. "What do I do now?"

"We have to stop her."

"We?"

"You're not alone in this. I can help."

"Oh, great. Well, grab onto that oxygen tank, and let's get after it." Jason stood.

"Jason—"

"No. Let's do this. Sadie can find something on the computer, like how to stop an insane parent from going after any more of her kids—Google that, okay, Sadie? And then we'll find Uncle Alexander a wheelchair and all go after her together. We'll take turns pushing." Jason spun and walked across the room.

"Jason."

He turned back to his uncle. "What? Don't like that idea? Maybe we can get an ATV instead, load your tank on that so you don't have to drag it."

"Jason." Uncle Alexander's voice was hard.

"What?" Jason yelled.

"Shut up and sit down." Uncle Alexander pointed at the couch.

Jason stayed planted for a few seconds, then stomped across the room and plopped into his seat.

"Thank you." Uncle Alexander scratched at marks left by the IV needle. "I talked to your dad, he knows you're here."

"Does he—"

"Ah." Uncle Alexander held his index finger high and shook his head. "My turn."

Jason nodded.

"He knows about your mom, and he and Grandma Lena are coming over as soon as they get Della. In fact, they should have her by now. They'll all be here soon and we'll figure out next steps."

Uncle Alexander's cell phone rang. "There he is now. Hello?"

A moment later, Jason's phone rang. Unknown caller. "Hello?"

"Hi, Jason." His mom's voice was sweet and sad. "I'm so sorry about Kyle." Jason heard a catch in her throat.

He moved across the room so he could hear over his uncle's conversation. "You did that to him."

"No, that wasn't supposed to happen." She started crying. "They weren't supposed to do that. I didn't—he must have—he was so angry . . . " She cleared her throat.

"He who, Mom?" Jason's stomach jerked in on itself. "Are you saying it was Kyle's fault?"

"No, no never. I was trying to get a message to Kyle without being seen. Those Skyfish were out of my control. He, whoever's behind this, manipulated them, made them go against my wishes." She whimpered. "And now I may have lost Kyle. We may have lost Kyle."

"Mom."

Her sobs filled Jason's ear. Sadie tipped her head toward him, one eyebrow arched.

"Mom."

She swallowed air. "Jason, they're trying to eliminate us all, as I suspected. I can't lose you. I can't lose Della." She sniffed. "Thankfully, she's here with me. Safe."

Jason heard his sister in the background, singing along to the radio. "You have Della?"

Uncle Alexander ended his call. Both he and Sadie watched Jason.

"Yes. I knew you'd be worried so I wanted to let you know. She's safe." She sniffed again and her sniveling eased. "And I want you safe, too. I want you here with me. Together we can beat this thing."

This thing? You're the thing.

"Are you still there?"

"Yeah, Mom."

"Jason, you and your sister have power. Not a lot, but definitely some. And I think we can combine our forces to win this, come out on top, get everything we want."

"All I wanted was you home with us."

"I know, honey, I know. And I've messed that up by not asking for help, by trying to do too much on my own, thinking I was protecting you. But help me now and we'll fix it, as good as new."

As good as new? "You're not the one trying to destroy the Rampart?"

"They're trying to make it seem like that, like I'm the bad guy, but you know I'm not. Honey, I'm your mom. You know me better than anyone. You know that couldn't possibly be true."

Jason scrunched his eyes and rubbed his temple. "Yeah, that's what I thought . . . "

"Good. I'm so glad. I love you so much, Jason. So you'll help me? We'll do this together?"

His gaze zipped between Sadie and Uncle Alexander then back to the floor in front of him. "What do you want me to do?"

She sighed into the phone. "Meet me in the parking lot behind the high school. Nine PM. I'll be in a red Subaru."

"Okay."

"And honey, tell no one. You saw what happened to Kyle when he told. You don't know who you can trust."

"Right. Okay. Say hi to Della for me."

"I will. She'll be so happy you're coming. We'll see you soon." She ended the call.

"She has your sister?" Uncle Alexander still held his cell phone in his hand.

Jason nodded.

"Dammit." He punched the arm of the chair. "I'll text your dad. What else did she say?" He typed into his phone.

"That she loves me." Jason backed to the wall behind him and slumped down. "That she didn't mean for Kyle to get hurt. That it was an accident or something. And that she needs my help."

Neither Sadie nor Uncle Alexander spoke.

"Oh, and she wants me to meet her at nine PM tonight and not tell anyone because *you saw what happened to Kyle* and *you don't know who you can trust.*" Jason dropped his phone and raked both hands through his hair.

Sadie and Uncle Alexander stayed silent, waited.

Jason swung around and punched the wall behind him.

"I say screw that. Kyle talked to me and to her, and I know I didn't attack him."

"I'm so sorry . . . " Sadie clutched the pillow tighter.

"She sounded so much like my mom, ya know?" He cocked his head to the side. "Like she really cared. But something was off, wrong, like I was having a pretend conversation instead of real one."

He stood and brushed off the back of his pants. "So, yeah, I'm not keeping her little secret, but I am going to meet her tonight."

"I'm not sure that's the best idea," Sadie said. "What if it's a trap to hurt you? To kill you?"

"If she wanted me dead, she could have done that when she attacked Kyle. And she took Della—she didn't kill her. She says she wants to keep Della safe. Maybe I can talk Mom into letting me take Della someplace else, convince Mom I've found an even safer place or something."

"I doubt she'll let you do anything like that," Uncle Alexander said.

"Then fine. I'll stay with her. At least I can make sure Della is okay, and maybe we can sneak out."

"She's not going to let you just hang around." Sadie's bottom lip quivered.

"Maybe she will. Maybe she really does like me. Even love me." Jason rubbed the back of his neck.

Uncle Alexander spoke. "She's ill, Jason. What she says, and what she feels may be two different things. It's too dangerous."

"You have another idea? We can't leave Della alone with her. And it's not like we can send the cops—we don't even know where she is."

"We'll have Sheriff Gunderson pick her up when she comes to meet you tonight."

"Oh, okay. He can arrest her for—what? Being alive when she's been presumed dead? Having her daughter with her?" Jason's tone sharpened. "Or are you going to tell him about the Rampart and Mom's part in some plan to destroy it? Coming from the town crazy dude, I'm sure he'll rally his troops. Or troop. What are there, like three deputies?" Jason paced across the room.

Uncle Alexander waved his hand. "Alright, alright. Point taken." He removed the air tubes and tossed them aside. "We'll think of something else."

"There is nothing else. I have to meet her."

"I'll go with him." Sadie scooted forward in her seat. "She knows me."

Uncle Alexander shook his head. "Not a good idea."

"Yeah, and I don't want to piss Mom off. She's freaky enough already." Jason remembered his mom's hugs in the dugout a few days ago. His heart choked in his chest.

"I'm going alone."

TWENTY-EIGHT
Saving Della

Dad and Grandma Lena arrived. Grandma Lena held a wad of worn tissues in her hand.

Dad hugged Jason hard. "Are you okay?"

"I didn't hurt him, Dad."

"I know. I know you didn't." Dad hugged him again and gulped in a breath. He released Jason and turned to Sadie. "And how are you doing?"

"I'm fine. You guys are the ones dealing with the super-hard stuff." Her eyes filled with tears.

Grandma Lena put her arm around Sadie's shoulders. "Everyone is. But we'll get through this."

Sadie gave two little nods and wiped her eyes.

"So, *everyone* knows what's going on?" Jason asked his uncle.

"Grandma Lena's known about the Guard since she met my dad, your Grandpa Tate." He nodded toward Jason's dad. "And Zachary knew about them even before meeting Adrienne."

"You did?" Jason's head cocked left.

"Yes. My family has a history with the League of Governors. But it's a long story."

Jason stepped back. "One that you couldn't tell me?"

"It wasn't time. We didn't know exactly what was happening," Dad said. "But we did know one of you would be chosen for the Guard. That's another reason why we—your grandma and me, and your uncle—decided it would be good for us to move to Salton."

Jason dropped onto the couch and crossed his arms.

"Jason, no one knew your mom was alive." He gestured to Uncle Alexander. "After we moved here, and before your uncle disappeared, I suspected him of killing your mom, and trying to manipulate you. That's why I didn't want you spending time over there until I knew more. It wasn't until you found Alexander that things fell together."

Jason scanned every face, landing back at Dad's. "And Mom—how did she die but not die?" His throat tightened. He shook it off.

"Mizu," said Uncle Alexander. "Kappas drink blood. They also have the ability to drink it but not digest it, like siphoning fuel out of a gas tank. Mizu bragged how he'd meet Adrienne during her walks in the woods, collect her blood and store it. On the day of her pseudo-death, Mizu extracted a large quantity of fresh blood from her and left it at the scene—that's what the police found. Mizu used Adrienne's stored blood to replenish her, to save her. I saw Ahool—giant bats—at the sugar mill. I suspect they used the Ahool to fly them to the blood stores."

"Sure. Giant bats. What else would it be? God, I really hate that Mizu guy. Or whatever he is."

"Hate is a strong word, but in this case it's justified." Dad squeezed Jason's shoulder and spoke to everyone. "We've got to get to Della. I will not let Adrienne hurt our daughter, too." His eyes were dark, determined.

"We need to stop Adrienne, protect the Rampart," Uncle Alexander said. "Even the destruction of one region means millions of deaths."

They decided Jason would meet Mom with his cell phone GPS activated. Dad would follow in his car. Grandma Lena, Uncle

Alexander and Sadie would listen in via Jason's cell phone and track his GPS on the computer. Dad argued against sending Jason alone, but what other option did they have?

* * *

Jason waited in the parking lot. Pools of light dropped from the streetlights.

Seven minutes past nine and no red Subaru. Maybe this was some kind of mean joke. He sat down on the curb.

"Stand up. She might not see you if you're sitting." The phone was in his shirt pocket, underneath his sweatshirt. It was connected to his uncle, his tinny voice carrying through the speaker and the fabric. Uncle Alexander was supposed to be muted.

"She's not coming," Jason said.

"She's coming."

"I don't think so."

"There's a car turning in."

Jason stood and squinted at the headlights headed toward him.

"Remember, she's smart. Clever. She knows what to say."

"She's still my mom." Jason stared down at his hands.

"Not necessarily, not really." Uncle Alexander paused. "Listen to her. But don't trust her."

Mom pulled up in the red Subaru.

Jason shifted his weight and forced his shoulders to relax.

She got out of the car, rushed over to Jason and hugged him tight. "I'm so glad you're safe."

Jason's insides jellied at the sound of her voice. *She sounds like Mom. Real Mom.* He slowly put his arms around her and hugged her back.

"When I heard about what happened to you at the sugar mill, and then your brother, I've been frantic trying to get to you."

"Okay. I'm here. Enough hugging."

She released him but held onto his shoulders. "Sorry. But I'm so happy to see you." She kissed his forehead. Her eyes were swollen, puffy.

She seems so normal. What if we're wrong?

"C'mon, let's go see Della." She put her arm around his shoulder and walked him toward the car.

No Della.

"She's not with you?"

"No. She's back at my place. Safe." She opened the passenger door.

Jason glanced at the shadows. For a split second, he thought about leaving, about running to his dad's car. But he had to get to Della. Jason climbed into the Subaru.

Mom shut the door. After getting in on the driver's side, she locked all the doors. "Put on your seatbelt."

They drove out of the parking lot. Jason gripped the armrest then relaxed his hand. He wasn't worried. Everyone knew where he was and they were tracking him.

"It's not too far. A little bit outside of town. Didn't want any nosey neighbors to worry about." She gunned it. Jason watched the headlights in the side view mirror. Dad was still there.

Up ahead, different headlights shone out of a field, as if waiting for Jason and his mom to pass. Once they did, the tractor pulled into the road, a wide trailer dragging behind it.

No. Oh, no. "What is he doing?" Jason jerked to look out the rear window.

"Probably moving equipment so it's ready for tomorrow. Why?" Mom glanced at Jason then back to the road.

Jason thought fast. "It's just—that trailer was so big. I haven't seen one like that before."

"The farmers know what they're doing."

"Yeah, I guess." The reflected glare of the tractor's headlights waned in the side mirror.

A few minutes later, Mom turned off the main road onto a dirt one flanked by tall rows of corn. There were no headlights behind them.

"This is all ours, Jason."

"The corn?"

She laughed. "The farm. I don't know if you remember me telling you this during our trips to Salton, but the Fallon family used to be quite the farm family, back in the day. This farm used to belong to them. They had to sell it when times got tough, but I bought it back. It's the Fallon Farm again." She turned her head and smiled.

"Great, Mom."

"Yes, it is."

A large white farmhouse loomed ahead. One lone street lamp bathed it in a minty green glow. There was a light on inside.

Mom stopped the car in front of a gate. "We're home."

Not my home. Jason followed her into the house.

Della clicked off the television and ran into Jason with a near-tackling hug. "I'm so glad you're here. Are you going to stay?"

"Of course he's staying." Mom mussed his hair when she walked past. It sputtered with static electricity. "Do you want something to drink?"

"Yeah, water." Jason licked his hand and smoothed his hair back into place. "What do you mean staying? What about Dad?"

"Dad's fine. Mom needs us. Right, Mom?" Della asked.

"That's right." She put three glasses on the kitchen table. "Have a seat."

Jason sat and took a sip of his water. *How was Della so happy and okay with everything? Our presumed-dead mom is alive, Kyle is in the hospital, and she's not worried?*

"Della, honey, would you mind checking on the chickens, make sure the door to the coop is closed? And refill their water? Your brother and I will talk and then we'll all watch a movie or something. Okay?"

"By herself? It's dark. Maybe I should go with her." Jason stood.

"No, I can do it." Della picked up her water and headed to the back door. She flipped a switch that lit a floodlight outside. "And now it's not dark."

"Okay . . . " Jason glanced at Mom who smiled and nodded at Della.

"I got this," Della said. "And I'm really glad you're here, Jason."

"Thanks, Dell. I'm glad I'm here, too."

The chickens cackled a moment later.

"You have so much potential, Jason," Mom said.

"Um, thanks." He sat again and took a drink. "But what is really going on? And how is Della so okay with this?"

"She's happy to have me back, like you are. Right?"

Jason shrugged. "Yeah, totally. She's not upset about Kyle?"

"She doesn't know what happened to Kyle. I didn't want to upset her. I told her he was injured playing football, the doctors told him to rest tonight, and he'd be able to join us tomorrow."

It amazed Jason how easily she related the lie, almost like she believed it herself. "So, what about everything else?"

"There's so much to tell, and you deserve to know. It's hard to know where to start."

"Start anywhere, I guess."

"Well, Della and I have been talking for a while now, and I've explained things to her. She understands that we're working to do something important, something extraordinary."

Jason remembered Della's chat sessions. More than once she'd minimized her screen when he'd walked by.

"You and your sister can do great things, with my help. Kyle too, if . . . when he gets better." She slid her glass aside. "We, as our own team, and part of a larger team, we can do great things."

Larger team. "Like save the Rampart."

"Like save the Rampart. Yes we could."

"And getting Kyle's attacker."

Mom's hand fisted then opened. "Yes. Definitely."

"I'm all for that. So who are we going after?"

"It's not that simple. There is a much larger group, a global team with forces all over earth. The leader is a visionary who wants to create an existence on earth that far exceeds any expectations."

"What are you talking about?"

"I'm saying it's much bigger than this region of the Rampart."

Jason realized what she was saying, that there was someone leading an effort to destroy *the entire Rampart,* but he couldn't think about that right now. He could only focus on Della, and Dad, Uncle Alexander and Sadie and her grandmother.

"Okay, but you don't want that to happen, right? Can we start here and keep our part of the Rampart safe? We can get Dad and Uncle Alexander to help, and anyone else we might need."

She half-smiled. "Oh, honey, he's not well."

"Uncle Alexander?"

She tsked. "I'm certainly not talking about your father." She carried her water glass to the sink and dumped the contents.

"He doesn't seem that bad to me."

"That's part of the illness, making people believe you're fine when you're really not. But I've known him a lot longer than you have and, sadly, he's a very sick man."

"Okay, Mom, whatever you say."

"Well, I should know." She snapped at Jason then shut her eyes for a moment. "I'm sorry. I've been so worried knowing you've been spending time with him. He's dangerous."

"He seems like kind of a pansy to me." Jason cringed a little. Uncle Alexander was listening. "And how did you know we were spending time together?"

She refilled her glass with ice and water. "I've been keeping an eye on you, even before you moved."

A memory flashed in Jason's mind. "You were there. At the house that day, the day we left for Salton. I *did* see you."

"Yes. And I had to work quickly when you jumped out of the van. It was too soon. I had to stay gone." She tucked her hair behind both ears. "I thought I wanted to say good-bye to the old house while you were all still there. I didn't want to do it alone. But that was stupid, especially since I almost got caught."

Jason wasn't sure if he was relieved or sad that he'd really seen her.

"It was so nice to have you here in Salton, closer to our work. But you spent too much time with Alexander. My brother is insane. I didn't want anything to happen to you. You're my son."

Jason swallowed hard. "And what about Kyle? Weren't you keeping an eye on him?"

She pursed her lips. "Please, Jason. Understand I can't control everything."

Jason shook his head. "Mom, I saw you. You were there, with the Skyfish."

"I told you, I was trying to get a message to him. The Skyfish went against my direction."

"Then whose direction did they follow?"

"The leader of our mission. He made the decision."

Jason huffed. "So you *are* part of this global team you talked about. You are working against us, your own family. You want to destroy the Rampart."

She pulled a chair around and sat next to Jason. "What we're doing is vitally important. Our leader, Sewell Kendrick, is a genius. This plan is his and I'm proud to be part of it." She paused. "But I didn't agree with his direction regarding Alexander. Alexander and I haven't been close, but I couldn't bear to lose him completely."

Jason's head spun. "This genius leader guy kidnapped Uncle Alexander? And you knew about it?"

210

"I wanted Alexander away from you. That's *all*. But after we had Alexander for a few days, Sewell ordered that Alexander be eliminated."

"As in killed?"

"I couldn't do it, but I couldn't blatantly defy his wishes. I needed to somehow help Alexander escape without being directly involved. I knew you cared about him and hoped you would help. And you did. I was so proud of you." Mom brushed Jason's hair out of his eyes.

He stared at her. "I almost died . . . "

"But you didn't. You saved Alexander." A small smile flitted across her face. "Sewell . . . he wasn't happy. He already suspected I had done something to help you get to Alexander, and then when he learned you and Kyle had talked, he was livid. He ordered the attack on Kyle."

"No one was there but you and those Skyfish." Jason leaned back, trying to distance himself from her.

Mom's eyes were fixed on Jason. She didn't blink. "I didn't want that, Jason. I didn't."

Jason's mind raced, tried to find logic and latch on tight. "Please, Mom . . . just tell me this is all some kind of sick joke, that you're on our side." His voice was almost a whisper. "That you don't want the Rampart destroyed."

She trailed her finger through the condensation on her glass.

Finally, she spoke. "What I've told you is the truth."

Jason's breaths quickened. His memory of his mom dissolved and he felt like he was looking at a stranger.

"I want to bring you in on this mission with me, with us, so you can help us do the right thing."

Jason's skin tingled. "Which is what?"

"To save the earth from destruction by the human race and become leaders. Innovators. How does that sound?" She beamed.

Sounds whacked. "What destruction? How would we be leaders?"

"Because tonight the Rampart is coming down and the earth will be saved. And you'll be the one to do it."

TWENTY-NINE

Dark

Jason's scalp creeped like spiders were spinning webs in his hair. He wanted to yell, to run, to get as far away as possible. But he squashed it deep. He forced his inhales to match his exhales. He planted a smile on his face. He thought about Della. And Dad. His uncle. And Sadie.

Everyone.

Everyone who wasn't a cryptid.

Every human.

"Why . . . how? How could I do that?"

"We'll do it together, as a team—me, you and Della. With our combined power, we'll change everything."

Jason's gut wrenched.

"My power as a Guard is unmatched. I can take down the Rampart on my own. But it would take time. Together we can bring it down in an instant, relatively speaking."

"But people would die. We'd die." Jason fingered the fabric over his phone.

"We won't die." She stood and walked to the refrigerator. "We're Guards. We live in both worlds. The Rampart means nothing to us." She waved her hand in the air, dismissing the shield that kept humans safe.

212

"I'm not a Guard. Neither is Della."

"Not officially, no. Not yet. But you'll stay close to me. I can protect you."

Like you protected Kyle? "What about Dad, and Grandma Lena?"

"Honey, I'm sorry, but sacrifices must be made. Besides, my mother wants me to do this."

What? Jason scrambled his brain trying to find a clue, something that said Grandma Lena was part of this.

Mom opened the refrigerator and took out cheese, mustard, bread. "Are you hungry? Want a sandwich?"

Jason shook his head. "Grandma Lena never—"

"Since I was a little girl, Mom and Dad taught us to value Mother Earth, protect the planet, recycle, reuse, take good care of her. Your dad and I taught you kids the same thing and we've done our best. But it's no use." She smeared organic yellow mustard on a piece of whole grain bread. It was the same mustard she used when she made sandwiches for him back home, before all of this.

"Humans are destroying the planet. They're leeches. They suck everything dry. They take and take and take and give nothing in return. They're useless, really. A waste." She stacked slabs of Swiss cheese between slices of tomato.

"So we should be wiped out?"

"Yes. My mom would say it's the only way to save the planet and she's right. Besides, cryptids are the superior species. They've lived on this earth longer, they've preserved and repaired her resources, they've lived peacefully. Mostly. They've had a few clashes over the years, but compared to humans?" She pulled a butcher knife from its block and pointed it at Jason. "They're pristine." She sliced her sandwich in half.

"But. . ." Jason rubbed his forehead. "Grandma Lena told you to do this?"

"She didn't have to. I know this is what she'd want me to do for the planet."

"To kill every human."

"Not all of them." She put the ingredients back in the refrigerator. "We'll keep some humans for guaranty purposes in isolated locations away from cryptids. There the humans can do whatever they want all day long, reproduce to their hearts' content, hunt, and fight, and ruin the landscape." She bit into her sandwich.

"Guaranty purposes?"

"To ensure the cryptids don't go back on their word." She turned toward him. "We bring the Rampart down and govern earth and all cryptids." She picked up the knife. "But if they don't keep their end of the bargain, we restore the Rampart and release the humans. They'll overrun the place in no time, like a super-virus. And the cryptids will have even less power than they have now." She dropped the knife in the sink. "We can't lose." She bit into her sandwich again and smiled as she chewed.

"And this Sewell guy?" Jason's head reeled.

Her eyes sparkled. "He'll continue to lead us all. You'll like him."

Like him? I'm never going to like some guy who ordered Uncle Alexander's death, and the attack on Kyle. "Where is he, Mom? Is he here?"

"No, he's at headquarters, in England, overseeing the global operation. You'll meet him once we've completed our assignment."

Jason took two breaths that only partly filled his lungs. He stared at the floor.

Mom knelt in front of him and lifted his face to hers. "We'll be together, Jason. You and me and Della. We'll be a family again." She stroked his face.

He'd missed her so much. He'd missed being a family. "Can we go home? Back to our house in Colorado?"

"Maybe we can live there some of the time, if that would make you happy." She stood and pulled a chair next to Jason's. She sat close.

Jason liked the idea of going home, to his real home. "And can we take Dad and Grandma Lena?" Uncle Alexander would be okay on his own, he'd survive since he's a Guard. "And Finn? Can we take Finn?"

Mom's expression changed. Her mouth still smiled but her eyes didn't. "Sure. They can come with us. But we have a big job ahead. We need to focus on that now, okay?"

Jason's excitement trickled out. He grasped at it, at its energy, trying to make something solid out of air. "But Sadie, and—"

"—Jason." Mom put her arm around his shoulders. "We are changing the world, making it better. We are doing something amazing. I know this is hard to understand, but making sacrifices is what makes you into a strong man. A better man." She kissed his temple. "I promise, it's the right thing to do. And I'm so happy you're here to do this with me."

She crossed to where she'd left her sandwich and tossed the rest in the garbage, brushing the crumbs from her hands.

It's the right thing to do. Jason repeated it in his head. He knew about global warming, and how polar bears are drowning because there isn't enough sea ice. The planet's temperature is rising, the ice is melting, there are huge islands of plastic garbage floating in the ocean killing animals and damaging ecosystems. Humans did that, and are still doing that, still destroying the earth.

It's the right thing to do.

Mom filled her glass with water. "Are you all right? You look pale."

He nodded but didn't look at her. The image of Skyfish slamming into Kyle filled his mind. *Is that what would happen to Sadie? To her grandmother?*

"We're leaving in a few minutes. You're sure you don't want something to eat?"

"I'm sure." Jason's palms tingled.

"All right. I'm going to get Della and we'll head out." Mom opened the back door.

"I can't do it." Jason mumbled his words, didn't realize he'd said them aloud.

Mom stopped. "What did you say?"

Jason sat straight in his chair. "Mom, I can't do this, I can't help you."

"What are you talking about?" She tensed.

"I can't . . . I don't have any power." *What can I say to convince her to stop?*

"I know what happened when you escaped with your uncle." She stared at him.

"I was lucky."

"Hmm. Well, I think it was more than that. And I've done some tests with Della. There's something there." The back door clicked shut. She stepped in front of him and leaned against the counter. "I am your mother. I'm doing all of this for you. Didn't you miss me?"

"Yeah, but—"

"—Of course you did. A boy needs him mom." Her eyes squinted then widened and she smiled.

"You were cool before you left. I want that mom, that family . . . " A knot blocked the air in his throat.

The light dropped out of Mom's eyes. Her mouth was taut, on the edge of a frown.

"I won't do it. I won't help you kill people." The words rushed out. Jason stood.

She stared, too long, too hard. After a long moment, her expression softened and a small smile came to her face. "It's okay. I understand."

"You do?"

She nodded and stepped toward him, arms out. "Yes. It was too much to ask."

216

Jason backed away.

"It's okay. I want to give my son a hug, to let you know that we're fine."

She wrapped her arms around him and Jason remained rigid. Would she crush him, or stab him, or burn him? But nothing bad happened. Her closeness felt good. He relaxed into her and returned the hug. She loved him. She'd come home. She wouldn't do this.

"My poor Jason. I should have known this would be too much for you to handle."

"It's not that. I just don't want anyone to get hurt—"

A needle prick bit into his neck. He sprang back and pressed the spot with his hand. He tried to talk, to yell, but nothing came out.

"It's a paralytic. Starts with your vocal chords, which is especially nice so I don't have to listen to any more of your whining." She took his water glass to the sink and refilled it.

"I really hoped you were ready to become something great, but I see that's not possible. Sewell told me you wouldn't do it but I didn't want to believe him. But he's right . . . there's nothing special about you." She set the glass of water on the table.

Jason's eyes blurred. Still holding his neck, he took two steps toward the door. His legs seized and he dropped to the floor. Air hissed through his narrowed throat.

"Make yourself comfortable." She pushed him onto his back. "You're going to be here a while. And I'll take this." She removed his cell phone and dropped it into the water. "The signal's been blocked since we drove onto my road, but no point in taking any chances."

Jason wheezed in oxygen. She knelt down next to him and brushed his bangs away from his face, stroking his forehead.

"Don't worry, this isn't going to kill you. I don't want that, you're my son. And as long as you're alive, I get a boost from your energy. It's not quite the same as having your cooperation, but I'll take what I can get."

She pulled his hand away and examined the puncture. "I should still be able to get the Rampart down by morning, only a few hours later than I'd hoped." She kissed Jason on the cheek and closed his eyes.

Her shoes clicked on the linoleum. He pulled hard on his lungs, willing his diaphragm to keep working, to keep sucking air in, to keep shoving air out.

Mom went out the back door and hollered for Della.

Jason fought with his body, fought for air. But each bit came slower, smaller, less than the last.

His brain sniped out signals to move, to gasp, to act. But Jason was locked.

Frozen.

His heart hurtled and blood crashed through his system, beating in his head, heating up his body. His neck swelled.

Choking.

Everything went dark.

THIRTY

Fighting Back

Needles of pain panicked Jason awake. He wailed and swatted at things that weren't there. He scrambled to his feet, stumbled to the kitchen sink. Cold water soothed his arms and hands and face. He turned his head and drank. Water gushed over his chin and soaked his collar.

The pain eased. The breath came.

Jason was alive.

He checked the time—it was past midnight. More than two hours lost. His cell phone dead, he searched for another phone. A computer.

Nothing.

He staggered outside to find a bike or a scooter.

Nothing.

No communication. No transportation. And no way to stop Mom. But maybe he could slow her down, or change her mind. He huffed, remembering everything she'd said before he lost consciousness.

There would be no changing her mind.

But he had to do something.

The sugar mill glowed dimly in the distance, a white aura hovering around its edges. Jason moved toward it but the lingering effects of the paralytic drug made his moves more zombie than sprinter.

He pushed himself through rows of corn and built speed with each stride.

When he reached the mill, Jason circled it and dropped into the hiding spot he'd used with Finn. Kappas guarded the main gate and front entrance. Only the security camera watched the back, sweeping left and right. Jason waited a few more minutes until his breathing and heart rate steadied.

The camera went left and Jason dashed right, his movement better, more in control. He pushed on the door handle—locked. The camera swept toward him and he scuttled behind a dumpster. A moment later, a furry cryptid exited the building and headed away from Jason. The door closed slowly but the camera's focus was too close to Jason's position. He couldn't move. He glanced between the camera and the door, the camera and the door, each moment moving the door closer to closed. One more glance, then a second later he raced to the door and tucked his fingertips into the gap.

He slipped inside.

Heat swathed him like he'd stepped into an oven. Sizzling noises rose from deep inside the building. He moved through a short hallway, one that hadn't been there the last time. A secret passage? It opened to a vast space full of cement pillars and steel tanks. A network of pipes snaked above. He ducked behind the vats and hugged the walls, sneaking toward the source of the sound, toward the center of the building. A few minutes later, Jason found himself on an overlook. He hid behind giant gears and peered through the spokes at the scene below.

A white flame with orange edges shot from a blue-hot pit in the center of the floor. The flame soared two stories and swept along the ceiling. A hole in the roof vented the heat. Cryptids of all types performed tasks at various stations around the base of the flame. A giant bat hung near the ceiling, moving its wings back and forth.

Ahool.

On the floor, a moat full of water dammed by a three-foot high hill of dirt circled the blaze. At a nearby bank of computers, two different cryptids watched the screens and typed on keyboards. One was short, with red fur all over its body. Jason didn't know what kind of creature it was. The other was someone Jason recognized. Mizu.

"How in the . . . " Jason whispered to himself.

Thick black stitches circled Mizu's head. His slimy hair hung long and stringy and skimmed his shoulders. He glanced up in Jason's direction. Jason shrank back.

But Mizu wasn't searching for Jason. He was looking at one of several monitors that hung around the space. A bar graph filled the screen. "We're making good progress," Mizu called out to the group. "Seventy-one percent complete and climbing."

"Shit." This was one of the Rampart access points Uncle Alexander had talked about. A vortex on steroids. Jason examined the crowd below. Where was his mother? Where was Della?

There were cryptids of various heights and shapes, furriness and scaliness. A couple had mouths that looked like beaks, but their legs were human-like. Another looked like a black dog, but its eyes were red. Jason spotted a huddle of silver Skyfish across the room. And another Ahool on the far corner of the ceiling.

And Haru. Still bald, still Kappa, and hopefully still on Jason's side.

Haru held a laptop and stared at the flame. He viewed his screen, then the flame again, shaking his head.

Jason twitched in his spot. Haru saw him. Jason locked on Haru and barely breathed. Haru moved his head the tiniest degree left, and the tiniest degree right. *Don't move.*

Haru handed the computer to another cryptid and walked away. A moment later, Haru's voice whispered behind Jason. "Stay as low as you can and move out of there. Slowly."

Jason belly-crawled backward, away from the edge. An arm linked under his and pulled him to his feet.

"What are you doing here?" Haru's voice growled.

"I'm trying to help."

"Well, you're not. You're making it worse. Your energy is boosting her power." Haru glanced at his watch. "It's already seventy-three percent."

"Jeez." Jason ran both hands through his hair.

"In the last twenty minutes, the progress has increased ten-fold. You have to get out of here."

"I can't leave. She has Della."

"Listen to me. Della is—"

"—Della is what?" Jason's sister stood a few feet away from them, her hands on her hips. Her smile looked like Mom's, before Mom disappeared, before she got weird.

"Della." Jason rushed over and hugged her. "I'm so glad you're okay."

She pulled away. "Of course I'm okay. Why wouldn't I be?"

"Because Mom, she, she's kind of sick."

"No." Della clasped her hands as if trying to warm her fingers. "No, she isn't. She's fine." Her voice quivered.

"She's sick in her head. You can't really see it. And it's making her do some bad things. Like this." Jason waved toward the flame.

Della crossed her arms and her face fell. "Now you're scaring me."

"I don't mean to scare you. But we need to get out of here, okay? Get you someplace safe." In his peripheral vision, Jason saw Haru shaking his head.

"Mom told me you'd say that." She turned toward Haru. "And she said you're bad. She asked me to watch you."

"He's not bad. He's a friend and—"

"—Shut up." She held her hands out from her sides. Jason

noticed a trickle of blue light around her fingers. "You hurt Kyle, and now you're trying to hurt Mom."

"No. No that's not—"

"—I said shut up." Della raised one arm in front of her.

Jason stopped. Instinct caused heat to rise in his hands and forearms.

"Jason, calm down. You're feeding your mother's power." Haru's voice was even but pleading.

"You shut up, too." Della swung her arm toward Haru. Blue waves shot into him, knocking him to the floor.

"Della!" Jason rushed to Haru.

Blood seeped through Haru's shirt. Jason pressed his hands against the wound.

"I will heal," Haru said.

"But the blood . . . "

"Not life threatening. I just need some time." He pulled at Jason's hand. "But you need to go, and the only way you'll get Della to go with you, quietly, is to knock her out."

"What? I can't do that." Jason said.

"Then you must leave her. She's too far gone. She belongs to your mother."

"Get away from him." Della sounded more robot than Della.

Jason glanced at her and back at Haru. Haru's eyes closed and Jason backed away. He faced his sister. Both of her hands were aimed at him.

"Della, you hurt someone."

"He's bad."

"No, he's not."

"Yes, he is." Tears filled Della's eyes. "And you hurt Kyle!" She yelled the last two words.

"No. Mom, her Skyfish did that." He took a step toward her. "I saw it happen."

"No." Della's hands twitched.

"Yes. I promise you, I'm telling you the truth." Jason took another step toward Della and her electrified hands. "I could *never* have done that to Kyle." He held his hands out to her. "Please, think about it. Mom left us. She didn't really die, she left us. She lied about it. And she's lying about Kyle, and me, and everything else she told you."

"She told me she loves me."

Air caught in Jason's chest.

"I love you, Dell. And so does Dad, and Grandma Lena." Jason felt his heart rate increase. He needed to get them both out of there. "And you love us, too, don't you?"

"Yes." Della's eyes flicked to something behind Jason.

"I wouldn't be so sure about that." Mizu grabbed Jason from behind and flung him to the ground.

Jason scrambled to get to his feet but Mizu was on him again, pulling Jason into a choke hold. Jason smelled the reek of Mizu's swamp-water stench.

"I, for one, am happy to be helping your dear mother." Mizu spun Jason around to face the flame. "Doesn't her work send a thrill into your very soul?"

The swirling center of the blaze smoothed like the surface of a lake on a windless day. Mom appeared between fire and sparks and flares, but not just in the flame. She *was* the flame.

"Beautiful, isn't she? Little by little she's sealing off the energy core deep in the earth that fuels this region of the Rampart. And you're helping her. We're already eighty percent done." His hold against Jason's neck tightened. "Too bad you won't get to see the big finish."

"Let him go," Della yelled at Mizu and pulled at the arm that choked Jason.

Mizu kicked her and she fell. Jason heard a crunch. "There there, princess. I'm not killing him. Only making him sleepy."

Blackness edged over Jason's eyes. Heat inflamed his hands. He clamped them onto Mizu's head.

"Gaaahhhh." Mizu shrieked and released Jason.

Jason turned and fired a bolt at Mizu.

Mizu dove right. The flash cracked a cement pillar. "Damn her orders to keep you alive. I'm finishing this." Mizu rushed Jason.

Jason darted sideways but not fast enough. A talon sliced into his chest. Jason skipped back and grabbed at the spot. Blood ran below his collarbone, flowed through his fingers. Jason zinged another bolt at Mizu. It skimmed his leg.

"You're weak, just as your mother said." Mizu sucked Jason's blood off his claw and charged again, carving into Jason's chin. "You bleed easily. It will be simple to finish you."

"Stop it, stop it. I order you." Della held her wrist and yelled at Mizu.

Mizu kept his eyes fixed on Jason but addressed Della. "Regardless what your mother told you, you're not really a princess, my dear, so keep your trap shut. I'm hungry." He hurtled toward Jason.

Jason fired, landing a hit on Mizu. He spun sideways. Jason shot fast and it reeled Mizu backward. He recovered quickly and stormed Jason again. Jason slammed Mizu with a hit to the throat but it wasn't fatal. Nothing was fatal. Mizu kept coming, kept swiping, kept slashing.

Would anything stop him? The first time they met, Finn had ripped off his scalp, but apparently that only slowed him down.

But at least it slowed him down . . .

Mizu grabbed a pipe and charged. Jason fired, missed and jumped backward but Mizu connected with Jason's leg. The metal pipe bounced off and the recoil threw Mizu to the floor. "What?" His eyes were wide and he shook his hand. "How is that possible?" He looked sideways at Haru then back to Jason.

Jason smiled. "I guess I'm not as weak as you thought." *Or that I thought.* Jason skittered to the right, leading Mizu farther away from Della. "Care to try again?"

Mizu bared his yellow teeth and streaked toward Jason, his deafening screech filling the room.

Jason raised his hands, focused, and zeroed in on his target. Dual bolts hit their mark and Mizu's scalp wrenched off. Slimy green liquid soaked the floor in its wake. Mizu stopped moving, stopped screeching. His dark eyes filmed over and he crashed to the floor.

Jason hunched, braced one hand on his knee and pressed the other into the large wound on his torso. He watched Della. She marched to Mizu's scalp, hovered one hand over it, and incinerated it.

"I never liked him anyway." She brushed her hand on her pants then used it to cradle her other arm.

Jason stood. "Wait, that's it? No scalp, no Mizu?"

"Pretty much. It holds in fluid from their homeland that keeps them alive."

"How do you know that?"

"Mom told me. That's what she wanted me to do to him." She pointed at Haru who still slept.

"And now?" Jason took a couple steps to the side, moving between Haru and Della. He eyed the other cryptids on the floor below and wondered why they hadn't heard them, why they weren't attacking. The cryptids stayed at their stations.

Della shrugged. "I don't . . . I want . . . " Della crumpled. She pulled her knees into her chest and started crying. "I don't want Dad and Grandma Lena to die."

"Me neither, Dell."

"But I don't want to leave Mom." The blue of her eyes blurred behind tears. "She needs me."

Jason knelt beside her and put his arm around her shoulders. "Dad needs you, too. And so does Grandma Lena, and so do I. I mean look." Jason pointed at Mizu's still form. "You just saved my life."

Della sniffed and cried harder.

"Let's not stay here, okay? It's too dangerous." Jason squeezed Della closer.

Between cries, she gasped air and her shoulders shuddered. "Okay."

Jason helped her up and noticed her wrist. It was swollen and purple. "Hey, are you all right?"

She lifted her arm. "Yeah. It only sort of hurts."

"It might more than sort of hurt later. I think it's broken."

Della sniffed and nodded.

"Do you think you can help me with Haru? Have him lean on your good side?"

She sniffed again. "Yeah."

They walked over to Haru. He opened his eyes. "You're still here."

"So are you." Jason hunched next to him.

"So it seems." Haru peeled back his shirt. The wound was healed. He stood and examined the gash on Jason's chest. "Mizu?"

Jason nodded. "And this one." He turned his chin toward Haru.

"It seems you've done a nice job cauterizing them yourself." Haru studied both lacerations.

"Huh. I'm full of surprises."

"May I?" Haru held up his hands.

"Della first," Jason said.

Haru turned to Della. She looked at Jason.

"It's okay," Jason said.

Haru held her wrist between both of his hands and closed his eyes. Della whimpered but didn't flinch. After another moment, Haru released her.

Della shook her arm. "It doesn't hurt anymore." She shook it harder, showing Haru, then Jason, then Haru again.

"It's not fully healed, so careful with the shaking." He smiled at her. "But as your brother has discovered, once it has healed, it will be better than new."

Haru returned his attention to Jason and placed one hand on Jason's chin, the other on his collarbone. Tiny electrical pulses pumped into Jason's skin and the pain flowed out. A moment later, Haru removed his hands and Jason's skin was smooth and healthy.

"Thank you, Haru." Jason clamped Haru's shoulder.

Haru checked his watch. "Eighty-five percent."

"Let's get out of here." Jason stood and pulled Della close.

Haru grabbed his arm. "I'll take her. You stay."

Jason's brows pulled together. "But I'm part of the problem. My energy . . . I'm helping her destroy the Rampart."

"Yes, you both are. But you're stronger than I thought, Jason. You defeated Mizu."

"Yeah, but I had inside information about the scalp thing."

"It's more than that. Your ability to generate power is extraordinary. You are strong. Like your mother."

Jason shook his head rapidly. "No. No way." He thumbed over his shoulder. "Have you seen her lately? She's a freakin' lightning bolt. How do I beat that?"

"With lightning."

"What?"

"She is pure electricity, and she's using that to destroy access to the core that powers the Rampart."

"Right. I know."

"It's a delicate operation. If she sends too much power into the core, it will bounce back, and destroy her."

"So that's it? I add some electricity to the deal and she's done?"

Haru sighed.

"Not that easy." Jason's shoulders slumped.

"No." Haru led them to a spot on the ledge where they could look down without being seen. "You see the moat?"

Jason nodded.

"The water is helping conduct her energy into the core. Do you see what is surrounding the moat?"

"The dirt?"

"Not dirt. Worm."

Jason focused on the ring. It was moving, undulating, pulsing in circles around the water. It had to be at least thirty feet long. "That's a worm? From where? Gigantica?"

"It's a Mongolian Death Worm. It's protecting your mother, and the core, from power surges. It redirects excess electricity to the ground."

"Mongolian Death Worm. No way."

"Yes."

"And I need to unplug it or whatever."

"You need to kill it."

"Right. And if I can't?"

"If you can at least damage it, there's a chance a surge will get through and ricochet back, stopping your mother. Saving the Rampart. Saving your family." Haru glanced at Della.

"How big of a chance?"

"I don't know, Jason." Haru checked the meter on his watch again. "Eighty-eight percent."

Jason ran both hands through his hair, tugging on it before releasing.

Haru pulled Jason away, to a spot where Della couldn't hear them. "I'm not going to lie to you. This isn't going to be easy."

Jason listened, his breath shallow.

"Mongolian Death Worms are full of acid. It's the acid that serves as the diverter for the electricity. They also spit this acid as a defense mechanism. It will burn right through you."

"Okay. Don't get sprayed with acid. Check."

"And they can discharge a lethal jolt of electricity from several feet away."

"Okay. Don't get electrocuted. Check."

"If you can at least inflict some damage . . . "

"No. I need to kill it."

"Jason—"

"No. I'll . . . .I'll be fine. Get Della somewhere safe . . . or at least out of here."

Haru nodded once and held out his hand. "Good luck, Jason Lex."

"Thanks, I need it." Jason paused. "And hey, Haru, how come Della's bolt hurt you, but nothing would stop Mizu short of scalping?"

"Because Mizu is . . . " he eyed Mizu's lifeless form, "was, much older than I."

Jason nodded. "You guys better get going."

"Bring Mom home with you," Della said.

Jason reached up and rubbed the spot where Mom had pricked him with the needle. "I'll try, Dell. I'll try."

"Okay. Good." She turned and left with Haru.

THIRTY-ONE

Battle For the Rampart

Jason watched the scene below. There were at least fifteen cryptids. How could he get past all of them, or enough of them, to do even a little damage to the Mongolian Death Worm?

He scanned the room, the walls, the equipment, hoping for an idea, an item, something that might give him a fighting chance. Even half a chance.

There was nothing. Only him and his blue-bolting hands.

His mother's voice rang out. "There's nothing you can do."

Jason inspected the white light that was his mother. Her eyes opened. She didn't search for Jason. She knew exactly where to find him.

She smiled. "You will fail." She closed her eyes.

"Maybe. But I'll do my best, Mom. You always told us to do our best."

She sneered.

Jason's throat tightened for a moment but he shoved the sensation back. He focused and headed toward the stairs. No use hiding. If she knew he was here, everyone knew he was here.

Two Kappas cleared the landing and rushed Jason. He raised his arms and fired. Blue bolts ripped off their scalps. The flesh stuck to the wall behind them. The Kappas collapsed and Jason scorched their scalps to smoke. The stink of burned fish wafted into the air.

Helps to know what I'm doing.

He raced down the stairs and met two more Kappas. Two more scalps slicked and fried. He spun toward the center of the floor where cryptids worked around the flame. He was ready to fight.

But no one came at him, no one attacked. Every cryptid stayed at their station, working computers, watching monitors, examining gauges. Some glanced at Jason but quickly returned to their tasks.

"You're not a threat and everyone knows it. Join us," his mom said.

Jason ignored her. He circled the room, positioning himself so he always had a line of sight on the cryptids, his mom, and the Mongolian Death Worm.

He moved in closer, circled again. The silver Skyfish pulsated faster in their cluster near the ceiling, but none approached.

Jason felt like a mouse trapped in a snake's den, wondering from where the snake would attack.

A small sound buzzed in his ears. Jason took another step forward, toward the cryptids, toward his mother. The sound increased. He reached a hand out. Vibration tickled his palm, building when he moved his hand forward, easing when he pulled it back. A force field.

No wonder they're not worried. I can't even get to them.

Jason made two more circuits, using his hands to search for gaps, breaks, anywhere the force field might not be sealed. No such luck. He leaned against a wall and watched the cryptids, watched them working to destroy the Rampart. Watched them working to kill Jason's family and friends.

"The force field . . . that's you, right?" Jason asked his mother.

She didn't open her eyes.

"I bet it's slowing you down. You have less energy to aim at the core. Good plan, Mom."

"It may take longer than I'd like, but it will be done." Her voice boomed.

"Then you won't mind if I do this." Jason shot a bolt out of his right hand. It splayed into a circle on the force field, burning white. He kept it flowing, kept it burning.

"You are no threat."

A segment of the force field disintegrated behind Jason's beam. He stepped forward and added his other hand to the fire. The edges of the field, visible in the heat, split, and folded, and opened. Jason sidestepped and redirected. He plowed his power into the Mongolian Death Worm.

The Worm arched and spewed acid, slicing through power cables on the floor. Alarms screeched and strobe lights flashed. Sections of the force field dissolved. Jason fired again and dove behind partitions of force field still intact.

The Worm reared and aimed at Jason. Acid ricocheted above Jason's head and zapped a computer bank on the other side of the room. Two cryptids fell. Others fled. Waves of water splashed from the moat and electrocuted cryptids.

Jason scrambled, fired, and ran again. The Worm chased him with acid. Jason pitched behind a pillar. The acid hit. The concrete sizzled.

Jason sucked in chemical-filled fumes. He rolled under a steel vat and slid himself across the floor. His lungs pulled at the air. Two big breaths and he pushed himself again, sliding behind another pillar. It cracked next to him when a gush from the Worm hit its mark.

Jason dashed, fired, ran to another pillar. The Worm flailed. Its body thrashed through the space, spraying acid, wrecking everything with burning and crushing weight. Cryptids fell around it. Cryptids fell from above it.

Silver Skyfish dodged sprays of acid and dove at Jason. He hurled himself sideways and onto his back, locking his hands above him. Shafts of blue merged and spread like an umbrella. The leading Skyfish hit and disintegrated. Jason rolled. Skyfish rocketed in from the side. Jason fired. More came. Jason's power surged. Skyfish dove, Jason battled. He finished them all.

The chaos subsided. Greenish-yellow acid flowed across the floor. Jason scrambled back, redirecting his attention to the Worm.

It moved but no longer thrashed. It puffed out then sank in on itself. Acid leaked out of gashes across its body. Faint sparks snapped on its skin.

Bodies of cryptids spattered the room. And body parts. A wing lay across a red furry leg. The scaly arm of another creature smoldered under a desk. A Kappa sat near the pool, eyes open, acid flowing down its face, now more skull than skin.

Jason's mother was gone.

A graphic on a slimed-but-still-operating monitor showed ninety-two percent complete.

"What? How?" The flame was gone. Why was this still happening?

Jason scanned the room. He crossed the space, dodging pieces of cryptid and bubbling pools of acid. Stepping on a bench, he peered into the hole where the flame had been burning. A bright gleam emanated from below.

"It's too late. You've failed. No surprise."

Jason leaped from the bench and spun around, hands up and ready.

"Oh please." Mom waved a glowing hand past her glowing face. All of her glowed like a neon sign. "Do you really think I'm afraid of you? You're a child." She walked to the bench and sat.

Jason stepped back. "You're still doing this."

"Yes, dear son, I'm still doing this. You've only made it messier."

"But everything's gone. Why didn't it stop?"

"Before you started your tantrum, I had enough time to connect to the core. Now I'm draining its power, little by little." She lifted a handful of her blond hair. It shimmered like melted gold. "Pretty, isn't it? Sadly, it's temporary. No more core power, no more sparkle."

Jason dropped to his haunches. "Please stop this."

"Can't you see it's useless? Join us. Be on the winning side."

"You're sick, Mom. But we can get you help. You can get better."

"*Get* better?' I've never been better. I have power, wealth, and I'm saving the planet I love, saving Mother Earth. It's everything I've ever wanted. Everything."

No mention of family, of kids, of me. Jason swallowed. "What wealth?"

"Once the mission is complete, Sewell is rewarding me. I'll have everything." She smiled.

She sounded like Mom, she moved like Mom, she smiled like Mom. But this wasn't Mom.

Maybe she never really was Mom.

Bile oozed up into his throat. The mom he knew was gone forever. "There's nothing I can do?"

"Yes. Join me. Join us. He can teach you, make you stronger."

Jason shook his head. "Any other options?"

"You could kill me. But we both know you don't have the power, much less the courage to try."

He stood. "You're right. That's not happening. So I'm outta here. I'll spend the rest of my time with my family."

Her smile switched off. "I'm your family, Jason."

"No. You're not." He picked his way through the mess toward the exit.

"I want you to stay here."

"I don't care what you want." He hopped over a spill of slime.

"You will stay."

A ball of energy slugged into him. His foot came down in the muck and he slipped. Jason fell in the crater that led to the core. His hands gripped the edge.

"No!" His mother screamed. She seized his wrist and yanked him out.

Jason skipped forward and braced himself on a pillar. His wrist sizzled where she'd grabbed him. Why hadn't she just let him die?

His energy. That's why she wanted him here.

And that's why she didn't want him to fall into the core. His energy could short out the connection.

He faced her. She was between him and the hole.

"Sit down." She pointed. "Sit down right there."

"You don't get to tell me what to do. Not anymore." Jason leaped to the right and zipped past her. Walls and pillars and vats exploded behind him. Jason zagged left, zoomed behind her and launched. He was dead on. He dove toward the core.

An orb of white smashed into him, whirling him sideways, crashing him to the floor, sliding him far from the pit. He swung his arm up and shot a blue bolt.

A thunderclap sheared the air when the blue hit the white of his mother. It boomeranged back and the force spun her around. A second shot from Jason knocked her into the shaft.

Jason scrambled to the edge. She had one hand, four fingertips, fixed to the lip.

"Pull me up." She gasped out the words.

"Promise me you'll stop everything."

"Or what? You'll leave me here? You'll let me die?"

Jason scooted back. All he could see was her fingertips.

"Jason, get me out of here."

Jason's heart beat hard and fast. There was only one way, one answer, one thing that would save everyone.

She called to him. "You don't want to lose me again, do you?"

Smash her fingertips. Push her in. Save everyone.

"Jason, you're my son. I love you. And we're so much alike. Help me." Her fingertips slid a fraction.

Jason crawled back to the edge. "I'm nothing like you." He reached in and grasped her wrist. His hand burned. He pulled but she didn't move.

"Pull harder," she yelled, her other arm flinging up, trying to grab onto something.

Jason hooked his foot around a chunk of broken concrete and added his other hand to his hold. He moved her only inches.

"The core is pulling me in." Her eyes were wide, wild.

His skin blistered. He pulled one hand away. Bits of skin stayed behind, bubbling on her wrist.

"Stop burning me, Mom. Turn it off." He blinked trying to clear tears forced by pain and fire.

"I can't. Don't let me go. Pull."

The smolder of his skin rushed into his nose, into his gut. Jason squinted and pulled with every ounce of strength, of adrenaline, of determination. His grip slackened.

"Jason."

His skin slipped. Her wrist slid. The pain seared his throat.

"Jason. No!" She scrambled, one hand trying to grab the rim.

It was no use. His skin sloughed away and she fell, screaming.

"Mom!" He flung his torso forward into the shaft, keeping his foot hooked. "No!" He roared after her.

He couldn't see the bottom. He couldn't see anything except a glow growing from the depths.

The ground rumbled. Everything around him rattled and shook. The edge of the pit crumbled.

Jason shoved up with his forearms and skipped backward. He teetered left, tried to find his balance. The ground bounced under his feet. A howl roared from the pit. Concrete and metal broke off around him.

He ran. He raced to the stairs and vaulted up the steps, some of them falling as he pushed off. He cleared the landing. He shielded his head with his arm. He dodged debris.

The din escalated and the mill shook. Jason turned down the hall and flew toward the exit. The door was open. He was almost there.

An explosion hurled him forward. Something slammed into the back of his head. He fell to the ground, took the impact with his shoulder. Pain cleaved into his arm, his neck, his back. He rolled, forced himself up again, pulled his arm to his side, and lunged toward the door.

Cool air hit his face. He was out.

He pressed on, willing his legs to stumble forward.

"Jason."

No. No more fighting. Keep running.

An arm wrapped around Jason's waist and heaved his weight off his feet.

Jason turned his head. "Dad?" A cold nose pressed into Jason's arm. "Finn?"

"Let's go." Dad kept Jason moving, practically carrying him across the ground, across the bodies.

Dead Kappas.

They cleared the fence and went right, away from the trees, toward the front of the mill.

"I've got him." Dad yelled to a shadow ahead.

"Get him in the car. We've gotta get out of here." Uncle Alexander opened a door.

Another explosion knocked them to the ground. A white pillar of light flared out of the mill, into the sky, making daylight out of darkness.

Dad yanked Jason up and forward. Pain mowed through him. Dad pushed him into the back seat with Finn. Uncle Alexander climbed into the passenger side and Dad stomped on the gas. They sped toward the road.

Jason watched the light burn through the sky. The flame was silver, like mercury, with flashes firing off it like fireworks. Crackling racked his ears. His neck burned, but the feeling dwarfed compared to the rest of his pain.

A moment later, the laser of light folded in on itself, dropped down to the ground and was gone.

Jason stared at the blackness. "She's gone."

"Don't worry. We'll find her." Dad reached back and squeezed Jason's shoulder.

Jason kept his eyes fixed where the light had been. He shook his head. "No. She was in the light. She fell in."

"Ah. Okay." Uncle Alexander nodded his head.

"What? What's okay?" Dad asked.

"Adrienne found a way to connect to the core, to redirect its energy away from the Rampart. But when she fell in, the energy she'd stolen reunited with the core. It was too much all at once."

Jason's vision waved and his head throbbed. His breaths were short and quick.

"And the Rampart?"

Dad asked the question, but Jason couldn't figure out where Dad was. In the front seat? In the back seat?

Uncle Alexander spoke. "It should be restored. But I'm afraid she's lost."

"I'm cold." Jason wasn't sure if he'd said that out loud. Something tugged on his eyelids.

"He's going into shock."

THIRTY-TWO
Awakening

It smelled like Band-Aids. Jason opened his eyes. Metal rails ran along the foot of his bed. A machine beeped and plastic tubes dripped fluid into his arm.

"Good morning." Grandma Lena sat next to the bed. She brushed his bangs off his face.

"Hey." Jason's throat scratched out the word.

"It's nice to see you. How are you feeling?"

"Like I fell out of a burning building and then got beat up."

She smiled. "Well, that's about how you look, too."

"What time is it?" Jason's words slurred.

"About nine in the morning. But the better question is what day is it? You've been asleep since they brought you in yesterday morning." She stood. "Your dad's in Kyle's room. I'm going to let him know you're awake."

Jason gasped. "Kyle . . . how is he?"

She smiled again. "He's just fine. He has a concussion, but he gets to go home this afternoon." She walked out of the room.

Jason sighed and lifted his right hand. It was wrapped in gauze and it hurt. His left arm hung in a sling, strapped tight to his body. Gauze peeked out where his fingertips should be.

The door opened and everyone came in: Dad, Grandma Lena, Uncle Alexander, Della, and Sadie. And Kyle.

They all clamored, asking how Jason felt, relaying information about his injuries, his burned hands, dislocated shoulder, his concussion just like Kyle's, broken collarbone, and broken ribs, and asking what happened. Jason told his story, leaving out the details about Mom's fall.

He told Kyle how good it was to see him. And he asked Dad how they knew to go to the mill.

"I lost your mom's car after I got stuck behind that damned tractor, and we lost your signal soon after that. We didn't know where else to go, so we decided to check the mill." Dad pulled a chair next to the bed. "When we got close we saw lights, and then noticed the Kappas on guard duty, so we figured we might be in the right place."

Uncle Alexander continued the story. "We watched the Kappas for a while, trying to devise a way in. They guarded the gate and the front entrance of the mill. There were ten of them and two of us. And Finn."

"Our secret weapon." Dad grinned. "She is one amazing dog."

"She's had excellent training." Uncle Alexander smiled. "We saw Adrienne arrive but there was no sign of you and we weren't sure what to do next. Then Finn started throwing a fit, trying to get out of the car, pawing at the back window. That's when we saw you go in. If it hadn't been for her, we wouldn't have known you were there."

"She is a great dog." Dad nodded his head.

"Okay, Dad, I think I understand that Finn is a great, amazing dog." Jason smirked and slowly shifted his right arm to a more comfortable position.

Uncle Alexander spoke. "We were going to make a run to my house for anything we could use as weapons, but Finn managed to open the back door and jump out."

"It was horrible. We thought she was a goner. At least I did. I didn't know she'd been trained for this sort of thing." Dad shook his head. "We ran after her. By the time we caught up, she'd grabbed a pant leg and pulled a Kappa to the ground. He was trying to slash her but she'd leap backward, dodge his swing, then bite down on his ankle again and shake him."

"The Kappa screamed and more came running. Your dad was attacked from behind. A Kappa knocked him to the ground and jumped on top of him. Zachary fought hard but the Kappa was strong. He slit your dad's arm—"

"—What? Are you okay, Dad?" Jason tried to sit higher and see the wound.

"I'm fine, I'm fine. Lie back down." He tipped his head to Uncle Alexander who started talking again.

"He is fine now but things didn't seem too good then. I couldn't get to your dad. But Finn could and did. She launched herself into the Kappa and ripped off the Kappa's scalp. Then she did the same thing to the one attacking me. She took out three more before she got slashed."

Every muscle in Jason's chest clenched. "Finn? Is she . . . "

Uncle Alexander put his hand on Jason's shoulder. "Finn's okay. She's with Haru."

Jason closed his eyes and sank into his pillows. He blew out air and opened his eyes again, directing them at his dad. "You met Haru."

He nodded. "He's got quite a talent."

"You have no idea." Jason closed his eyes for a moment, trying to clear the fog in his head.

"Haru was our second hero. He came out of the mill with Della and ordered them to stop their attack. Most did. Two didn't but Haru eliminated them. And he healed Finn and your dad." Uncle Alexander sighed. "He's a good friend."

"I like him." Della climbed onto the end of Jason's bed. "He's nice. And pretty tough."

Uncle Alexander jumped back into the story. "Haru gave us his access key and left with Della. We tried to get into the mill but every door was locked and Haru's key didn't work. The windows were inaccessible without a ladder. There was nothing we could do until you came out." He patted Jason's leg.

"How long do I have to stay here?"

"A couple more days at least. It depends on your hands and how they're healing." Dad ran his fingers through his hair. "Do they hurt?"

"Yeah, but I'm okay."

Sadie, who'd stayed quiet until now, moved to the end of the bed. "Jason, how did you burn your hands?"

Jason shook his head in small, almost unnoticeable movements. "Just, you know, fighting and stuff. There was acid."

"The doctor said they weren't acid burns." She kept her gaze fixed on him.

Jason shrugged. "There was a lot going on." He closed his eyes.

Sadie paused a moment. "It was your mom, wasn't it?"

He looked at her and shrugged again.

"Your mother did this to you?" Dad pointed at Jason's gauzy hands.

"No, I did it to myself. She was hot."

"What do you mean?"

"She was glowing, burning white. She was hanging on the edge. I grabbed her. I tried to pull her out but I couldn't. She was too hot and I couldn't hold on." Jason swallowed. "She fell." His voice was quiet, less than a whisper.

Everyone stared at him. He felt hot, like he was under the glare of a spotlight.

"I killed her, okay? I killed her." Jason's voice faltered.

Grandma Lena stepped forward and sat on the edge of Jason's bed. He leaned back into his pillow.

"You listen to me and you listen good." She looked into his eyes. "You did not kill your mom. You did not fail to save your mom. The only person responsible for your mom's death is your mom."

Jason didn't know what to say.

"What you *did* do is save your family, save your friends, and save the Rampart. I am proud of you, Jason, very proud. And so is everyone here. Always. And don't you forget that." Tears brimmed her eyes.

"Thanks, Grams." Something gurgled in Jason's throat. He gulped air.

She kissed Jason on the forehead. "Now, I think we should let you get some rest."

She turned and hugged Dad and Alexander. Sadie hugged Della. Everyone sniffed and sobbed as they said their *feel betters*, and *see you laters*. All but Dad left Jason's room.

He moved over and put his hand on Jason's head. "I'm so sorry for everything you've been through, son. And I wish I'd been there for you earlier, listened to you earlier." He gently brushed his hand through Jason's hair.

"It's okay, Dad."

"No, it's not. But that's going to change. The best thing about mistakes is that you can learn from them. And I've learned plenty." Dad wiped his eyes. "And one thing I know for certain, you are an incredible, strong, courageous young man, Jason. I could not be more proud of you."

Jason's chest tightened and goosebumps skittered across his skin. "Thanks, Dad."

He smiled and squeezed Jason's good shoulder. "We'll save hugs for when you're feeling better, okay?" Jason nodded and Dad left the room.

Jason soon fell asleep. He dreamed about Haru. They were in a fire. Then they weren't. And Haru said *it can't be too good* and was gone.

A nurse woke Jason a few hours later and asked about Jason's pain, asked him if he needed more meds. He flexed is fingers and carefully stretched his palms. He declined the pills.

Thanks, Haru.

THIRTY-THREE
A Name in Gold

"Miraculous," the doctors said about Jason's injuries. They were healing rapidly, especially his burns. The doctors had been worried about infection and permanent damage to his hands, but they were healing as if he'd suffered only second-degree burns.

After two more days in the hospital, Jason went home.

The next day, there was a small gathering at the Lex home. It was the Lex family, Grandma Lena, Uncle Alexander and Finn, Sadie and her grandmother, Willene, and Haru.

Willene cooked and filled them with a hot meal. The adults lingered at the table. Jason signaled Sadie and stood. He walked out into the backyard, followed close behind by Sadie and Finn. They went to a far corner and sat in the shade.

"Are you okay?" Sadie asked.

"Yeah, I guess. It's weird." Jason rubbed the top of Finn's head. "I mean, I know everything that happened was real but it doesn't feel real, ya know?"

"I know. It's totally weird."

"I wish I could feel normal again."

"But you're not normal."

Jason huffed. "Don't remind me."

246

Sadie picked a nearby dandelion and smelled it, then twirled the flower in the palm of her hand, watching its head spin. "You did a really good thing, a really brave thing."

"Then why do I feel like shit?"

"Because what happened with your mom sucked. And it's hard and horrible and stupid. And you'll get through it, Jason. And you'll be better. And *not* normal. You already are better." Sadie held the dandelion under Finn's nose. Finn snorted. Jason smiled.

Dad came out the back door. "C'mon inside. We want to talk to you."

Jason stood and brushed grass off his pants.

Everyone, except Uncle Alexander, waited in the family room. Della sat tucked under Dad's arm, sharing the recliner. Kyle plopped into a beanbag. Everyone else sat on the sectional.

"Did Uncle Alexander leave?" Jason and Sadie sat on the ottoman.

"No," Dad said. "He's getting something."

The front door opened and Finn's head perked up. Jason turned. A second later, a speedy ball of fur with four legs and floppy ears peeled around the corner and barreled at Jason, leaped through the air and missed the landing, sliding sideways off Jason's lap. The puppy rolled and scrambled and raced to everyone, flew up on the couch, clambered over laps, vaulted off, sprung onto the recliner, fell off the arm, tumbled over the back of Finn then slid into Jason's feet.

Jason scooped her up with one arm and she launched into a frenzy of licking, and licking, and licking his face. "Who are you?" Jason tried to dodge the puppy-breath kisses near his mouth but failed and laughed.

"That's for you to decide, Jason." Uncle Alexander sat on the arm of the couch. "She's yours."

"What?"

Dad nodded, smiling.

The puppy climbed into Sadie's lap and bathed her in kisses then hopped back to Jason. She circled three times, curled herself into a ball, sighed, and closed her eyes. He moved his arm around her so she wouldn't slip off his lap.

"Clearly we'll have to work on increasing her stamina," Uncle Alexander said, only half-seriously.

"We?" Jason shook his head.

Uncle Alexander frowned. "Yeah, there is a catch."

"What catch? I have to train her? I'll do that."

"Actually, we'll be training together." Uncle Alexander pursed his lips for a moment.

"Training . . . with you?"

"And Finn."

The puppy opened one eye at Jason, then closed it and sighed again. Jason stroked the top of her head.

"Jason, your name is in gold. You are the next Guard."

Jason's mouth dropped open. He looked at Della and Kyle, then back at Uncle Alexander.

"But Della . . . at the mill."

"Adrienne was likely feeding power through Della. Nothing more."

"Wow." Jason inhaled deeply and blew it out. The puppy's ear twitched at the feel of his breath. "Why did it take so long for my name to turn gold?"

"Remember at my house when you . . . died—" He shifted his focus to Jason's dad. "—Don't worry, Zachary, as you can see he's perfectly fine."

Dad opened his mouth to speak then thought better of it.

"The Skyfish that did that, that was part of the test. Your athleticism in trying to outrun them was a test. And your ability to connect with them, to absorb their energy, to advance your power because of that connection with them was all a test."

Jason looked at his hands and willed them to glow blue.

"One that you clearly passed with flying colors." Uncle Alexander leaned forward and rested his elbows on his knees. "So only one question remains."

Jason raised his eyes to Uncle Alexander. "What's that?"

"Are you in?"

Jason grinned. "Yeah, I'm in. Me and little . . . little . . . " He examined the puppy's patches of white and black fur. She had one white ear, one black ear, and they were pointed but flopped at the tips. One eye was framed in black. "Shay."

The puppy opened both eyes and popped up to a sit. She started licking Jason's face all over again.

"I guess she likes her name," Jason said.

THE END

Chapter One

The first few weeks back at school were weird, uncomfortable. Jason had battled his own mother to stop her from destroying the Rampart, a shield that protected humans from the energy of cryptids, and the battle resulted in his mom's death. He discovered he was a Rampart Guard and now spent hours training every day. But no one at school, besides his older brother, Kyle, and his best friend, Sadie, knew any of that.

To everyone else, Jason was the new guy who attacked his brother on the first day of school. Jason couldn't explain what really happened. Who would believe Skyfish and electrocution when all they saw was Jason slamming into Kyle?

Weeks passed and the whispering and pointing faded, then stopped altogether. Jason and Kyle made new friends. And Jason and Sadie ate lunch together whenever their schedules matched.

"Ugh." Sadie rolled her eyes. "Here comes Derek Goodman."

Jason looked over his shoulder. His lip curled when he caught Derek's eye.

"What are you looking at?" Derek and two of his friends stopped behind Jason.

"I was trying to figure out what smelled so bad."

"Well, it might be you, the slime-ball that beats up his own pansy brother."

Jason bolted out of his seat and faced Derek, standing only inches away from him. Jason's hands were hot. "Take that back."

"Or what?"

Jason pressed his fists into his thighs. He moved closer to Derek. "Take. That. Back."

"No way. For all we know, now you've done something to your sister, too. My little sister hasn't seen her in school for like a month."

The sparks zapped inside Jason's hands. His chest thrust forward. He battled the urge to singe Derek Goodman. And to slug him hard in the gut.

"Jason?" Sadie's voice was half-anxious, half-warning.

Jason shook his head. "You're not worth it." He glared at Derek.

"No? How about now?" Derek shoved Jason into the crowd.

Jason sprung into a fighting stance.

"What's going on here?" Coach Martel grabbed Derek's shoulder. "You. To the principal's office. Now." He turned to Jason. "Are you all right?"

"Yeah. Fine." He straightened and relaxed. His hands cooled.

"Okay. Good man." Coach patted Jason on the back. "And don't forget basketball tryouts are in a couple of weeks. I told Coach Thomas to look for you."

"Thanks, Coach." Jason wouldn't try out for the basketball team—he wanted to stay focused on his training for the Guards.

Coach Martel nodded. "Now, if you'll excuse me, I have a problem to escort to the principal's office. Again."

Jason returned to his seat. The adrenaline eased. Lunch period was almost over and most of his friends left for their next class.

Sadie remained. She leaned across the table. "Della's still not in school?"

Jason wadded his trash and hooped it into the nearby bin. "No. She can't deal. She's awake half the night, she starts crying at the weirdest times. She was playing fetch with Shay yesterday and lost it when Shay wouldn't drop the ball for her."

"Is there anything I can do to help?" The bell rang and Sadie picked up her lunch bag.

Jason stood and looked at his hands. The skin on his palms was shiny and tight, newly healed after he'd burned them trying to save his mom. "Nah. Dad's trying to figure it out. Thanks, though." He turned toward his next class. "See you later."

❄ ❄ ❄

After school, Jason and Shay headed to Uncle Alexander's. Jason opened the front door, and Shay rushed in and tackled Finn. They rolled and lunged and growled, sounding like they wanted each other's blood.

Jason checked their body language. This was all fun and games. Reading the dogs' signals was one of Jason's first lessons as a Rampart Guard. Shay and Finn continued their wrestling match with a slam into the leather couch.

"Hey, Uncle A." Jason collapsed on the couch.

Uncle Alexander poked his head out of the kitchen. "Did you study the guidelines and laws of the League of Governors?"

"Yep. Until I fell asleep. Which took about five minutes."

"I know it's not the most riveting read. But you have to learn it."

Jason leaned back and closed his eyes. "I will, I will. Maybe this weekend when I'm not so tired."

Uncle Alexander walked in and tapped Jason with a water bottle. "What about the Rampart distress signals?"

He sat up. "Much more interesting. I'm now on the lookout for sundogs, moondogs, rings around the sun, changes in electromagnetic field noise, extra-bright double rainbows, and a few more things I can't remember at the moment. And Sadie's going to keep an eye on the Internet for any hey-look-here's-a-picture-of-me-with-Bigfoot or whatever postings so we can check them out."

"Good. I'll quiz you while you work the bag. Let's head downstairs to the gym."

Jason kicked and punched, defended and attacked, and practiced methods to escape choke holds and bindings. During breaks, he rehearsed Shay's basic commands and started her on cryptid scent identification. Finn assisted when Shay was stumped.

When they got home that evening, like every evening after training, they headed to the kitchen. Kyle sat at the table doing homework. Shay bee-lined to her water bowl, slurped up a sloppy drink, and caved onto her kitchen bed—one of several dog beds placed around the house.

"Must be nice." Jason plunked down a pile of books on the table next to Kyle's stack. "No homework for you." He bent down and rubbed Shay's cheek.

"Seriously nice," Kyle said. He stretched his arms overhead.

Dad walked in. "I'm glad you're both here. We need to talk."

"What's up?" Kyle asked.

"Della . . . the League of Governors. They're worried."

"What do they have to do with anything?" Jason took leftover chicken out of the refrigerator.

"Because of the Guards, because of the power she still has since your mother used her as a conduit," Dad said.

"Okay." Jason bit into a chicken breast, not bothering with a plate.

"I'm taking her to them."

"What? Why?" Kyle asked.

"They may be able to help. They may be the only ones that can help."

Jason shifted his weight and swallowed. "I don't get it. Why them?"

"She needs to talk to someone but she can't meet with a regular therapist. Plus, the League, they're worried that she may be going down a path like your mother's."

Jason straightened. "Della is not crazy."

Dad shook his head. "No, I know. But she needs help. You two and Shay will stay with Alexander, okay?"

"Yeah, that works. When are you leaving?" Kyle shut his notebook.

"Tonight. Three-hour drive to the airport then we catch the red-eye. GQ is picking us up at Heathrow tomorrow."

Dad's anxiousness quashed the amusement Jason usually found when he heard Grandad Quentin's nickname. "Wow. Okay. I'll get my things together." Jason snagged an apple and scooped his books off the table. He headed toward the hall.

"Me too." Kyle followed.

Shay led them upstairs and leaped onto Jason's bed. Jason tossed shirts and pants and underwear into a duffle bag. He packed his bathroom stuff. At the last minute, he remembered socks. He yanked open the drawer.

A T-shirt was stuffed in the corner. He pulled it out and the broken rook and the old metal coin fell to the floor.

"I forgot all about this." Jason set the coin on his dresser and examined the two parts of the rook. He slid the notch into its matching slot. The pieces locked like they'd never been apart.

What the . . . why didn't that work before?

He twisted the rook, trying to remove the base again. He pressed on the bottom, he pressed on the top but the pieces held fast.

Weird. Jason returned the rook to the chessboard and slipped the coin in his pocket.

"Ready, Jason?" Dad called from downstairs.

"Yeah. Coming." Jason grabbed his bag. "Let's go, Shay."

Shay jumped off the bed and trotted downstairs. Della, Dad and Kyle were there with their suitcases. Della's eyes were puffy.

"Lucky you, Dell, going to London." Jason rolled his duffle behind him as they headed to the garage.

Della sort of smiled. "Yeah. I guess."

"Well, I'm jealous. You and Dad get to have fun, and I get to go to school."

Della nodded. Jason wondered if she was about to start crying again. He wanted say something, try to make her feel better, but everything seemed to make her feel worse.

Dad loaded the bags into the van. They arrived at Uncle Alexander's a few minutes later. He and Finn greeted them in the driveway.

Dad got out. "Thanks, Alexander. I appreciate this."

"Anytime. It gives us more time to train." Uncle Alexander winked at Jason.

"Cool. I can help toughen him up." Kyle smirked and punched Jason in the arm.

"So not funny." Jason faked a punch at Kyle's gut.

"Boys, please behave yourselves and don't torture your poor uncle. I'll call you tomorrow, as soon as we arrive." Dad hugged Kyle and Jason then patted Shay's chest.

A late-October wind whisked into Jason's shirt and goosebumped his skin. "Okay. Have a safe trip." He reached into the passenger window and mussed Della's hair. "Talk to you soon, Dell. Have fun."

"Not the hair again. Now it's going to be all staticky." Della batted at his arm and raised the window.

Dad backed out of the driveway. Jason, Kyle and Uncle Alexander waved them away.

Jason slapped the front pocket of his pants. *Crap. I meant to ask him about the coin.*

❅ ❅ ❅

The next day, Jason woke early and ran with Shay, a ritual they practiced every morning. He and Kyle went to school, Jason completed his afternoon training, and then they sat down to dinner with Uncle Alexander.

"Have you heard from your dad?" Uncle Alexander passed a bowl of roasted veggies to Jason.

"No. I thought maybe he'd called you or Kyle."

"Nada on my phone," Kyle said.

"I haven't heard from him either. I'm sure he'll call soon. He probably got sidetracked with something. The League has a way of doing that." Uncle Alexander offered to serve Jason. "Salmon?"

"Yeah. Thanks." Jason's mouth watered as the scent of maple glaze wafted up from the fish. He dug into the meal and tried to ignore the jitters in his stomach.

"Do you want more? How about some bread?" Uncle Alexander picked up a loaf of garlic bread wrapped in foil.

Jason waved. "Nah, I'm good."

"Jason, you're training a lot. You need more food, more nutrition." Uncle Alexander took a piece of bread for himself. "I'm concerned about your weight."

"I'm fine. I'm strong." Jason glanced down and admired the veins raised above the surface of his forearm.

"Looking strong and being strong aren't necessarily the same thing. Please eat something more."

"No worries, Uncle A. I'm fine. Eating plenty, I promise." He took a drink of water. "Hey. Did you ever find out anything about that guy Mom kept talking about? Sewell Kendrick?"

Uncle Alexander shook his head. "Nothing at all. There's no record of him in the system, and none of the other Guards have ever heard of him." He stabbed lettuce and tomato with his fork. "I suspect he was some kind of construct of your mother's, a way for her to do the things she was doing without taking full responsibility for them."

"So, she made him up," Kyle said.

"I think so." Uncle Alexander ate the bite of salad. "And the number of disruptions in the Rampart have dropped significantly, back to normal levels. That's another indication Adrienne was the driving force behind the attempted destruction. Since she's been gone, there hasn't been anything unusual to report."

Jason picked out the green beans and pushed them around on his plate. "Well, great. She was the big bad all along." He shoved back from the table and took his plate to the sink, rinsed it and put it in the dishwasher. "We can stop worrying about it and all go back to being normal."

✳ ✳ ✳

The rest of the evening passed without a call.

Jason dialed Dad's cell. It went straight to voice mail. "Hey, just checking in. Hope the flight went well. Give me a call . . . whenever. Love you guys." Jason disconnected and crawled into bed. Shay curled up close.

"They must have gotten busy with something, huh girl?" Jason stroked Shay's fur from nose to forehead. "He'll call tomorrow. Right?" Shay wagged her tail. "Good girl." He switched off the light.

✳ ✳ ✳

Heat broiled Jason awake in the middle of the night. He kicked off the covers. His T-shirt clung to him, sweaty and soaked. Shay panted hard.

Intense light caught the corner of Jason's eye.

Fire?

He grabbed Shay's collar and scrambled away.

He turned back. He saw the source of the heat, the light. But it wasn't fire.

It was the coin.

The coin from his pocket, the coin with the initials L-E-X, the coin once hidden in the chess set that had been in the Lex family for generations, which sat on the nightstand next to Jason's bed.

It glowed bright red.

Continue Jason's adventure in
The League of Governors.

ACKNOWLEDGEMENTS

Writing a novel can be a solitary process. After all, it was only me sitting at the keyboard, typing out the words, making them into a story. But transforming that story into something worthy, in my humble opinion, of launching into the world, took a universe of family, friends, and talented professionals.

Jan Kays used her career coaching skills to kick me in the butt and reawaken my writing bug. When I said, "But I can't be a writer," she continuously asked me why not until I didn't have any more excuses. Without her, writing would be far from my mind rather than lighting it up every day.

Lisa Miller entered my life when I believed I could write this story as a pantser—one who writes by the seat of their pants, no outlining or planning required. The story will just flow. But then it didn't. I signed up for Lisa's workshop, Story Structure Safari, and wowie—it was one of the BEST classes I've ever taken. She stretched my brain and my story, and she is awesome.

Rocky Mountain Fiction Writers and Pikes Peak Writers provided (and still provide) learning, and support, and guidance as I navigated my way through the writing and publishing worlds. And it was through these groups that I found my fantastic critique groups. Many thanks to Tattered Cover writers, Mark Lehnertz, Matthew Woolums, Bob Biniek, Sue Loeffler, Chad Mathine, and Tim Curtis who listened to me read my book one chapter at a time, one week at a time. And über thanks to my Coal-Fired Writers group, Judy

Logan, Kim Byrne, Terri Spesock, and Becky Clark who read pages and critiqued pages and read them again. Everyone's input has been invaluable. Thanks, too, to Tattered Cover Bookstore, and Racca's Pizzeria Napoletana (formerly Marco's Coal-Fired Pizza) for sharing your space with us. It's a privilege.

So many beta readers at different phases helped me in so many ways. Big thanks to Meghan Mortimer—beta reader and personal cheerleader for my story. She helped keep the motivation fires burning. And to Kelly Hindley for your feedback and forever friendship which are both treasures to me.

Thank you to beta readers Corinne O'Flynn, Sue Loeffler, Matthew Woolums, and Aaron Spriggs. You all made this story so much stronger. And extra special thanks to Jack Blowers who took time from his summer break to read *The Rampart Guards* and provide insightful and eye-opening feedback I couldn't have received from anyone else. You rock, Jack.

Stephen Parolini, also known as the Noveldoctor, provided keen developmental edits and even saved a life in this story. And Susan Brooks at Literary Wanderlust made copyedits extraordinaire.

If you love the cover, all the thanks goes to Steven Novak at Novak Illustration. And if you don't like it, you should totally blame me since it's likely because of something I insisted on having, or not having, in the design. And kudos to Dale Pease at Walking Stick Books for the sharp interior design. A valuable talent indeed.

Thank you to my husband, Kevin, who took a huge breath and said, "Yes, you should do this." And to our three rescue pups, Maggie, Shea, and Boon, who delight and de-stress me every single day.

Unending gratitude goes to my friends and family who, when I announced to my world that I was pursuing a writing career, sent me positive emails, and texts, and cards. Even gifts to help me along my journey. You all transformed what was for me a scary leap off a cliff, and made it a jump into a kiddie pool filled with colorful balls and wonderful moments. Not that this journey has been easy—I've been challenged time and again. But knowing your support was there was immeasurable. And I love each and every one of you that much more for it.

And finally, thank you to every reader of this book. I hope it brought you something good, something positive, something fun. May you all be surrounded by golden Skyfish ready to fight by your side.

ABOUT THE AUTHOR

Wendy Terrien has been writing stories since she was in grade school. Her debut novel, *The Rampart Guards*, is the first in her intriguing urban fantasy series.

Inspired by an episode of *Bones* that suspected a killer to be a fabled chupacabra, Wendy was fascinated and dove into research more about cryptozoology—the study of animals that may or may not exist, or cryptids. Pouring over stories, videos and photographs of creatures others had seen all over the world, Wendy developed her own story to share with middle grade, young adult and grown-up readers.

Raised in Salt Lake City, Wendy graduated from the University of Utah and soon transplanted to Colorado where she completed her MBA at the University of Denver. Having applied her marketing expertise to the financial and network security industries, it wasn't until a career coach stepped in that she fully immersed herself in her passion for writing. Wendy began attending writers' conferences, workshops and retreats.

She regularly participates in two critique groups and is a member of Rocky Mountain Fiction Writers, Pikes Peak Writers and the Society of Children's Book Writers and Illustrators. In 2014, she was a finalist in the San Francisco Writer's Contest and in March 2016, will release a novella in the anthology *Tick Tock: Seven Tales of Time*.

Wendy lives in Colorado with her husband Kevin and their three dogs: Maggie, Shea and Boon. All three of her dogs are rescue animals, and Wendy is passionate about promoting shelter adoptions. If you're ever in Colorado, you may even be able to spot her by her "Adopt a Shelter Pet" license plates.

Visit Wendy's website at wendyterrien.com

Sign up for Wendy's newsletter at: wendyterrien.com/new-page

Twitter: twitter.com/wbterrien

Facebook: facebook.com/wendyterrien

Instagram: instagram.com/wendyterrien

CPSIA information can be obtained
at www.ICGtesting.com
Printed in the USA
LVOW12*1547070416

482603LV00006B/15/P